GALA

/

BOOKS BY PAUL WEST

Gala

Bela Lugosi's White Christmas

Colonel Mint

Words for a Deaf Daughter *(nonfiction)*

Caliban's Filibuster

I'm Expecting to Live Quite Soon

Alley Jaggers

Tenement of Clay

A Quality of Mercy

Paul West

GALA

HARPER & ROW, PUBLISHERS

New York, Hagerstown, San Francisco, London

Portions of this work originally appeared
in *TriQuarterly 36*, Spring 1976.

FIRST EDITION

Designed by Dorothy Schmiderer

Library of Congress Cataloging in Publication Data

West, Paul, date
  Gala.
  I. Title.
PZ4.W5192Gal3 [PR6045.E78]   813'.5'4   76–9212
ISBN 0–06–014569–2

76 77 78 79 80 10 9 8 7 6 5 4 3 2 1

AUTHOR'S NOTE

Asked for a brief preface, I oblige.

Readers familiar with an earlier book of mine, *Words for a Deaf Daughter,* will recognize, or think they recognize, two of the characters in this one, and with reason. But Milk and Deulius, as such, exist only within these pages, whereas whom and what I extrapolated them from exist non-fictionally, as do others of this novel's characters, while yet others are outright imaginary. The mix, as sidewalk colorists declare, is all my own work, a mix—or tapestry, mosaic—that was in my head long before I wrote *Gala* and even before I wrote *Words.* Both books came out of the same ferment, and the present one, in its different register, is a true emotional sequel to the other. What I have done is to stage in fiction a desideratum that didn't happen. *Gala* is thus the scenario of a wish-fulfillment; the wish abides, and the book partly fulfills it on the level of imagination. I have often thought that one should be able not only to describe something but also to recover (or create) anticipations of it. Here, as best I can, I make a pipe dream into prose.

The traditional prefatory note to a work of fiction denies

that the characters resemble people living or dead. In this instance I am obliged, selectively, both to deny it and admit it. I have tried to invade imaginatively situations I know quite well, and in so doing to win a freedom of response, of conjecture and intrusive epitome, of license to transpose or combine, otherwise illicit. That is in part what art is for, as well as being a means of trying to create something perfect. I think of this book as an "auto-fiction": its stimulus, or occasion, I know profoundly at first hand; its pattern is a dream that I have signed.

Any sequel to *this* sequel will probably be neither memoir nor novel but a prose poem dense as a neutron star, one flake of which, metaphorically speaking, would weigh a million tons and cut through any of us as if we were air.

P. W.

We'll meet again, we'll part once more.
The spot I'll seek if the hour you'll find.
My chart shines high where the blue milk's
upset.

James Joyce,
Finnegans Wake

ONE

Canis Minor to Cassiopeia

Can a human being hide? Not like a god, at any rate. You skulk within the theater of your various selves, though doomed to one esophagus, one brain stem, one ration of threescore years and ten (plus any bonus from prosthetic surgery). Speak in tongues you may, but with one tongue only. Your only hiding place is arithmetical: you will always have thoughts that pass unrecorded, even by yourself, and so, over a lifetime, you build up into an incalculable sum. You will know yourself only through samples, factors, predominances, flashes of ore in rock, and this is how others have to know you too. A man's mail isn't addressed to all of him. A human is a breeding tribe; and of the Mohicans, say, who compose him, the last one's never known, not even after death, nor even before it by the executioner who's handcuffed you behind and stuffed a soft rubber ball into your mouth to quell the sounds. The universe that a human is expands indefinitely the further he, or anyone, probes it. Outward, ever outward, alas, until out of sight.

Actually, I have just penciled the above on a green-lined pad of disinfected-smelling yellow paper: my contribution to

3

identity as an art of fugue. I so often feel as if someone, some puppeteer, is working me, writing me down, someone who is unknowably in charge, even if not in the right. No atheist I, but an anti-theist, that most reluctant of witnesses (as if the difference made any difference). It is almost eleven P.M. and Vega is on the meridian. Do I keep astronomer's hours, until four in the morning, because I can't sleep, or is it the other way around? I no longer pose the question with hope. For the past year or two, I have been working up to a visit, a reunion, with my sole offspring, not that she knows it, not in so many words. I would like to feel wholly behind my motives in that act, but I'm torn: as many voices urge me back as forward. I heed them all, acting when in doubt and brooding while action is under way. It will no doubt always go thus.

And so? I, Deulius, novelist, can no longer back down. I return to the entry I began with and add a sentence that reads, *I am in trouble again,* only at once to distract myself with an allusion to the Radiant Point of Giacobinids, a meteor shower of 1946. Exactly where was I? On the point of taking an aspirin or six. If headaches are grace, I'm multiply blessed. Mind made up, I'll write as if for publication (that dubious hoist to one's spirits), as many times before. I intended otherwise, but what's to lose that isn't lost?

According to the legend on the back of my planisphere, thing which omits the Moon and rotates beneath a hand-sized ellipse cut into a square of celestial blue card, if you learn the stars' positions, the planets become the strangers. A neat reversal, isn't it, there being so many more stars than known planets. But it's a hard way to make the familiar strange, installing it thus in some unthinkable vastness. It's perhaps even a way of universalizing human hurt or joy, just think of that. Doubtless the Edgar Telescope Company, from whom I bought this thin astrolabe for the price of a flashlight battery, means Venus, Mars, Saturn, big Jupe, the four most

4

easily seen of the local crew, but the maxim fits Earth as well. As if to say, bicycling toward the Statue of Liberty, with eyes firmly fastened on her crown, the rider finds his leg motions incongruous, and even more so the chain, the frame, the wheels. Or, reassured by the electric-blue Pleiades, he fidgets at what he stands on, the arches of his feet aching while he cranes his neck. Something such. A useful, fortifying idea worthy of an incantation: Altair, Deneb, Mirfak, I say, choosing the most foreign-flavored names for intimates, while New England, the Gulf Stream, Daylight Saving Time sound inexpressibly remote, nothing to count on. Maybe it works, over a span of years, but only if you try harder than is decent, and by that time you're nowhere at all.

Ultra-fondness, then: love of the distant, that's for me, not an astronomer royal but an astronomer ordinary, seeking out the constellation into which pain, or mortality, fits without fuss; into the jazz of cosmic chemistry. At least, perhaps, it mitigates the abiding headache I've spoken of, that goes away as if winked at only to return recharged, more elaborately nagging, all the way from brainpan to "heartspoon." But, to get on, my matter properly begins as follows: IT IS A MARVELOUS NIGHT, THE SORT OF NIGHT ONE ONLY EXPERIENCES WHEN ONE IS YOUNG. THE SKY . . . or: SO, THEN, WE ARE HERE IN ORDER TO LIVE; I WOULD SOONER HAVE THOUGHT . . . But it can't, of course, any more than it can begin, I SAW ETERNITY THE OTHER NIGHT. As a matter of fact, I can see it, or some of it, almost any summer night, cloud permitting, which is why I have come to loathe that substance, anxious to be out at my post on the balcony, eye to the Astrax eyepiece, with Penderecki's *Auschwitz Oratorio* or Ives's Fourth Symphony pouring from the stereo through the screen door behind me, and the merest first pile of imminent middle age itches from the cramp I sit in. The only way to do it is to transpose organs, or instruments, and talk directly into the tiny pupil of the lens itself, projecting the words across the Atlantic and the Pacific, even to Andromeda and the Islands of Langerhans. Thus coming full circle. After that, I shall look with my mouth, read with my ears. Calmly, I say to her, in rehearsal, In a manner of speaking we have spoken before, under so-called difficulties which we still share. At once the headache lifts, I am once more crystal-headed.

Going on, I enter the swim of things with a voluntary, a speech suite: On behalf of you, in your deafness, I spoke, as much in your absence as in your presence, shifting every now and then from plain talk into peacock bravery. And you rarely answered, hardly then having language although a coffer full of forbearing smiles. Response I found in your thrusty drawings done with a never uplifted fiber pen, in your big-lettered versions of your name, even in the curved graph of your hearing loss, its abscissa the core of a brutal riddle. Years ago, like accomplices face to face, we mimed and mugged, and now you know getting on for four hundred words, the fruit of endless echolalia, year upon year of hard-driving school.

Unkindly kind, the situation now is that visits are allowed, she to me, I to her, as if either of us were in the lock-up, some Lubianka of the kinship state. Prisoner of February 23 awaits arrival of prisoner of October 18, as simply as that, except of course that she has to be fetched, like a baby giraffe or a box of new-cut lilies. No matter how big she has become, on womanhood's edge (on a bigger nothing's margin), she entails preparations, logistics, goods, befitting one who steers at the Magellanic Clouds, as if her own planet were hostile to the very life-form she represents, as it almost is. What a commotion, what a marathon of getting ready. Tickets, schedules, emergency numbers and remedies, calendrical affidavits, all I haven't consulted being the sun dial, the almanac, the *I Ching*. Were she slinking out from behind the Iron

Curtain, it would seem easier, except that we don't need guns or darkness. A bit of a gantlet to run, all the same, what with time zones, jet lag, international variations in fodder, lefthand drive for right (I can see her now, scowling because the driver's on the wrong side), ninety degrees in the shade for sixty-five among the dogs and the mad English, and her own private metabolic clock, working as usual on sidereal time, though that isn't the only reason I call her Milk.

As for the conventions of this autofiction or interior deluge, they're few. (1) Everything permitted. (2) No obligation on her part to answer, collaborate or read. (3) Two weeks allowed for composition, say a dozen pages a day while she tries to tear them up, or while she sleeps. Neither enueg (word for a long medieval bleat) nor a put-up job (such as staging the Week of the Creation twice over in six rooms). It's going to be more like my eavesdroppings on our behalf on what we might have said had things been otherwise. And this will survive, a lexical echo of where she was, and what.

As I read through, even so early, I find every C and G, A and U, a textural obbligato to what went wrong at her vagitus, or even before, as many as nine months earlier, when, as the books tell us, the DNA of the sperm unites with that of the ovum, and that is that, beyond revision. Occasionally nature makes a mistake and binds the wrong molecule into the chain, the result being that, when splitting occurs, the two molecules that form won't be identical, and, as the books calmly enough point out, there will be corresponding changes in the code of instructions and the individual will deviate from the original pattern. Clinical horror-story I know by heart. If she could understand that explanation, she might not need it. So let me pay my dues again and again to C, G, A and U, the gods of the copybook: to cytosine, that sounds close to trigonometry; guanine, evocative of bird-droppings; adenine, almost a girl's name; and uracil, which might almost be the magical toothpaste of the year. Grand committee of teleological agents, they'll never be far from mind, heading each thought, steering each fit. I'll stop, and then on.

Graffias in Scorpius, Cheleb in Ophiuchus, Unukalhai in Serpens, Almach in Andromeda: uncouth-sounding stars which, in no special order, keep coming to mind and hinting at unmentionable monsters as I pore over the grease-thumbed tar black of the star charts lined in Euclidean white. No matter: with each paragraph I lose a little of me to chemistry, a little of chemistry becomes my own. Win a few, lose . . .

Uncanny that tomorrow's the day, confirmed expensively by telephone, and all I need to do, having readied the house, vowed to change my sleeping habits, is to clean up the strategies of this, the intended remnant after she's come and gone like a nova that bursts forth and fades, even if to erupt again years later, like RS Ophiuchus, 1898, 1933, 1958, 1967. Here's hoping, I tell myself (there is hoping here indeed), it won't ever be that long for Milk and me, who have never been able to exchange letters, what with her being incommunicado (unlettered and unphonable) as well as in a non-stop category called constant supervision. No postscripts to her presence, then, not from her anyway; hence my need for verbal spoor, something beyond the school's guarded reports (She is making progress and learning to recognize coins). *That* when she was twelve. And now tomorrow has come I see myself setting out full of giddy foreboding. An arch, as Leonardo said, is only a strength caused by two weaknesses. Draw strength from that thought, I tell myself. Draw from it now.

Abbreviating chores, I'll record only that I'm driven to one airport, where the handwritten country menu reads Dough-nought with an Oops! above it and a line through the second *ugh,* then fly to another that has a long arcade of display cases

8

crammed with trash, then cross several thousands of miles, in the course of which a home-bound Englishman reading a journal about metals spills whiskey on my shoe and I decline to dab it or kick aside the fallen ice. I avert my clogged gaze from a South African film about a patrician former Olympic gold-medalist who wants his son to win a local marathon, and, instead, while music, on channels (or canals) obedient to a rotating wheel under my left thumb, flows into the stethoscope I rent for the price of a paperback, I observe the dawn's vertical spectrum as it fattens behind my Plexiglas porthole.

Approaching her at over five hundred miles an hour, though much slower than Earth spins, I divide the sleepless hours between Classics in Stereo (2) and the Jazz File (9), which is to say between hosts Carmen Dragon and Leonard Feather, unlikely-sounding watchmen whom I splice back to back, Cain and Abel of the ether, in the violet night sky. Here is how the menu of the earphone reads: two movements from Tchaikovsky's Suite Number One, music of soul vermilion, while the horizon flickers (what on earth the time is, I have no idea, but I'm sure *she* isn't watching the dawn); then Mozart's Serenade Number Six in D Major, in which a chamber group seems to be counterpointing a full ensemble. What appetizing euphoria as the east blisters white.

About the time that Ellington's "Johnnie Come Lately" thumps forth with flaunting fused brass, the dawn is a visual scald, the pastel spectrum has almost gone.

"Go Back Home," a raucous percussion from the Don Ellis orchestra, comes almost as a hint while I tug down the plastic shade over a window brimming with eye-wounding silver. But I've seen the day come up like thunder, Rudyard Kipling's fetish; I've scanned Earth's drowsing meniscus; I've felt like a returning astronaut aloof behind the heat shield. Leonard Feather says goodbye: "Take care of yourselves and of each other," which sounds like an intrusive rebuke. Or was that Carmen Dragon? I don't care as I sip the orange juice an alert hostess delivers. Airmaid, I think; she's an *airmaid*.

Already past more time zones than birds allow themselves in one go, I walk down the steps from the jet in clubfooted reverie and show passport in a country other than the country of origin (as the inside cover of my ticket says in a tart addendum concerning the Treaty of Warsaw). I was born here in a season of fogs. All I have to do now is wait an hour or two, shave because I won't have a chance to do so later on, come round enough to collect one tall girl infatuated still with planes, and (if not in this order, at least in this approximate dimension) lunch awkwardly as part of a disbanded trio at the airport restaurant, check documents and cabin supplies, and hope to board the 1300-hours departure without too much fuss, streak back along the great-circle route before local time takes hold, yet not before general fatigue sets in. I'll be setting a retarded child five hours further back, a grimmish thought on which I cannot linger.

An impossible enterprise? Of course. Akin to recovering a space capsule? Nearly. There yesterday, here today, there today, and gone tomorrow. Not quite, but close enough to it. Where, I'll be asking, did the day get lost? Arrive there at 1530, which is 2030 here, and settle down to five hours by car. The logistics are special, are they not? More like logarithms. She cannot, ever, travel alone, even with a label round her neck like the schoolchildren whom the hostesses, airmaids, ply with tiny pilot's badges, flight logbooks scaled down, coloring books, soft drinks, and daintily wrapped candy. And you can't drive alone with her because she might leap out or seize the wheel on a turnpike at seventy miles an hour. But at least we two get to board first, along with the elderly and parents with toddlers. My twitching mind strays to the Epstein bronze marooned behind the terminal's giant picture window; commemorating Brabazon, patron of aviators, it's like a lava flow frozen in mid-air over its pedestal. Supposedly Icarus, or the spirit of flight, it appears to unfurl untidily above the passengers' and watchers' heads. My mind makes common cause with it and goes null, hovering.

Uh-huh, the bar is closed, but what care I, having no need of it, as for several years now. A bar to moan at, however, that might be something worthwhile. The restaurant is stalled between the end of breakfast and the start of lunch. I exchange a few Washington-headed dollars for the Queen-embossed pounds that seem smaller yearly and a handful of outsize Britannic coins that buy too little considering their weight. A telephone call later, the experiment is on, and this piece of its raw material is already wincing at the prospect. I lap up the phenomena of disorientation: coffee tasting of cocoa, Muzak from the Sixties, flight announcements in an accent so fastidiously muted it might be a laryngitic sloth, an aroma of cut roses from the flower stall, one of leather from the gift boutique, a gust of hops as the bar seems to open and close again like a bloom of evil, a reek of kerosene from the runways, even a whiff of vomit from under the seat. Somnambulistically patrolling the imitation marble floor, which makes each footstep glide a fraction as if I'm walking gingerly without meaning to, I buy English and French newspapers, note the headlines, fold the stack double into my bruise-black flight bag, and go to eat haddock with an egg, refusing the always-offered french-fried potatoes. This country's future will be found to have been long behind it, spurned in the 1890s when it showed its face. Unfair? I know it is, but this morning I'm hardly capable of balanced thought.

Communiqué: the pair of them, it seems, will take their lunch at home, not ten miles away as the swallow flies. An elegiac repast. So be it: I'm guaranteed a minimum of unrelished contact; I'll have time to brood on the status of this reverie, the thing which is assembling itself within the cerebral illusion I've made. I can only call it the pre-written enactment of what hindsight knows took place today in Utopia, meaning Nowhere. It's the past written in the present prophetic tense, as befits. I plan. I go. I claim my Perdita at this distant terminal, whizz her away, will have to ferry her back again, after which . . . there is a metal fatigue of the mind: a wing falls off, the nose splits, the tail crumples up. I do these words to draw my line through time, across the Mercator quadrants, to prove it all happened, was capable of happening, and so can go on happening. Saying it, I do it. Saying I do it, I'm planning it. Planning it, I do it. Having done it, I keep it in the present tense to make it last. I know that to write in the past tense confers an illusion of command and fixedness, but the future tense is just as final. For instance: *I bought her a doll,* a second ago, and now the sentence is cold. *I buy her a doll,* am buying it now, and already the act is over as the hasty, never-quite-simultaneous sentence that almost sheathes it dies. *I will buy her a doll,* and the act is over before begun. Something always keeps the rhetoric from coming true. Something always keeps the truth from being rhetorical. Better, perhaps, to kiss events without thinking at all.

Clearly, there are subtler ways of living than writing things down, *whenever.*

Aramaic? No. Ogham script? Never. Linear B? Hardly. Then what? Just allowing the electrical scribble of cognition to fizz and fade out.

Going to hell on an abacus, mouthing prayers in code: that might describe me.

Urging on my mind's eye without looking at the outside world.

Careful now, I instruct myself. Be tactful. You'll soon be

high over the ocean again, watching Milk grin at the cloud floor.

Arrange, arrange, arrange. Reconfirm pre-reconfirmed reservations.

Calmly take over when that iron-clad umbilical has to stretch, and reassure the girl as best you can. That she'll get her mother back in fourteen sleeps. "Vordeen zleep."

Get her aboard fast, beguile her with aeronautics, the up-ness of the plane she has always called "abbala," stress on the first syllable, please.

Check that her two hearing aids aren't on the blink (and abstain from awful metaphors). Then let her shed them for the trip, if she so wants, what with her lip-reading so demonically accurate. See all, hear nothing. What else? Tranquillizer at the ready, one she won't reject.

All ball-points, fiber-points, puzzles, crayons in the status astronauts call Go.

Get mentally ready for custodianship, and urge whatever beneficence warms the cosmos not to make her run amok, ripping out the flotation cushions, fisting loaded plastic trays of near-computerized food, clamoring for snow, or TV, or a ride on her swing, a slide on her slide, a sleep in her very own bed. All that up there, among the invisible stars.

Going westward in daylight (which precedes going west and gone west), we won't see Jupiter, as I did while coming, but we'll certainly be flying to an intenser summer than this gusty carbon copy, copyright by the temperate zone. In her lingo, summer is "when the moon is hot," season in which she likes to ford rivers, romp in her plastic pool outside on the lawn that I no longer tread. She still has no word for sun.

Count out the time for her, I remind myself, and mark her

face when, after two mealtimes, she arrives almost at the hour she took off. Where, I wonder, will she think the time went, she having no abstractions. Entering into the anomie of travel, she may well laugh, loving an uncontaminated surd; or, aghast, she'll rip the cabin apart, given a chance, as her true old circadian rhythms tell her she's been betrayed, it isn't 1530 body time at all, it's half past ten, two hours after she goes to sleep.

Going to sleep on board, though, she'd come to life at midnight Eastern Standard Time, just when she should be dropping off, as I. Helpless, I leave it to nature, which . . .

A lottery, as everyone has told me. Play by ear and expect a crisis somewhere along the line of flight. I'm just tempted to fly back empty-handed, having anticipated enough in the past hour to fuel a month; but no, I'll go according to plan, hoping she's been as fully briefed as possible about the day's and the next two weeks' events. As it is, she'll have more sense of going from than of going toward, more of being severed than of being reattached. Surely thought has now canceled itself right out?

Greenwich time is creeping up to embarkation time. My head fills with bags for motion sickness, glibly dubbed. My sinuses hold isinglass, dark and cold. My third coffee sets up an old familiar tremor in my wrists, and, just as I light up a cigarillo in the shadow of Epstein's Icarus, I see them across the hall at the head of the escalator, loaded with bags. Why did they come upstairs? Rendezvous was ground-floor, at the check-in point, and not for another fifteen minutes. Now we'll have to go down again.

At an enormous distance I hear my friends' voices, expostulating, analyzing, adding diffident riders. Pi: "Is it worth all the emotional turmoil? Won't it upset her more than it's worth? And you?" (She is usually right in her level-headed acuity, born under Libra, like Milk herself, like my mother.)

And Chad: "Leave well alone, my friend; distance is the healer. Out of sight, out of trouble. Absence makes the heart grow stronger." (Facetious-sounding, especially when I try out on him prospective titles for some new stars, he's at core serious, a postgraduate in both marital and cardiac attrition.) The legal opinion, as so often, leaves it up to me, cautioning me, however, that what one is legally entitled to isn't always a joy. Why, then, am I committed to this high-wire act, this emotional binge, when the reward is only scars made wounds again, the final catch an exhausted goodbye at this very airport? Pride, paternity, curiosity, masochism, involuntary defiance: my hand includes at least these cards, as well as one that lengthily reads: Addiction to ontological ground floors, the presentation of things in their most horrible aspect. At bottom, I find a passion for disharmony, because harmony there is none, and anyone who thinks there is has another think coming. All that hubris in a dunce's cone upon my head, and then some.

Consider, though, her accreted beauty, which exists, is just now a few yards from my suntanned hand. A Nordic elf, brunette where she once was flaxen, but with the same wide pale blue-green eyes. Pubescent, long, and given to agitated skips while her head rakes sideways in bursts of eager curiosity. My long-distant heavy-featured face she knows; this extended smile is no pretense after diligent briefing. She *has* no pretenses: she knows what she knows, knows not what she doesn't. "Yah," she says loudly, meaning not *ja* but me, and with her usual ritualized protocol asks for a present, an "ooba," as of old, ostentatiously shielding one eye with a cupped hand. "Soon," I mouth, exaggerating the vowel to her, frontface (I'm saving the doll for the crisis). Does she know she, and she only, will soon be in the *abbala* with me, up high, fourteen sleeps, water, swim, where the moon is hot? Then home again? I ask, and she gives an affirmative, impatient nod. This has never happened before, not to her, so let there be light and sweetness indeed. Once upon a time, to all such novelty, or to an unknown person, she would say her imperious, conclusive "No," followed by her "bye-bye-bye." Now, though, she awaits the next step, grinning almost slyly, all mercenary sheen. Encased in the strictest of demeanors, her mother gets the show on the road, anxious for the anesthetic to be given, the first incision made, and aching already to come to in the recovery room in a fortnight's time.

Check in, show documents as if in iron mask; people stare at this girl, and not always unkindly. She spellbinds with her looks, her bravura symmetries. Too soon to board, so helplessly I agree to coffee, more of it. "Beebee," says Milk, meaning she's lip-read that much and wants some too, using her generic word for anything to drink, anxious never to be left out. For no solid reason, an ad comes to mind: "Any fluid you can find in nature, we can deliver by flask or trailer, plus an almost infinite number of mixtures." One day I may need them, royal plural and near-infinity and all, even if only for something to metabolize while being nervous.

Grope up the escalator again, which Milk adores, has always called "bo."

God (that clutch of ions or steam), the goodbyes have been said, and I escort my backward-frowning child through the door to motherless limbo. From now on, screams or fits or mayhem notwithstanding, I have to see her through. *Eureka,* I have found it. Found what? The daring to go on. Oddly, she faces front, a little as if I am going to back her to the wall while the firing squad waits to one side (an image *she*'d never supply), and we arrive at the duty-free shop, which has an oddly liberated sound. I buy her some toilet water, resisting the connotation, and a blue silk scarf in which dragons are evanescing, and (since she hasn't one, is bound for the country where every second counts) an inexpensive watch. Erratically I read the signs behind the counter, marveling at one bit of irrelevant pageantry saying, beside a scarlet flag imprinted with crescent moon and a star, both white, "Turkish currency is *not* accepted." Had such currency *ever* been proffered here, at this secondary although international airport? Milk's big teenage hand is a vise for mine. I walk her to the toilet, just in case, then realize I've taken her to MEN. There is no one to embarrass, or incite, with my young and busty Viking with her two microphones against her canary-yellow jumper and her sizzling earpieces tuned in to phenomena she usually likes to do without. A bud of euphoria starts to peel open, but I nip it: we're not even on the way. No tears, though, no frenzy. After all, she is fourteen. I remember her first pun, akin to an esoteric allusion to Galileo from an Easter Islander, calling her then thirty-four-year-old mother *dirty-fork*. To the lip-reader the sounds look alike, but Milk relished the difference. An inborn wit among the garbled engrams painted that distant day in gold.

Conversation piece while waiting: "Abbala," I say (it is blue and white out there, all its refueling done, its tail fin high as a tree; I've already spent half a dozen hours in it today). She utters nothing, but hungrily points, eyes nacreous with the old aerial craving. She thinks she's going, but isn't sure even now. "Mickel *up?*" Fanning her fingers at me, she again checks that figure of fourteen sleeps that will restore her to mother, and I confirm. If an expression can be of disgruntled complacency, she has one, wears it with potent will. Off soon, we're travelers from an antique land setting out for a peak in Darien, hands linked in First Class (an innovative extravagance), with nothing to declare except each the other. Mickel, she calls herself, rarely Michaela, and never knowingly Milk, which is my own private tag for good and sentimental and almost religious reasons. Perhaps Milt would have been as good. No. If parents knew beforehand their child would be damaged, they'd perhaps choose more suit-

17

able names, easier ones at any rate, like Beau (easy for the child to say) or Bab (almost as easy); but if they knew beforehand, they'd probably get as far as passive euthanasia. Christ's blood clots in the firmament. Gynecology in the stirrups howls. And these are not thoughts to fly around with.

Untold prevarications dog me now I've thought that. I wish, I wish, I wish.

Calmer, just a bit calmer.

Good going, I've cheered up again; I'm on my way to a classical reunion. I'm nearly *there.*

At long last we obey the manicured glottals directing us to gate something-or-other, the ramp, the steps, the ribbed platform at the oval door into Kubla Khan's anteroom, a-sprinkle with a new batch of white-gloved debutantes in freshly sprayed aromas. Two of them coax her into the broad window seat, exclaiming and cooing while she scans the tarmac for mother. I, Deulius, feel like a rejected sponsor, or a used-up battery, or a flipped-off seatbelt. The air in the cabin is crisp and even, has just been beautifully manufactured; and how coolly the airmaids bow, unfurl their apple-firm arms, pirouette, adjust, succor, calm. We have been taken in by a hospice of the sky. We are almost home, in this six-hundred-mile-an-hour living room. Milk's entranced, kneading a royal-blue cushion, while I, I'm unwinding so fast I almost fall asleep. As a turbine faintly revolves into life, she unplugs her hearing aids, unbuckles their harness, and hands it over, microphones and all, like so much bungled knitting. I transfer it to an airmaid, who pretends to put it on, causing Milk to laugh aloud at one so hindered. Tribute to this airline, its light militia has cool; but, then, they can take almost anything for seven hours and a half, and for the nigh-mythic price I've paid I can tap their spines as well. I wonderingly await catastrophe as we taxi out, strapped in.

18

Alert to the straight-line takeoff (an obsessed-feeling trundle that might prove Einstein's propositions about rectilinear speed), Milk smirks like a maenad, giving herself over to upholstered vibration and the back-thrust phases of landscape. Her lifelong love of violent motion—being swung around by the shoulders, being carried upside down, or of handstanding herself against any available wall—takes over; this best roller-coaster of all drives her into a broad uncaptious grin that lasts until we leave the ground. The abrupt shift to smoothness piques her at first, but a thump of upfolded wheels renews the grin. If only, I think, we could cross the ocean at takeoff speed on terra firma all the way, or on ice, stampeding past polar bears and earthbound whales, careening past bergs and frozen waterspouts, while the tremor in our feet goes on and on. If only Hendrik Hudson and his crew would keep on creating the special thunder of playing bowls, then she, the Rip Van Winkle of learning, would never sleep again. Clearly, though, we have taken off right on time, which she at once, with newly developed skill, tells me as I adjust her new wristwatch. "One and a half," she mouths, juicily oblivious of Earth's rotation and west-east headwinds at bitter altitudes.

After that, the cornucopia of executive luxury (doesn't the *consultative* echelon ever fly?) breaks open, and a menthol-fresh airmaid facially not unlike her plies us with carbonated drinks while another, dusky with Romany curls, demonstrates the ocher life-jackets, a charade which Milk enjoys, chortles at around her two barber's-pole straws, as if the airmaid in question is a hopelessly discombobulated goon, victim of her own truss. Quizzical, Milk looks around for hers, to don and then top up by blowing through the mouthpiece. Again I thank the deity of ions for not allowing oxygen masks to flop down before us from the overhead compartments. When they do, we'll need them; until then, if you please, no circus rehearsals.

Comes a headset each. What a lark. To Milk this is like shelling peas. On goes hers, like a parody of what she wears daily, except this doesn't prod deep, in toward the drum. After a sly frown at the head-brace, she plugs into the chair-arm socket and happily spins to maximum volume the wheel I show her, getting 110 decibels with luck. Spinning the channels as I too listen, I see one of her biggest smiles, even a tiny flush, as big-band swing slams out, Count Basie to be sure. This is Leonard Feather's Channel 9, where I came in, and I time-travel back to my own teenage record collection, which included such other samples of Basie's raucous ping as "Basie Boogie," "Pound Cake," "The 9.20 Special," "Clap Hands, Here Comes Charlie," and "It's Square But It Rocks." Briefly I yearn for the amplified farts of Gene Krupa's "Tuxedo Junction," the demure stomp of Goodman's "Jumping at the Woodside," the motoric jam of Herman's "Perdido," and other rhythmic gems. My teens are meeting hers; she has just heard, says Leonard Feather, "Everyday" (sic), from Basie and Joe Williams, and the critic's voice goes on within that vacuum fastness, invulnerable to the roar and cold of half a thousand miles an hour as we go on climbing over Ireland. She pouts questioningly, can hear nothing now, until Miles Davis' rendition of "It Never Entered My Mind," and I dumbly applaud the abstract quality of music which, titled something like that, or "Copenhagen" or "Mission to Moscow," makes the maximum style out of a minimal allusion, whereas words, my own envoys, need to tell so much. And while Milk attends to music (that notorious stimulant to the brain's subdominant hemisphere) with befuddled-looking calm, not tapping her foot of course (her only rhythms are her own), I let my mind roam as it wants, marking the aroma of lunch from the microwave ovens, wondering if scraping potatoes makes the airmaids cough, and thanking more than a few of my lucky stars.

A nothing, like that which reasserts itself through contrast after words have been used, now includes us, unlikely-looking pair of fellow travelers, though with the same nose, mouth, and shape of eye. Chances are she'll listen to the one channel all the way, her tastes favoring sameness, patterns, constants, each time finding Basie, Davis, or the Don Ellis ensemble not so much new as still at a distance, unappraisable as time itself, a camel through a microscope, or blood spilled on a galaxy. Divided-up noise, *that* she hears, however, and relishes the bombardment next to her stirrup and cochlea, making something fidget in her middle brain, her teeth tingle, maybe, her head at length, as almost always, ache with an ache she's learned to confide about: "Ah, sore!," indicating temple or scalp in its bush of tropical-thick hair.

Aspirin is easily procured in this high-altitude cul-de-sac, where we shirk the natural context of ice, hydrogen, and sun, that much nearer the neutrinos raining through us every second like mortality itself. I light another cigarillo (cigar privilege denied you in Tourist Class), and Milk poufs the match as an airmaid with wings and patented smile hands me a handful of book matches that image Africa, Singapore, Rome: inflammatory tabloids with which to undermine the domain of Uncle Sam. For some reason Channels 7 and 3 are blank and I shake my First-Class head at the technical explanation I'm given. Damn the Norns of audio. Damn the Norns of cinema—man who make round trip, same day on same plane, see same movie. But no: not again the marathon about the South African Olympic-medalist patrician feuding with his sons, but *The Way We Were,* picturesque at least, a campus abscess lanced. Milk will yawn of course, but might even pick up Barbra Streisand at her plangentest, in which event she will flick an eye sideways like one discovering an elephant's tusk in her ice cream. Is this OK? says the look. Is it often thus? Is this how *you* hear things? One of her least respectable habits is to leer in ridicule at her handicapped

21

compatriots, caricaturing the spastics and the truncated-fin rhetoric of the thalidomides, all the time asking in dumb-show what the hell is *she* doing among schoolmates this ungainly. Why, look at them, there's something wrong; whereas . . . She evokes that old chestnut of the philosophers, the class of all classes that are not members of themselves, and she will probably find Streisand just as impeded, stunted, halt, victim of macrorhiny or whatever nose-blight's called.

A cruel pair, we'll wound even the caviar, the plaice, the tournedos, the Roquefort fresh from this morning's Paris plane. As for the wines, so help me, I'll curb her: the girl's a compulsive bibber, forever in those old days hunting the key to the liquor cupboard in order to settle down to a good long splash with the rest of us. And what am I going to tell her, I whom she'd ply back then with Dry Sack, when I show my non-drinking colors, intact these last three years? Will she force-feed me from a bottle or, like a mother penguin, squirt into my mouth what she's squooshed around in hers?

Unabashed in the toilet, she helps herself like a Hottentot to all the cosmetics Elizabeth Arden's powder cottage has provided. She insists. We emerge reeking of ambergris or civet, but my main thought just now is that, when I pee, I'll do it alone; her predatory curiosity, fanned on by immodest boys at that superb school, is worse than ever; she'll try to seize and tug until life is over. Foul and feral games we may have played in an almost mythical past, when she was a hooligan child, but now she'd better turn on some decorum. Some, at least. Now she gets a cabin bag, the sac of status complete with the airline's acronym, and she jubilantly finds within more toiletries, akin to those in the pure-pure rear cubicle we've just left. Again she makes up her face, again a shade tartish, but with exemplary finesse; the motions are deft, the results loud. "Yah?" she suggests. Not today, I inform her. "Ankew no?" she snaps, to confirm my aberrant refusal, and she echoes the negative, her headset on, blotting out whatever is playing with an exquisitely tapered diphthong, an orchestration all her own of the rounded vowel, that makes everyone look, even the intensely preoccupied carnation-sporting VIP with his thirty-seven global newspapers. Sir Fitzcontumely Rex-Relish, was it? (What did the fawning senior airmaid say?) He looks as if he has just seen an engine rip away from under a wing, but then he recognizes it was only one of the semi-aphasic unmentionables next an unkempt barbarian oaf with a suntan and glazed eyes. Back to his *Paris-Match* he turns with an Etonian grunt, while Milk ransacks the bag for something that isn't there, then pitches it beneath her, as if into the cloud clumps themselves.

Champagne has me saying oh-to-hell-with-it, I'll-drink. We'll arrive looped and be taken away in cuffs to Rikers Island or wherever the sauce-afflicted go. Sipping, with a fistful of smoked salmon, Milk looks suave and wise, for once in a world (other than school) where earpieces are worn in autistic raptness. She lip-reads the cabin staff, who clearly are used to being read thus by sybarites aloft not only in sky but in an enclosed continuum of private sound comparable to her own non-stop tinnitus of seashell surf. She has more in common with them than she knows, as if the Monte Cristo chocolate tart had made the Many into One. Plied, we take. Half tipsy, we tremble with expensive mirth, not least, in our very different perspectives, at the non-communication for years (no letter comes; one cannot phone) right next to this Lucullan reunion in a zooming tube. Vicissitude undoes me quite, and I release a long-saved tear that Milk espies, deplores with a vehemence befitting an aunt, and blots with tissue. Under control again, I let her puff my cigarillo once, which cures her for hours, and blithely take aboard another thousand calories with the fish, a sauce like vermilion-streaked cirrostratus. Among these colors, in this cabin dedicated to Joseph's coat, the gray line is the present (as it said under some cosmogonical diagram I somewhere saw), and the present is at the moment hard to see. Refraction through a small tear. We're living in animated suspension in a churn of cream embedded in royal-blue velvet, and I half-ban the future, near and distant: if this be altitude euphoria, let it never end. All I'll ask is a little sleep, like Milk, who's succumbed to Mumm's, alcoholic strength by volume twelve percent. Good night, imminent lady, you've almost gone a thousand miles, with only the headwinds retarding us.

According to Leonardo, among the "great" things to be found among us the existence of Nothing is the greatest. This unimaginable entity, he says, dwells in time, stretches into past and future, swallows up all, but is not the essence of anything. I like reading that old polymath, whose brain must have been the bulbous shape of the old-style Göttingen airfoil section, but I'd rather he'd hit on something useful, such as lion manure for scaring predatory deer away from crops. *Next*-to-nothing: that I can just about fathom, whereas Nothing, which I've pondered for more years than I remember, is it simply theoretical absence (a thing in air; the thing removed; and then air again), a vacuum, extinction of the soul by death of the body, or nirvana? Or is it what preceded the first appearance of energy that became matter that later became ourselves? In my book, Nothing's my imagining of my own absence in any of the places I've been: the omitted relativistic ego, which has little in common with Taoist notions of pure emptiness or with Kuan Yin's view of nothing's being established in regard to oneself, the result being that, identityless, one becomes a model of the universe. Much honorable sleeplessness has gone into whatever thoughts I have on this, forever envisioning myself next to Milk, whom the universe bungled into an unselfconscious surd, and wondering how much accommodation a mind can make. For instance, saying: she belongs more to the universe than to me, has more in common with the streams of hydrogen now flowing back from the Clouds of Magellan to the Milky Way than with me, for all my own bizarre metabolism. For instance, saying: there are miracle cures, or even miracles, but these will take a half-century to come, and I contrast her fate with that of the latest maltreated famous Russian, his balalaika on fire, asking myself what is remediable faster, *en bloc,* brain damage or totalitarianism. The former, I imagine, because the second isn't remediable at all: the brain-damaged are retarded, the commissars are not. One day we shall all grow up, when the hippic and the reptilian brains have withered away, then solve everything with nothing but the fairly recent neo-cortex. I can't finish the thought. Nothing, I begin dimly to see, corresponds to my not knowing what part of nature to blame for making her the way she is, or just recognizing one can't bring a case for damages against the internal compulsions of the DNA chain. Paired base and triple coding: what kind of a scapegoat's that?

Canted sideways, her broad but fragile-skinned face has the flush of winy slumber. I guess at dreams I'll never hear about: a candy-stripe avalanche or obsidian blank. And it becomes easier to possess her mind on her own behalf, in default of discursive conversations, than to stomach just the minimum she thinks. Hence, then, galas that implode: silver charms (Lisbon Fado Singer, Atlanta Cotton Bale), the penny gumball machine that doubles as a lamp with bright-checked gingham shade, the kaleido-go-round clock of pastel-colored disks, all culled from the in-flight gift catalogue. Or others, verbal mainly, from sickening pun (the Cyclops' favorite musical note is Middle C) to pyrotechnics (of which I find no sample currently available), as if coincidence or wit gave us a contributing editorship to the tears of things. There's the absurd you find, and the absurd you invent to hurl at it in therapeutic feud. I've only ever understood one form of art:

expressionistic, in which how you feel about things out-weighs how others do, in which uncurbable sensibility junks the camera, the calipers, and Copernicus, for what? The throb, the getting-it-off-the-chest, the sentient mutilation of what placid people see and count on. How many of us are there left? Life's extremer than most folk's images of it, so most folk skip the image altogether. Or most folk have just become so plain adjusted they feel nothing at all, just routine indignations, routine bliss, Our Father Which Art, death and taxes, trust the nation's elected leaders, and hire the handi-capped. Depiction limits rage, does it not? The agreed-upon, the classical, shuts out an I.

All right, one signals with what one has, and one doesn't vent what's already in another's possession. Phrase-making's the only poiesis: delicate pandemonium in the eyes; the heart's gristly *love-you / love-you-not;* and all unfelt form is mere refrigeration. Half my thinking is epitomistic blazes amid a linear mosaic of the not-me, yet I dearly like to outline Africa on tracing paper and mark in the rivers and the ports. The ordinary's no mere launching pad, is the miracle itself of course, once deep-inspected: blood cell to nebula, brain cell to neutron star.

Umpteen miles high, seven of air, above the mid-Atlantic trench, in the pell-mell capsule of the maniac's haven, I'd freeze this expedition, halt us here forever, given enough fodder, toys, and toilet tissue, until it all came right, and, imagining we were en route to Alpha Centauri, four and a half light-years away, yellow and red, age not a jot during the sixty-two-billion-mile trip. Our cosmic Lourdes. A hyperboli-cal way of putting it, of course, but nowhere near as frighten-ing, in the spectrum of outlandish wants, as the sentence in which you express your feeling so well you feel it no longer. Better perhaps never to say it thus palpably perfect, with always new reaches of the lexical superb to aim for; better to hold tight her hand, dab her sweating hair, and choose a fresh channel to listen to after switching hers off while leaving her headset in place. I do, and hit on what I discover was "Gimme a Pigfoot and a Bottle of Beer," hardly First Class, but of the Earth earthy, and pertinent when I recall how this child used to eat, more grossly than any wild child of legend, her feet a-wave over her naked belly, a hambone or drumstick in her paw.

Good: there is a high-wire act of trying to keep our every minute together from becoming a high-wire act. We ate lunch absent-mindedly, right on top of one she'd only just had, oblivious of such shudders as the plane gave. Like a team chosen for difficult assignments. Shoulder to shoulder, we fueled up, and now I have the stretched-tight cobweb in the head that comes from no sleep at all, while she, frayed with too much emotion and not enough understanding (a blend of parcel, waif, and heiress), grows little blebs of tissue over the splintery nerve ends, perhaps to storm furious or jolly among us while the most elaborate afternoon tea in the world is served by the same, but even fresher-smelling, girls. My mind, on strike, knits a puzzle that unravels thus: *gala:* a holiday with sports or festivities; *gala: galaktos,* Greek for milk, hence *galaktikos,* whence galaxy; Galatea? statue whom or which Pygmalion brought to life. Am I engaged in some unwitting triple play that converts bringing this girl to life into a galactic holiday? Taking my own hints like one obsessed? Perhaps not, but that is much how it would feel. In a blue reefer, she. Jaw, chalcedony cool. A fleck of mustard at her mouth corner. Book open on her knees. Albatrosses flying through the cabin. Heavy squawks. Followed by a glazier, bearing a sheet of glass five feet square. Now she reads out, not end-stopping the lines, Shelley's *Ozymandias:* "I met a traveler from an antique land / Who said: 'Two vast and trunkless legs of stone / Stand in the desert. . . .' " Then says, "A bit grandiose, isn't it? The poem that poetry-haters

27

love." Thus the dream within the dream.

Undying afternoon light over mid-Atlantic is the slaty blue of the Siberian cat, or the blue-bonnet salmon in its first few months. Reflying back into morning (an abstract one to be sure), we're only just a bit more ourselves than we aren't. A flat-out Vikingess tests the webbing of her safety belt, flicks an athlete's shoulder as she moves against the buckle, blinks, blinks, blinks. My headache's gone.

Unnumbered minutes later, the wheels go thump in the day above the eastern seaboard. I haven't even bothered to crane out over Labrador or the Hudson valley. A refreshed but bewilderingly peaceful Milk has stuffed herself with tea and buttered scones, fruit cake and Danish pastries. We have accomplished our toilet together without mishap or insult, lurching and laughing. She has proudly unearthed her supply of sanitary napkins right there in the cabin, setting one muslin-wrapped wad alongside an outsize éclair. I have taught her how to play ticktacktoe and, in trying on the quiet to lose, have mostly won. Stomach-twisting anti-climax sets in as we lose height, until I think: this is where the trouble starts, pax's tail in uproar's mouth, but all she does, for now, is beam condescendingly at the drab, hot terra cotta as it soars out of storage. Our cards and customs forms are ready for the groinch-groinch of the inspectors' stamps. Her hearing aids she's rejected, maybe anxious to make an unencumbered entrance into the New World. I feel as if, all night, I've been squinting into my telescope, foolishly neglecting to use both eyes and staring, as one should not, into the moon at full. I'm amazed; she's not. We're there. We're here. The one country has become the other. All is ground.

Grounded, out into eighty-five degrees Fahrenheit and then inside to a frosty sixty that sets her shivering at once, we call at the toilet in limbo, a DAMAS without a suffixed CUS, between gate and immigration, where she deposits a first

Columbian trickle. I'd like to patent whatever's kept things going this smoothly: no scenes, no incontinence, no demands for what's nearly four thousand miles ago. For one panicky moment I think she's decided she's back where she began, after a lavish circular trip. Then she asks, with bright candor, "Where?" and includes in a festive hand-sweep the terminal, the state, the nation. "Meriga!" she hoots, in frisky postscript to Vespucci; and, where I had expected bureaucratic obtuseness at the entry counter, a man in a pale-blue shirt decaled with his chore looks hard at her when she says her new word for the dozenth time, and sternly answers, "It sure is." We are through. Customs here is more wearing than in that other country, where, if you've nothing to declare, you follow the green signs, otherwise the red. But even this costive local apparatus spews us out and free after fifteen minutes. When we are met, Milk sees an ebullient woman with black waist-length hair (such hair a fetish with Milk since childhood), who confronts her with her first pair of polaroid sunglasses. "This is Pi." We all laugh. In my pocket I press the tube of sunscreen balm she has to wear. I remember the doll, forgotten. Five minutes later, with our introductions made, we follow a redcap's trolley into the burning air of the first day.

Consider. One can reach forty without having seen the Milky Way, without even noticing it when casually gaping at the night sky. Of course, conditions have to be right: no moon to speak of, a certain frosty scintillance going on, and eyes attuned, best shut for several minutes in private rehearsal while the big colander of light wheels overhead. Then look up at Cygnus and wait for the clustered star-stuff to bare its shape, a belt of crystalline shingles reaching high across the sky and down to the horizon: gigantic, variable, frail, no one's, everybody's, quite without design or mind, and dumb-foundingly lustrous.

All this I'd never seen, part of the trouble being you have to know what you're looking for. Unprimed, you register some silver haze that might be atmospherics or wisps of stratus cloud, not the real thing. But when you know, there it curves and you can get quite giddy just peering as your pulse thumps, Earth spins, this or that first-magnitude star blazes forth, then seems to quiet again, Sirius babbling white, Betelgeuse droning orange-red.

Unbelievably, the first time I saw it, I thought I'd never breathe again; but you do inhale again, of course you do, almost always. Aghast, I nonetheless felt a twinge of partnership. The thing was so inclusive; there was nothing of ours, down here, that wasn't in it, hadn't been, wouldn't be; yet it occupied only the most minor band of the heavens, there being a vast amount, even of that visible from about 40° North latitude, which was nowhere near it. Mind pulped, I went inside and with aching eyes pored over the page called Astronomical Geography in my atlas. There it was, pale blue on dark, sprawled narrow across two disks representing the northern and southern heavens, a fuzzy circlet crammed with dots like a photograph reproduced on newsprint. If I looked hard at the dots, they seemed to swarm, in both atlas Way and newsprint photo, yet stayed more or less within the lines. And it was as if, having never known it, I had found my address. It isn't everyone who locates himself by staring into vacancy, but I did, mumbling in the night air little fragments of relevant poetry, from Ammons to Zukofsky; even mouthing *Eureka!*, I have found it!, and *Mehercule!* rustily kept Latin for *Oh gosh!* Half a lifetime gone, and I'd only just had the wits to look a few seconds longer than usual, somewhat southward, letting my gaze meander down to Aquila, then Sagittarius, where, at its thickest, the Way seems to develop an elbow, which I now know is the galactic center. It was as if, having gawped my fill at Nelson's Column and Westminster Bridge, I heard myself asking, Have you ever noticed London? That kind of de-blinkering.

Although, as I later realized, it was one in the morning, I telephoned Chad to tell him; I had to give out my news. Awake and watching television of some sort, he humored me, clucked a little and said, of course he'd seen it, where had I been all my life? Good question. When a dealer in rare books can say that to you, you've certainly been idling. I had. But from that May morning I have been infatuated with the sight, angry when cloud or moon or the long winter hid it. High on my list of lifetime's joys, that luscious vertigo of looking up spills me over every time. I'm home, I say, eyeing it across the welkin. It's a chiffon filament of uncorrupted light: they can't damage it, they can't do it in, they can't do anything about it, it's eighty thousand light-years long and eight thousand wide, as many deep, and here I am, thirty thousand from its elbow, looking along it, into it, beyond it, with grand impunity. The cost of the view is just one's death, it's cheap at the price; or so I think until I cool off, and then am tempted to settle for a feebler, cheaper show, a poorer address. Yet luck one has: Earth might have been swathed in perpetual cloud, in which event there would be no galactic view at all, as from Venus. I thank not so much my stars as my planet for being in the clear.

Granted all the foregoing, what, I disembodiedly ask myself, am I to make of that chunk of the universe in the context of Milk herself? An old question, unanswered but repeatedly put, so much so that interrogative speculation has almost ousted any need for answer. Bold questions, yet somehow always askew or ill defined, come and go in my mind like sharks which cannot stop. As part of that, I ask, is she so extraordinary, so spoiled? Is there not, up there, a malformed, ill-functioning star to partner her, just as much as she a result of casual formation? This I ask, of course, while scorning the self-accusation that I'm just after a convenient vastness that dwarfs, minifies, not her only but Buchenwald, Hiroshima, pestilence, mayhem, flood, and madness. It's not a sedative ratio I'm after, no fear! Indeed, it's not hard to see my fumblings, the fumblings of us all, as trivial, a fluke. What, in my devious way, I want is a physics of the permissive, in other words a technique for accommodating the whole of nature, not just our ills, our doom, but our freaks, our flawed, not just our orthodox performers such as Vega and Sirius, intact in the mainflow of healthy stars, but also our Crab Nebulas, which are exploding stars, our peculiar or irregular galaxies, which are neither spiral nor elliptical but untidy, or galactic nebulae ragged as those in Cygnus and Crux, not to mention horseshoe-, dumbbell-, and owl-nebulae, morphic only through metaphor.

Groping? I certainly am. And finding, at length, instances of natural disorder, my head haunted, as ever, by the notion of harmony as the condition into which everything fits, the whole mass of life, nothing skipped. According to Leibniz, who intermittently knew everything, harmony's what God set up at the Creation between mind and matter, as if over the long haul mind mattered at all compared with hydrogen or methane. That mind is redundant I suspect, yet won't admit. At least Man's, at most God's. It exists only to discover and rediscover the absurd and to make plaints about it. I know only that harmony, convenient word, comes from the root *ar*, meaning: to fit. And, whether or not she's fitting, Milk is here, not to stay, but to figure, in the universe as in many lives, and I trouble myself, write down thoughts, about what's at hand. It would no doubt be more impressive to come out with a streamlined, flawless account of why things are so and not otherwise, but I can't, I can only go on thumbing a celestial lift from this or that star, one or another bit of terrestrial foul-up, a waltzing mouse here (some defect of the inner ear), a *gentian acaulis* there (refusing to flower in good soil). I've done it before, I'm doing it again, and no amount of societal good works is going to distract me for long from the appalling, outlandish macrocosm, although deep down I'm willing to see corrective education as teleology's true badge, what the mind is for. That said (and far from done with), I come back to cosmics, can't help it. That a universe, if it ever did, began; or if it ever will, ends; and, in all the unthinkable vastness of its predictable particulars, on-goes, erupting or cooling, expanding or shrinking, I find worthy of a lifetime's amazement, one of the most horrendous things being how named and mapped the skies are, pat and domesticated, thanks mainly to Arabs and Greeks. It isn't just physics up there in the Way, fixed patterns after random heavenly ballistics, but myth-opera and cozy anecdotes through which the dust and the fire and the gas, and heaven knows what savage span of the electromagnetic spectrum, all zoom congruously together. Perseus still "rescues" Andromeda, daughter of Cepheus and Cassiopeia, but Cepheus's a sentry box and Cassiopeia's a zigzag. No, I don't relish the narrative heaven I've inherited, or even see likenesses in the outlines named, but I sympathize with those ancients' wanting to humanize the star-stuff, carve commemorative initials on the astral bark. Just as logical, now, in any newly found constellation to see Albert Einstein rolling up his socks into one ball, or call a new star Bohr, Lenin, or Keats.

Unhappily, I am fetched low by other comparisons, in which my sense of awe equals my sense of pity, or of indignation, while my paltry awareness of physics just beats out my appetite for myth. And that's the only answer I have to those who chide me for so avid an interest in what's impersonal. Indeed, no, there's nothing societally useful in the sense of wonder, no matter how highly developed, unless the sense is harnessed and applied; but even that's not true on the plane of poetry, or dream, or vision, as distinct from the plane of the laboratory. Why, even observatories aren't useful, as first-aid stations are, or cancer research clinics. I can only say: It's there, I'm here, I'm in it, it's in me, and many other conscienceless assents. In the end, one's head includes what it can't keep out, and the gain, like the predicament, is as much metaphysical as not. At the universe briefly, I mean consciously, I'm trying to attend; yet what a speck one's total knowledge is, and what a trifle the Encyclopedia Ecumenica. Better, sometimes, to play than to complain. As it is, though, before waking her from a sleep already eleven hours long, I spend, am spending, a while on those English newspapers I bought (ignoring the French), tear sheets from a tribe famous in history. And yet after fifteen minutes I know of a French-born wife who, with her two young sons, has died from the fumes of a lawn-mower left running full blast in an upstairs room while her husband was on a business trip to Sweden. No suicide note. A former chief of British Intelligence, who vanished three years ago, has turned up in a locked attic in his own house: a seated skeleton in a dark-brown suit, a note in his pocket and, beside him, an empty bottle of unspecified size and a bin full of cigarette butts. A young nurse has been found dead in her nightclothes, lying between the speakers of her stereo record-player, dead from an overdose of some barbiturate; the last record she listened to being "Paranoid" played by a group called Black Sabbath. A young salesman, whose attentions a young café-manageress spurned, has pitched sulfuric acid at her in the public street. He later said he felt he was being slighted, laughed at, smirked at; and he felt hatred. The young woman now wears a thin, high plastic shield to keep her clothing away from the graft area on her chest; the fingers of one hand are slightly webbed, there is a cavity beneath her chin, and much of her epidermis resembles tissue paper. Further afield, a malcontent in Brunei has threatened to mail the heads of British officials to the U.N. Secretary General.

Grossness, grief, I've had enough.

As for us two, we seem to have got off lightly, have behaved with laudable decorum, abstaining—I especially—from power mowers, locked rooms, barbiturates, acids, and decapitations. My own mayhem stays rhetorical. And Milk, who in her time has sharpened the little finger of her left hand (the one she writes with) in a pencil-sharpener, filled her mouth with broken glass, and leaped through a picture-window like a thwarted Alice, is bizarrely sedate. It must come with the menses, must it not? Part of the mighty female web of the blood knot, which she neither asked for nor disdained, and not realizing it's aught but another of the jinks her captious body indulges in, maybe even thinking there's a big sore, inside, that will soon scab over, or half-believing in her twilight logic that she's cut herself on something while squatting, sliding, or in mid-wrestle. Trapped between thoughts of such a beauty going to waste, non-starting although biologically average, and a certain possessive satisfaction that the manchineel (sap and apples) of marriage will never claim her, I light a cheroot over my third mug of viscous tea, deciding to let her sleep it out, saving the novel-ties—chipmunks, cardinals, outsize robins, the telescope, the neighbors' pool—for later, *after* later, and especially those supplies in the basement: table-sized rectangles of fiber-board, rolls of mat black paper, pots of gorgeous poster color, brushes big and tiny, a rainbow of Scotch tape, the bulbs and screws, the chalk and the cardboard patterns. Perhaps she will never quite know what we've made, but it will at least amuse her, addicted as she is to the big and gaudy, and this mural will be eighty thousand light-years wide, whether or not we use all the materials. Hardest of all was finding orange-red bulbs for the likes of Betelgeuse; I didn't, so Milk and I will paint a few. Ocher enamel paint awaits. All I don't want is an orange daughter, descended from the one who, in the old days, soaked herself with what she worked in: not only paint, but cement (both house-builder's and aeromodeler's), plaster of Paris, and even varnish.

God help us. As a figure of speech (I was almost going to say); as a figure of minimal speech, rather, she works her hands a lot, so that talking is for her as manually busy as tennis or typing, though she signs, does not finger-spell. Yet her mouth moves all the time, meticulously enunciating words she's learned to *see*. Indeed, at times she over-communicates, doubling into faint enigma what singly would have got through. Never mind: Milk the carpenter-cum-handyman is going to have a field day with her big, dry paws whose heavily etched palms are those of a grandmother. On the southern wall of the basement, a large reproduction of Tintoretto's "Juno and the Infant Hercules" (depicting the legendary origin of the Milky Way) will oversee us, in its unscientific fashion, while we build our two-dimensional effigy, which will look something like an untidy airplane propeller, curving up and down on either side of Sagittarius, the hub. Another version, curling against an invisible celestial sphere, might be more accurate, but harder for Milk to make and enjoy.

Going into the bedroom, I audit her mild snore, remembering that you can make any amount of noise provided the floor is carpeted; what wakes her is vibration or, sometimes, light, but not today. It's almost one P.M., and I can see the faint speckle of wet on her brow, as if there were no air-conditioner at all. This head sweat she has in common with alcoholics, but then I think back to mid-ocean champagne, rebuke my own grandiosity, and go out to do some lethargic unpacking. Outside it is almost ninety degrees, humid among the thick green of trees. The house is almost a tree house, in fact, all you see through the picture-window to the balcony being a dried-up fir, several maples, and an apple tree already globed. It is above these that I aim the telescope at night, sometimes cursing the literal ramifications of summer

36

as they blot out this or that star, sometimes even a low Moon. I could sit out now on the long chair in shorts and panama, dip-reading in whatever's at hand, until she stirs, but if I did I might miss her eruption from that uncannily cool room into the tropical fug of the main house, with both panic and stupor in her gaze. In her day, out of gusto or rage, she has ripped doors off their hinges, whereas now, bigger, she's hardly a destroyer at all, more a respecter of edifices, iconoclast turned guardian. With a thumping, heavy-footed slither she will come, and no doubt with a hoot or two, but fast as a scout in enemy terrain, hunting the toilet, some toy or dress that's four thousand miles away. Until then, I settle for tea at the kitchen table, skimming an astronomy pocket book that tells what I already know, about our galaxy's being shaped like a double convex lens, thin at the edges and thicker toward the middle.

Closer at hand, like a critique of pure reason, the *rex begonia* is putting out baby leaves from its hairy, spider-leg stems; the refrigerator has developed a new, cylindrical-sounding buzz; and a new bird, whose call is a grackle's but more syncopated, is drowning out the groomed threne of two doves. A hundred miles away, Pi is getting her beauty sleep too, at her parents', after delivering us, the goods. No, they will have awakened her hours ago. I shall report by telephone tonight, report an event: a *levée*, a day of uncontaminated novelties, a juvenile field of the cloth of gold as Milk discovers cable TV, twelve channels in lurid cathode-color (the result of some flaw in the red gun, so that from time to time the screen has a cochineal flush, menopausal even, and consistently creates wrong color values), none of which ought to disquiet her. Lifelong she's exclaimed a jubilant "ho!" as things have gone wrong with appliances, weather, or hobbywork, a bit glad the macrocosm has its off days too. To an addict, but a repressed one such as she, about twenty-five movies a day means life is too short, one's screen is a needle's eye. With the rest of our day in mind, I roll the chances through my mind, then asterisk in the TV guide all movies having to do with water (2), the Arabian Nights (1), and aircraft (2). Westerns with Indians she adores, biting the dust with each and writhing in counterfeit agony all over the room. Of such films I lose count at seven or eight, noting that Westerns without Indians excite her less. It isn't going to rain, but she mustn't get too much sun, or too much TV, or too much—sleep. Then I realize I am three years out of date on how she lives, having had little news.

Uplifted by half-watching Van Heflin devegetate a golden idol of the Incas, I hear a click and a shuffle not from the jungle and she appears, a somnambulist Viking, her eyes almost concave with inertia, her legs flapping untidily, her face all of a sudden puce with heat. She bays, coughs, goes back into the bliss of air-conditioning. In that instant I shake free from my own heat trance and wonder if, whenever she emerges from whatever private state she's been in, it's a figure coming out of a ground—the hurt girl out of the universe—or vice versa, the hurt universe coming out of a reasonably intact specimen. Perhaps I'll never know, here in my eggshell of cranky pensiveness, as baffled as at ten years of age, when I first discovered sperm.

Confronted ten minutes later with a befitting tall glass of cold milk, she swigs a few mouthfuls, then points at the outsize blue teapot on its tile. So I put the kettle on, thanking my stars she has preferences; there were days, years, when she had none, would have eaten meat raw, eggs at hatching point, a brisling live. No, not quite: the one thing she has always refused is cheese, from whose evident stench she recoils in histrionic aversion. Her eyes devour the house, no doubt comparing and appraising, an enormous question full-blown in her befuddled head: *Is this where he's been all this time?* Not knowing what she's been told, even within the near-incommunicado enforced by her four-hundred-word vocabulary, she is in the unspeakable predicament of being unable to receive multiple notions, or qualifiers, so everything she's told is a simplistic absolute whose causes can only be dreamed at, not discursively spelled out. What little she has gathered she can only parrot, but not to the person it's about, because she can't manage the switch from third-person pronoun to second. For example: told that Santa Claus is away at the snow (in answer to one of her summer inquiries), she'll nod and be satisfied; but, meeting him in some store, she won't query his previous whereabouts to his face. In a sense, all his previous aspects will have vanished in that instant. Away from something, someone, she'll allude, all right; but, confronted, she loses abstraction in eyeball fact. So there's always this paradox to her: if you want to discuss your presence, you have to be absent; or rather, to have your presence discussed, you have to go away, which as often as not, I conclude, gets her citing absence above all. There is sometimes no way to win. Or even to control how you lose. In her shrunken cosmology, beings go, from time to time, into abeyance, she knows not where, though I've tried with maps and globes, guiding little metal planes across blue-tinted Atlantics, but she hasn't yet grasped that the model corresponds to something bigger; the plane might, but the ocean not. I intend to show her the full-size Way at night in order to explain the mural. No, *can't:* she'll be asleep, of course. I decide not to worry about that just now, otherwise I'll be in a bind as bad as the one at Christmas, years ago, when it wouldn't snow, and she ran outside, beseeching the sky with "Where?" and *"Hnow!,"* and in desperation, after she turned hysterical when she saw it snowing fast and thick in a TV movie set in Sun Valley, Idaho, I thought of flying her up to the Hebrides, where the weather was doing what it should. She still inhabits such a frail world of iron-clad connotations. Of chance, of the random, of the very element that fouled up her own brain chemistry, she knows nothing, and doesn't want to. Like an inquisitor that Christmas, she marshaled the evidence: snowy seasonal cards, illustrations in her reading primers, the white fungus on Santa's own chops, all the time yelling *"Hnow, hnow!"* to make the atmosphere be good. Could I have arranged for a ton of the stuff to be dumped over the yard, she would have objected that it still wasn't on the trees or the visible hills. In the end, after getting on for a day's upheaval, she accepted the helpless promise that it *would* snow in three sleeps (the longest time span she could then grasp), and the very next day it did, a bit, and she was pleased enough not to denounce the false prophecy. Out of such inabilities to explain to her came, I think, my own newer, stronger sense of surds in the ordinary world, which we claim to understand when we're only taking it for granted. A Saint Sebastian of a snow maiden, she feels chance's every shaft. Or felt. Dare I optimistically update her? I am going to find out.

At brunch, though, I am not. She polishes off eggs and ham, toast and jam, like a recanting starvationist, with four cups of tea, silently smiling in her perspiration, her nightdress damp, her hair an unharvested crop.

Calm, she seems even resigned: *things* happen, and this is another of them, so who is she to resist? She requests ice cream, gets it at once.

Aplomb of a different kind, unknown in her. I welcome it for what it is: an agreeable contemplativeness, with just a touch of the old effusive leer.

All her favorite goodies have been stockpiled here, against such a day as this. Suddenly she gets up from the table, vanishes into the bathroom, chuckles loud. It's the toilet that's got her, the first she's ever seen in the same room as the bath; in that other country they arrange things otherwise. Yonder the toilet is a monastic cell; here it's part of the open-plan apparatus of feeling easy. Whatever it is, Milk uses it for ten minutes behind a slammed door, occasionally giggling and uttering a few fluent-sounding comments in a tongue I think not even she knows: a parody of Romanian or Erse, maybe. I've heard it before. It's gibberish, beautifully intoned, a rehearsal for the day when she moves into suave society. Talking to herself, she seems to be alternating between irascible query and soothing reminder, the first high in pitch and swift, the second contralto, rather leisurely. As often, I feel shut out, unworded, aspirant to a secret society whose membership is one. And my truant brain switches to more morbid topics, runs riot thus: the parent will not know how the child will die, probably at any rate, and his ignorance grieves him as much as knowing would; the child will know how his parent dies, probably at any rate, and his knowing grieves him as much as ignorance would. In our case, however, only the former holds; the latter not, because she knows nothing of death, hers or mine, but only those chronic abeyances in limbo. She rarely asks for those who have not come back, perhaps having written them off as people who behave as comets do, reliably but very long-winded about it. May she fecklessly go on, smirking at people who've vanished, as if it's their own incompetence that's the cause.

Guessing how the dialogue with herself is going, I invent, as I almost always have, unless I've been happy to accept such bald exchanges as: "One more face," at which one pulls the expected grimace. "Yes," I answer, "I have just pulled one more face for Milk," knowing she must always be addressed in complete sentences. "More beebee," she might then add, and I fetch her the drink (her word for potables already being dispensed; otherwise, she names water, milk, or pop). A more complex effort will run: "In three sleeps Milk and Yah will go out in the car to see the airplanes," which she'll garble back as "Dree zleep, Milk and Yah ou i gar zee abbala." But there are thousands of things she will not understand, including my compensatory version of what she's presently staging in the bathroom:

"Down toboggan, whisper? Giraffe? When?
"No! Corn violet thumb antler, and hot soot.
"When then? Men in ten? Out.
"No. Grump simba antiquary. No. No.
"Loop? Dammerung, bondsman, Attaturk.
"Never. Slain lisp. Carl, school, shove-ark!
"No, n-o-o. Bangladesh. Card, howler, do. Water. Soap. Baba."

I have crept up behind her, watched her lip-read herself at a mirror, or, with her dolls arranged in chairs in front of her, play teacher, haranguing her pupils with a wealth of threatening tones I never knew she had, occasionally even picking one up to thrash it and thump it back into its chair only to ask it then some awful, elaborate, twenty-syllable question all over again, which it can't or won't answer, its being a doll no good excuse. Hence it gets another blistering onslaught before a second thrashing. A syllogism has gone wrong. Milk can't hear, but she tries to talk. The doll can't hear, but doesn't try. Milk's world is all interrogation: knowing she's forever asking and rarely knows an answer, she transposes her fix into almost voodoo terms, and one day that maltreated doll may scream out the sphinx's answer with its death rattle, and Milk will go forth equipped with her own version of the philosopher's stone, omnicompetent, vatic, sly, having got the dumb to speak. Now, however, she is still rehearsing:

"Goon Angkor, milt scabbard?
"No, dun apple Monday cinder.
"Brow, tongue, eye, ear" [she's at the mirror mouthing].
"Water, no!"

The sound stops, the shower starts, she screams with mirth, and I go in, find her naked, flashing the plastic curtain back and forth on its rings with one foot in the empty bath.

Cold showering sends her into an ecstasy. She soaps her blebby bosoms with self-conscious lewdness and puffs hard into the outfoaming rain from the nozzle. She comes from the land of sit-down baths, a slow sort of country where a shower is what comes from heaven. A bidet would drive her into impossible bliss, I think; she'd straddle or side-saddle it, getting gratifications no Parisienne ever knew.

Already she knows how hot the hot is, can gauge the two faucets, flip up the plug lever. She towels herself with insolent brio, as if she knows she is guest of honor and the only one of her kind. Time was when she'd spend half of every day in the bath, tootling and warbling in rapt hydrophilia, the water ice cold. I bring her shorts and blouse, careful not to hand her the swimsuit yet, because that bit of gear's the signal for instant action. In pink and white she looks eighteen, tall as I, less a hostage to fortune than an irresistible bribe.

Casing the house gluts her with mundane wonders. A refrigerator so big invites her to enter it, and she tries to, with mock naughtiness, withdrawing her leg from the low-level freezer compartment only when her hand extracts a can of carbonated beverage from the shelves higher up. In turn I have to demonstrate for her the blender, with a powdered lobster-bisque soup which with water blurs into a pale-pink cream; the switch for the garbage disposal, whose grinding she can't hear, though I caution her in mime not to stick her hand into this outsize pencil-sharpener; the synthetic moonlight of the neon tube inside the stove's control panel; all other light switches; the screen doors, which she finds an enormous joke, even trying to spit through the mesh; the indoor plastic garbage can with its fitted buff condom inside; the little broiler on the counter, whose red glow excites her to toast a slice of low-calorie bread, actually made from car-

43

rots, and munch the result as she prospects about. As kitchens go, it isn't a gadget paradise by a long way, yet each bit of machinery appeals to her as an object of contemplation, as if she's tuning in to the miracle of power, the dark nothing from which the universe was made. Her relish is enviable: new every morning, the world to her is genuine treasure which she eyes with murmuring awe. I join in the fun, especially when she makes a few dud phone calls, stabbing the dial at random, or so it seems until I detect more 2s and 0s than other digits, and I realize she's dialing the number of the house in the other country, not its telephone number but that in the address, announcing herself by name and saying repeated hellos.

Cryptic SOS? I doubt it, hope against it, ascribe it rather to happy bravura. She coos and exclaims her way through the other rooms on the same upper floor, grinning as she samples with her palm the one air-conditioner still running, and she caresses the pumped-out flow of cold, half-seeming to mold it as it comes. I nod at her pleasure, wondering if she thinks it synthesizes snow or popsicles. The vacuum cleaner, propped up in a closet, wins only a brief, bored stare, but I know she has registered at least one of the household gods as present and correct. No doubt she has a session with it in mind for later on; she loves to clean and polish. The white plastic Parsons tables, all got with green stamps, intrigue her: she strokes the surface, taps, listens, knowing at once the legs are hollow, thinking what might be inside: mice or alcohol? Into every drawer she goes foraging, claiming as a trophy a new pair of gleaming pliers, a see-through envelope of tap washers, three tapered purple candles wrapped in cellophane, and the unused UHF aerial loop the TV's never worn. Plus ten yards of neatly folded cord, which she unravels as if already in the labyrinth. The old thirty-dollar telescope, a three-inch reflector that wobbles on a wooden tripod and would deter anyone from star-gazing for life, she pats affably on its tube, as if detecting *its* handicap, and gently shoves until it keels over against the bed. (The big one, the eight-inch, I've locked away in a basement closet for later sorties when she's more adjusted, more scientifically attuned; some hope!) The books give her pause, but she goes by them with a minor heel-tap against the case's bottom, and skips out to the long balcony and its tubular chairs, which also get her listening, auscultating them, like some convict receiving messages in stir. Perhaps when she hears that a war is over, or that summer will end, she'll say so, glad to bear news.

After the balcony, she visits the bathroom again, teasing me by slicing air with my razor, which I decide to use fairly soon. Gaining permission with a rearward look as she squats before the screen, she flips the TV channel selector round and round, chortling at such visual plenty, almost all of it in color, and then turns the volume up loud, no doubt missing the special box which, back home, amplifies sound for her in headphones, nearly to the threshold of pain for those with normal hearing. Twenty minutes she sits there, rapt, sipping fizz from her can, then with politely imperious hand-wave calls for more. I flip the lid's tab and she begins to drink from the keyhole in the top without even looking. She might last all day like this, under ordinary circumstances, but fidgety curiosity sets her off again, as it must, and she rises for more touring, her eyes a touch glazed, her mouth mobile with accelerated murmur. I find her hearing aids, offer them, but she spurns them with a snarl and heads for the stairs down, there being no door.

Cooler at once by fifteen degrees, she smiles appreciation backward as I follow, and just about loses her footing, at which she lets out with a several-syllable curse. We swing open the downstairs screen door, check the box for mail (only a bill), then turn left into a room that's instant bliss for her, containing as it does an old refrigerator whose inside reeks of moss or mold, a defunct stove drooling a congealed brown, about twenty big cardboard boxes stacked ceiling high, the furnace capped with soot, and a heavy white homemade bar on which I've stacked relegated books, a model of a Lear jet whose door swings down (she pedantically closes it), a dead toaster that she gives a hard slam for reasons unknown, and an old-fashioned tall table lamp with a white, upturned bowl like a rain gauge. This she flicks expertly on and then stares onto the bulb's top by standing on a chair, an old trick that seems to recharge her mental batteries and cheer her up, whereas it would blind anyone else. Milk, though, devours light, always has, and she peers away into the heart of the hundred-watt filament as it tells her something intimate. I've read somewhere that it works for anyone, this bright on-slaught on the retina, accelerating mental processes no end for a short while, and I envision examination candidates raid-ing the absolute for three hours with a flashlight to either eye. Not for me, the almost photophobic one.

Undone by bulb-gazing, she straightens, scowls at the fur-nace and its Laocoon of pipes, dismounts from her chair, then flits into the basement toilet, a scruffy little cell but equipped with a washbasin, both of whose taps she cranks on, and a shower stall behind a dingy plastic drape. She gingerly starts the shower, yells as a house centipede an inch and a half long streaks down the wall and vanishes into a crack in the floor, yet without more ado downs her shorts and sits to pee. Dur-ing this, she notices through the open right-hand door of the toilet the stacks of supplies in the basement's other half and scoots to check it all out, hauling up her shorts as she goes. I hit the flush in my bourgeois way, follow her gladly. She marvels at so much to saw, scissor and fold, daub and arrange. "Wynd," I tell her (her all-purpose verb for manipulation): "we are going to wynd a big sky." A movie comes to mind in aberrant flash. She wants to start right now, but I've re-served this day for a swim at the neighbors' pool, who oddly enough have gone to Miami, leaving the key that unlocks the door in the redwood fence. *" 'Wim!"* she bellows when I inform her, and all thought of a big sky goes. She's up the stairs, unearthing her suit, a canary-yellow bikini. First, though, I smear her with sun-screen ointment and myself with routine oil. I change before she realizes what I'm doing (she'd love to watch, ogling) and casually stuff one of our airline bags with towels, pretzels, cold cans, a box of cigarillos, and (something atavistic) an inflatable foot-wide beach ball, a similar duck or swan, and a brand-new lifebelt for Milk to wear; she loves water, but cannot swim, not even as badly as I. We set out in straw hats, off her coming the cupric aroma of ointment mixed with her own of fresh-cut corn and minty perspiration. If only all the world smelled as good. The sun thumps us. The tall maples bulge. The birds heckle us the whole way as if we are cats. The world smells fine.

About thirty yards away, blue rocking water, sharkless and disinfected, awaits our jumps. Its very look soothes her from effusive jitteriness into grand patience, as with myself by the sea, at the Gulf of Mexico when I stand on an empty beach among stranded jellyfish, like experimental jet planes cut in plastic, and surrender to the lazy drum of water sliding down from Galveston. There are those who lack this quiet sea-fever or water-craving, and it's hard to explain to them. I end up mouthing Greek to myself: *thalassa, hudor,* in much the same mood as when I peer up at the Way. Lovers of the future yearn really for nature, whereas misoneists yearn for a pastoral idyll, a state that exists no more in time than, whatever my ostentations in these sentences, in space. Oh, I write in the present-past, confecting a spell of now inside a husk that's always too late. *Not long for this world,* runs a formula for someone moribund, meaning us all; but it fits language too, and each person's talk or writing even more. Compared with how old the universe is, language is a stop-press novelty. I sometimes think, in Milk's wake, how everything may in the long run dwindle to this: saying precisely how one feels about things, having one's say, then slow-motioning back into nature, the mind's few watts earthed, while the say stays behind, like a star named. Alkaid, for example, in the Big Dipper's handle, is Benetnasch to some. A brief ghost of someone called "Bennet Nash" hovers, spawned by connotation, among the perdurable chemistry of what isn't on the human scale at all.

Gooneybird in three feet of slop, she floats. Hurrah.

Unsteadily in her blue lifebelt, she starts to laugh, signing the water with expansive rings. "Yah?" she invites.

At bottom near her, I dunk my head, nose held, and emerge to see her doing the same. She comes up fast, airborne, jackknife in a bathing hat.

Uncouth grackles harsh-calling across the pool seem to chide. To hell with them.

Couple of squirrels chase along the redwood fence, doomed to quadrilateral boredom. Up into the trees they fling themselves, making debris fall into the pool.

As tame as wet paper, we float about together under the baking sun, Milk entranced, no doubt feeling jet lag, I at a contemplative halt.

Up goes the ball and lands without seeming to touch: air snubbing water through a thin skin of plastic.

Anti-climax I suppose I call it. Here she is, as if she's come thirty yards from the other country and could go to Hawaii in thirty more, just so long as water tided her over. Pun, I know, but over eight thousand miles earned. Not in blood, but lymph.

Cackling, Leda rapes the floating swan or duck, upends herself in shallow water, and I right her, wondering at her lightness. The bird, of course, has righted itself and can be relied on all over again.

Going over like a drogue towed, one cloud makes me shiver, her too; then we both warm up again, unconversing. An aquatic pact confines us to eyes, looks, a yard apart, a foot above the trembling water in which our limbs camber and trail.

Charitably or not, I think of all the manic sportspeople at this moment hitting balls into squares, holes, and nets: swatting them, clubbing them, toeing them, heading them, and I look at our own, floating free, unplayed with, random in a universe of its own, alone with one monumentally silent adolescent and a zonked adult who no longer has to talk, which he has sometimes done for a living, with always the frightful clack-echo from what I said on the previous occasion on the same subject.

An insignia for us comes to mind, culled from the star charts: where two stars are too close to be shown separately, a single disk with a line through it stands for both. Thus: Ø, a fisherman's float. Floundering to the edge, I draw it in wet on a dry patch while Milk cruises over to look, grins sarcastically as if I have to be indulged, gives me then a grown-up shove. Down I go, at the gulp, blinded by chlorine. When I clear my eyes, I see the splash has wiped us out, in symbol at least.

Used pearls, these eyes (I grumble) aren't what they used to be.

United we stand without even being able to converse. We never do say much.

Genially she points at the deep end, starts to paddle toward it, knowing what it is. Expecting me to follow. I don't. She shouts. She slams both arms against the surface, a banshee. I go, willing to drown, but by the time I'm there she's floated back to the other end, windmilling like a seed, and alive.

A small high-wing monoplane goes over, drifting as if to land. Seeing it, Milk whoops, waves, tells herself some anecdote, mouth close to the water for the echo effect. All I can do is helplessly eavesdrop, fitting the sounds to what words I can: band, banana, needle, Maori, sleigh. An old predicament. I miss her usual, all-invalidating "no," then it comes in an attenuated bray whose shading I construe as doubt, as if for once she almost agreed with herself, whereas two more degrees Fahrenheit, or one mile an hour more wind speed, or twenty extra calories to burn, might have made her affirm outright. Or just more command of the sound *s;* she was six when she first said "yes." Of her other negatives I long have known the one that commands all phenomena to a distance; the one that's elegiac, an aborted brainchild; the one that's rampant Hun, when her brain feels scalded and she wants folk to bubble and melt before her eyes. And other variants.

A "no" of Garbo dismissing the entire Ruritanian cavalry. A "no" of someone, grievously ill, almost giving in at the sight of another rainy dawn.

Guttural "no" powered by a small turbine that hates.

And noes that, as the saying has it, are beyond description, begotten by despair upon impossibility. These noes are absolutes from the gut, skull explosions which I haven't heard in years, having had little opportunity, but which doubtless still exist in all their miserable completeness. That smiling mien of the teenaged water baby belies her thunder, unheard for the past two days at any rate, and I'd do almost anything to preclude it, such as agreeing to forgo noes of my own, including the *no* to emotional blackmail attempted on me year after year through the hapless pawnship of an only child. And the *no* to increased blood pressure, to galloping pulse: I run a mile each day, round the basement, eighty laps, or round the baseball field, or jog the equivalent. An automaton for health.

Good old Milk, she is still in the hermetic reverie I left her in, chortling to her favorite element. Out of the pool she climbs on cue, with nauseated histrionic gasps. I know she must have peed. Down the ladder she comes, waved back in. A tiger prowls the water's edge, but we hiss it away. An eagle swoops low, but we rip its head off. The pool empties in a trice. An anaconda writhes up from the concrete. We climb out, board a low-flying air bus from Samarkand, get off at Thule, camp there the night in an outsize market bag, and spend the next day cramming tiny red spiders into the tube of an old telescope so as to barter it for lemon marmalade.

Gee, she'll do almost anything, always at her own disposal, a Curie, a Phaedra, an Amazon; a self-impediment, a victim, a slave; whom I revere-deplore, so far having failed to find or invent a philosophy that includes her, something that runs: "All things bright and handicapped, the good Lord made them all." A natural anthem everyone would learn in school and sing when the national flag is raised, the real enemy being not behind the Curtain but within the cell. What's the score, Adam? What's the human program? What's its point? Answer: there's no fool like a human fool, especially one with two legs, a daughter, and a dictionary, plus a compulsive habit of star-gazing (as if the answer were Out There, so many thousand light-years off-shore). I cannot believe that some vast Inconceivable, with foresight, oversees the All. The only message that keeps on coming through is light, radiation, and neutrinos. What happens when the speed of light is cubed?

Among scores, nay, hundreds of recurring wishful thoughts, all gently fanatical, there is above all one: let there one day soon come another bit of serendipity like that which yielded penicillin. Son of an Ayrshire farmer, Alexander Fleming, eventually working in the inoculation department of St. Mary's Hospital, London, was an untidy man apt to leave cultures exposed on his laboratory table. One day a spore of hyssop mold, the *penicillium notatum,* wafted in from Praed Street and landed on a dish of staphylococci. It remained only for a girl in Peoria to scrape a mold from a canteloupe melon, and the mass manufacture of pencillin could begin. Not a bad bedtime story for Milk, for whom I'd wish any such freak-of-circumstance discovery, one part of my mind saying: The answers lie all around us, the universe is complete, as time will prove. All very well, until another part of my mind says: It may be incomplete after all, some ills being incurable. A third part of my mind says its own unlucky thing, simply that a lack of oxygen made her the way she is: her defects indict no virus, no jumping of the track by RNA, but a merely mechanical mishap, like losing your thumb in the ejection chamber of a submachine gun. A baby suffocated from sleeping on its face might be a better analogy. Bad luck.

Cavorting at the pool's edge, she lets out one of her delirious high-pitched warbles, the terror of dogs, and then keeps it going in abstract celebration, a hydro-anthem or a utopian riff. A couple of neighborhood dogs respond with panicky crescendos, and then birds, chipmunks, even a squirrel, maybe acknowledging one of their own, more probably issuing an all-points warning against an alien in the vicinity. She toots on, hop-dancing to a private rhythm; the neighborhood soon sounds like a zoo. A hopping motion that marks time, her dance addresses itself to a dimension unavailable to most of us, in which perpetual motion is only an aspect of style. Dimly I think of the goose step, human version, frenetically accelerated, and of my own jogging trot; but no human movement quite matches this whirr of limbs while she aims her gaze at the zenith, as if some deity without portfolio were beating time for her. Mysteries she makes. Mysterious she began, mysterious she goes on, a cordial abstracted person from whom there must be much to learn, could we but tap it.

Gaily she hops closer, with a fistful of cubic red candies, like a piece of rhodochrosite, in hand. She has filched them from a high cupboard. Ah, she still raids with uncanny skill, she still caters to her oral compulsions with a kind of sucrose-radar; she knows where the stuff is, even before you've hidden it, and has never yet been caught in the act of helping herself. I look away into a vacant space, half-hoping to see her arrival in it, such is her unhearable speed. When I see her next, she's on her back under a colorful pool umbrella, sunglasses off, a large seashell cupped on each eye. I see a face with two blisters, looking at the sea as others listen for it. One day I'll try her out with amplified whale cries to see if she'll answer them. Where the shells came from, unless they happen to be part of her permanent equipment, I have no idea.

As I try to anticipate the old woman in her, a Milk of advanced age—like my mother, sitting for preference on a small-topped stool as if she were a medieval examination candidate, and speaking of the Wimbledon tennis players familiarly as Ken, Virginia, Evonne, while she nibbles a digestive biscuit—I see nothing of the kind, only fractional differences, a Milk unchanged, as when you see the Big Dipper from different latitudes or, more theoretically, after a hundred thousand years. I view her growing up, but not down, which perhaps means only that I can envision what I can expect to see, but not what, unless we manage to tamper with the aging process better than hitherto, I can't. I do, however, predict for her a permanent youthfulness of mind: at fourteen she's mentally a seven, I suppose, and how to pro-rate that, who knows? Maybe she'll feel twenty-one at forty, vernal in mid-career, something I feel myself, I,

Deulius, who never very young will never be very old. Unless . . .

Coming to a halt, I remind myself that this, the first of our two weeks, is ours alone, whereas the second will bring Pi back from her parental orbit, as well as callers of varying persuasions who aspire to meet my guest. A Hope Diamond of girlhood. The first week, centripetal, the second, centrifugal. For the first time I see the petal in the one, the fugue in the other. Milk's asleep, better thus than in some hyperactive trajectory based on burned-out nerves, with the vagus above all acting up. So I won't have to barbecue the local dogs on the lawn, wreck the TV with a catapult, sit on a homemade iceberg waiting for the mailman on a Sunday.

Cheered, I adjust the umbrella, set a towel over her legs to keep the ultra-violet at bay, then slither back into the pool as if into preservative brine. It's almost three P.M. At four I'll wake her for tea and muffins. Limping time now rests. Birds quit. The lull doesn't even feel the jet burrowing across, five miles above us, the silverfish with passengers.

Curious how words such as these function as retrievers, pulling the present of the writing act into the recent present of what was done. I am writing this sentence now, or nearly now; but when I write *we swam,* or *she danced,* I'm implying the habitual, which is tenseless since we go on swimming, or she goes on dancing, in my mind. These ephemera are forever, more or less. So what I'll end up with won't be quite like Stockhausen's composition "Out of the Seven Days," with himself locked up alone foodless in his house for a week, but in its way just as performative, planned to be unplanned, an experiment in tropism, growing toward the Galaxy together while we pick up the threads of each's being the other's child.

Crude oblongs of light arrive on her outflung arm, so I twist the umbrella. We spin so fast while circling the sun, which itself is headed toward Hercules, that I think the mass of all human movements only a fidget, a footnote to unlettered eons whose chances of having so-called intelligent life we sum up in some formula I can't remember. There is no formula for calculating the chances of eventual, wholly intelligent life in her, whose chemistry's as impersonal as the Way's itself. But when I reckon up how much more personality she has, compared with what I've nicknamed her after, I wonder at the superplus. No star can read, make puns, dial a channel on TV. She's a piece of the Sun with charm. Ten years old, at the bank, she studied the performances of everyone, on the next visit tried to deposit one of her baby teeth, recording it on a deposit slip in her own spiky hand, *Michla, 1 toth,* then handed both to a grave clerk, who stamped the slip and passed it back. The tooth he refunded to me as a bonus.

Unique, the trigonometry of that, making me swallow hard. Depositing her tooth was a spherical triangle whose angles added up to more than 180 degrees: a feat worthy of John Goodricke, deaf-mute astronomer who lived 1764–1785, not very long as lives went even then, yet long enough for him to decide that Algol, the so-called demon star, was periodically eclipsed by a dimmer partner that passed in front of it and cut out its light. A century later he was proved right. She's awake, talking again, in sounds that travel eerily over the pool from where, on her towel, she orates into the concrete with her mouth almost touching:

> "Un-banana, egg, witch.
> "Caramel, dreck, snood.
> "Ulan Bator, Bator.
> "Bugle-weiss. *Home. No.*"

I get her drift, I think. I would rather say anything to her than hear that. Oh, what a chubby vulva. Oh, for a beaker full of the warm south. Oh, so you'd like a ton of ox tongue in the shape of a whale?

Anything to shut out such desperate-sounding code that's mostly no more phonemic than the chaffering flick-flack of quasars, receivable by many, thought by none: alpha zigs next to omega zags. I take her to the house I call home.

Carpentry's one thing, like origami or painting unmimetic if needs be. Just saw and chisel away, making nothing at all; fold paper into abstract shapes or whiten four walls and a ceiling, even a plywood panel. But explaining the Milky Way, justifying its facsimile, to her, is nothing like. No use prating away about how Sir William Herschel, prince of observers, claimed 116,000 stars passed in review across his telescopic field of vision in fifteen minutes. Nor invoking Rifts, Coal Sacks, nebulae and star-clouds, or mankind's lazy switch from an Earth-centered to a Sun-centered view, from that to dim intuitions that Sagittarius is more or less the center of just one spiral galaxy among a million or more which have no central reference point and of which the nearest is 850,000 light-years away. Stellar nuclear furnaces, transforming hydrogen non-stop into helium, are nothing to her, and the Way's infinite profusion of dazzling suns is hardly more. Useless even to call on ancient metaphors that make the Way a long bandage wrapped around the skies (partial as she is to wound-dressings, even to the point of prurient interest); or the road to the palace of heaven, trodden by departed souls whose campfires mark their progress; or as a belt of corn grains, Winter Street, Silver Street, Watling Street, Asgard's Bridge, the path of white ashes, the path of Noah's Ark, the path of chopped-straw carriers. William Langland called it Walsyngham Way; the French peasantry the Road of Saint Jacques of "Compostella," a word invented by Bishop Theodomir, who

56

was guided by a star in 835 to the bones of Saint James composted in a field; and the Polynesians call it the Long Blue Cloud-eating Shark. All of little use. I'd just as well bake her a raisin cake to demonstrate how the galaxies, like the raisins in the cake, are all moving away from one another.

Curdled or flaky, the Way's thick white is beyond her ken as fact or metaphor. Shown it, if she can stay awake so late, she'll make a moue at it and then wonder why our model-to-be isn't on the ceiling, above us. One word she does know, though, and often use: *lots,* which coupled with such others of her favorites as *small* and *moon* might work the trick. "Lots and lots of small moons, very long, and up high, over" (word she adores) "o-ver the dark: Milky Way!" Such the theory. Now follows the actual first conversation as she rubs her eyes. I envy the ease with which Geoffrey Chaucer was able to explain the astrolabe to Lewis, his son. I try: "Lots and lots of small moons . . ." "Milk?" she queries. "Beebee?" (She is proposing to drink it.) Then she giggles at the notion of numerous Moons, when all along she'd thought there was one only. She even grasps the distance, saying, "Long way," which brings to her mind a thought I gave her about the size of the ocean. "Downstairs, one sleep," I tell her, "Yah and Milk will wynd Milk's Way, with lots and lots of small lamps: white, blue, yellow, red." "Green?" she chides, so I begin racking my brain for stars truly green. Now, Zuben Es Chamali, Libra's northern claw, is pale emerald, not in the Way at all, even though part of her so-called sun sign. Try again. There are faint greens in the Jewel Box in Crux. Sometimes, as Tennyson says, Sirius "bickers into red and emerald." And giant Antares, partly red, is partly green as well. "Yes," I announce, "green moons as well," knowing she will hold me to it once we begin the work. She might also want to color the stars according to her own ideas, and to hell with patient astronomers. It's Milk's Way, after all; and had the hydrogen atom borne a minute charge, with electron and neutron not quite canceling each other out, whole regions of primeval hydrogen in the universe would never have condensed into stars. Why they are equal we do not know, but if they weren't there'd be no galaxies, stars, planets, no Milk, no me. A narrow squeak, life has had, in a universe designed but not guaranteed to breed life, natural selection being in the long run a business of editing, not authorship. Why, Milk and I, ourselves made of star-stuff, are just a star's way of knowing about stars. We're entitled to our vagaries, she especially, whose narrow squeak goes on, in chemistry at least. So why quibble about a few tints?

Upstaging Arthur Rimbaud (who wrote: "A black, E white, I red, V green, O blue") as well as the *Harvard Star Catalogue,* which says: "O white, B blue-white, A blue, F yellow, G red," I write, as she might prefer, O stars crocus yellow, B stars pale rose, A stars garnet, F stars ashy lilac, G stars smalt blue. Two chromatic rebels, we write with birds' beaks, running toy trains powered by our brains. So long as she doesn't fret, she can play fast and loose with the Galaxy, convert the Sun into an optical binary of purple and maroon, give Earth itself a counter-spin just to wake everybody up.

Getting there, slowly, I'm amazed to say. A datum step, like the longitude of the star Regulus in Leo.

Going on with confidence, like an eighteenth-century eccentric building a folly.

Chances are she'll lose interest after four or five constellations. After all, dots don't have names. Then we'll be restricted to swimming, TV, and games of mad pursuit up and down the stairs. If only there were talk above and beyond the minimal, even a chance to share with her the vast amount about the stars there is to know, the surfeit about the surfeit, the chemistry, the myths, the sheer unmitigated guessing about Cygnus X-1 as a possible black hole. But no, I talk of necessity to myself, address all of my mime to her, chatter in, gesture out, as if we both were tongue-tied mummers with no ideas but in things, no things except in movement, no movement that's not one of energy's illusions, none of energy's illusions that isn't in the beginning an idea. Reminded how the heavens wheel, or seem to, only because Earth does, I let my head spin, still though it sits. I would really like to talk to her, as to a girl indeed fourteen, about disasters not in space but in adult and infant lives; discuss the art of swimming, the use of deodorant sprays, the caliber of store-bought apple pie.

Unerring, she slaps black paint on the lower panel of fiberboard while I do the upper one. Flop-suck go the big brushes against the sounds of our breathing. Her panel is the northern Way, mine the southern. Thank goodness the basement wall is wide enough, easily forty feet. Our mural's background looks like an enormous door to a non-existent barn. Spilled paint from her generous sweeps goes squittering on the newspapers I've positioned underfoot, marring ephemera with a darkness we're going to load with stars. She seems to understand. Shown my big sketch of the whole project, she grinned, lovingly uttered the word "black," and reached for her brush. All we have to do now is let it dry. Half an hour. Except that the floury-linseed aroma of the paint will be with us a day at least.

Uniform mat black soon absorbs both kinds of light, summer's natural and the artificial from four different lamps, without giving it back. It's really as if we have created space, a Stygian blotter of the far wall. "Pretty," she trills, one of her best-enunciated words. I concur while she tests the surface and indignantly holds up smeared thumbs.

Canis Minor, I say to myself, we're doing the Little Dog first. See if it laughs to see such fun. The last thing it resembles is a dog. I'll ask her when I draw it in chalk, before drilling the first hole, for Procyon's yellow bulb, which soon will flash along with, oh, fifty others, while stars of lesser clout will just be studs cut off a wooden dowel, painted, and stuck on. While waiting, we paint meter-long rods of half-inch boxwood, blue-white for the hottest stars, white for those with dominant hydrogen, yellow for metallic ones, orange and red for so-called cool ones ranging from 7,500 to 5,500 degrees. With a fine saw we slice off small lengths, then paint the tops to match the sides. I even, for double stars, have rods of smaller heft. Dabbing away at several dozen stubs of stars in different cigar boxes on the table, she seems engrossed, and I have a chance to sort the stack of shirtboard templates in which I've cut holes through which to mark the stars' positions on the black, all that remains being to chalk in the lines between, later to be gone over with a felt-tip marker. Now she sets the lesser stars to dry while I return to the Little Dog, one of Ptolemy's old groupings, the junior of Orion's brace of hounds, not much to it really: a yellow-bulb Procyon eleven light-years off, plus a white-stud white-hot Gomeisa, almost twenty times as far.

Galaxy calls. Moving from left to right, north to south, we thumbtack pre-cut pieces of shirtboard to the black, their inner edges tracing the Way's contours as it shrinks, bulges, even splits. I must, during the preparation phase, have used up a three-year accumulation, saved from the laundry as it came back weekly, not with this in mind at all, but for writing notes on, protecting small manuscripts in the mails, wedging into gaps around the air-conditioners, leaving messages for garbage men and friends. We soon have a mural patched dun gray or off-white, just a little like one of those composite pictures of Mars made with a hundred overlapping photographs transmitted back in series. But what's black and in the middle, roaming across the wall, is the Way itself, secret in black, as if unborn, still in Juno's breasts.

60

Can in hand, she sprays silver at the space between the shirtboards, making even, careful motions back and forth, as instructed. An inch a minute, the Way shows up, as on a totally clear night, here an estuary, there a curling promontory; here a piece that might be the Wash, that big bite out of Cambridgeshire, there an isthmus stolen from Central America. How geographical it looks, how unheavenly, a vast single spiral of Jutlands, Manhattans, and Britains, now frail, now burly, sinuous or muscle-bound, a bracelet of stuff upflung.

Comes the unveiling: we peel away the silver-splashed cardboard, rectangle after rectangle, and the Way shines forth untrammeled while I absently collect up thumbtacks, check the floor for them (our feet being bare as often as not), and dispossess her of the spray can, with which she might otherwise coat us both. A lovely sight, as if some giant snail had tracked across the wall, first going straight, then down, doubling back on itself to create the rift in Cygnus, then soaring slow to the ceiling before lapsing down to Canis Major, where I've arbitrarily chopped off to begin again, at the other side, with its junior sibling. She has, however, sprayed silver beyond the galaxy, beyond the masks, making satellite galaxies where none can be unless obscured by dust, as well as a few clusters far out in impenetrable space. For all I know, she may be right, prescient, but all the same I black them out, having gained her consent, and feeling a twinge of de-creation as the Amerigo Clouds, say, or the Columbus Clusters vanish never to shine again, and the heavens come to heel. The pungency of the silver keeps her wrinkling her nose, but the full sprawl of the Way has won her quite. Not that she's ever, as far as I know, seen the original. *Time out of mind,* I tell myself: that's what we've just made. Shining fit to beat the band. Yet that's not the half of it. Now for the dramatis personae, after some fluid refreshment, which I fetch from upstairs: two condensation-speckled cold cans that slip and glide against the palm.

Using the template made for Canis Minor, I mark the sites of Procyon and Gomeisa (at eight and two o'clock respectively) with a dab of pencil, then power-drill the hole. It would have been easier to do the carpentry, such as it is, with the whole mural horizontal; perhaps not. As things stand, it swings out into the room on sturdy hinges, so it's not hard to fit the bulb-holders or the wiring. From now on, we'll drill a dozen at a time; this is just the demonstration star, proving the technique is just the same as that for Christmas trees. I chalk in the short line connecting the two stars, then fit the yellow bulb, glue on the white stud. A moment later, as much to have fun as to test, I plug in and Procyon does its stuff, blooming saffron just outside a spur of the Way, amid the glare of downstairs. Out go the lights. The star beams. Milk claps, skips in delight. I unplug, swing the mural back flush with the wall, and point at what we've got, asking her in the long-standing formula of outflung fingers, histrionically raised brows: "What? What is it?" I draw it on a handy piece of shirtboard: a stick with a big star at one end, a smaller at the other. "Lamp," she says, getting the hang of it. To her, it's a flashlight, "a small lamp," and not a little dog. I look forward to her next analogies, especially because the constellations only rarely look like what they're called. In fact, the Greeks as often as not were merely commemorating, not likening. Henceforth, Canis Minor is a light to steer by when getting to Monoceros, the supposed unicorn next door. It has two nebulae, but not much else.

Unstable stuff, these stars: they don't figure in her view of the Way at all, and even less as what they are to me, who spurn the Greek alphabetism of astronomers and relish names: Procyon, *the foremost dog,* coming at us two miles a second; Gomeisa, *the watery-eyed,* next to those perfunc-

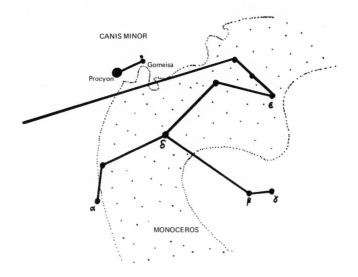

63

torily called ξ, θ, o, and π, but once grouped by the Chinese into Shwuy Wei, A Place of Water, being so near the river of the Galaxy.

Addressing Milk, I try on for size, just to give her a taste of the luxury she's denied, *der Kleine Hund, le Petit Chien, il Cane Minore, Catellus,* Puppy, mouthing as unexaggeratedly as I can. And then I roll-call to myself the other names of Procyon: Antecanis, Al Shāmiyyah, Algomela, Kak-shishka, Singe Hanuant, Nan Ho, Vena; then of Gomeisa: Al Gamus, Al Murzim, Gomelza, not having the heart to perplex her with tales of the Hunter Orion's little dog, or the faithful dog Mera, or the hounds of Actaeon. Hard as I ponder such estimable tales, I can foresee no chance of telling her, even in dumbshow, about Orion's vanity punished by the gods. *Gods?* No more does she have that notion (how lucky she) than that of Mera's master's undiscovered murdered body, or that of why Diana should resent Actaeon's seeing her in the buff. A few switches—Orion, Mera, and Actaeon's hound installed in the heavens—she might find amusing, but the plot, the concordant dovetailed incidents, the cumulative interstices, are quite beyond my power to say. Try it anyway. SCORPION KILLS MALE SUPERMODEL AND DOG-LOVER. DOG FINDS MASTER'S CORPSE, DAUGHTER HANGS SELF. VOYEUR TURNED STAG SLAIN BY OWN DOG PACK. It won't do at all. One day I'll try again, when the right narrative part of the Way comes to hand. We'll act it out together, and I'll be tale-telling to keep yet another Scheherazade, though mighty different, from another death among these Arabian-titled stars. Of the same myths' silence to the stars themselves, as of the stars' near-silence to men, I'll say less than little, just now having no stomach for the tacit. Like Don Quixote, having unsuccessfully tried to provoke the lion in its cage, I copyright the non-event, just in case. It might come in, like the lion, it just might.

Used up an hour, that did, but no more. Not bad going for two amateurs. We now have a little dog with a flashlight. There's nothing for it except to sally across the edge of the Way into the middle, where Monoceros sits, a different kind of problem. How much the outlines vary: my own attempt, as exact as I can make it, delivers a stick glider, left wing poking a strut forward, right wing poking one back, whereas another version shows the profile of a sitting, sharp-nosed dog. Egging me on with mellow war-whoops, Milk disappears into the basement toilet and returns at such speed the flush develops full hydraulic force only after she's left. Stabbing her hand at the background, at the silver splash of the Galaxy, she conjures forth form. "More," she sighs. Again I pencil through the holes in the shirtboard, connect them up with chalk, am glad I chose the sharp-nosed dog. Then she seems to spot something familiar. I ask what, but can't at first decipher her runic vowels. She does a three-step dance of celebration: a hop, a double stamp, a pirouette, all five feet of her, then yells, as only she can, peering at me from under the visor of her hand. "Wuff." Is she impersonating the sharp-nosed dog? I ask. No, she is not. That would have been "dog-wuff." Glory be, she means *wolf.* Yet, as I again look at the outline, I see only a bird, at rest, one leg thrust far forward. So let it be wolf, I am not the master of the bestiary here. We have just had a golden moment. She has to make sure the blockhead has understood. She does. He finally has. Now she demands lamps, little knowing that Monoceros, our second step on the Galactic great white way, has no notable stars, just some that have been impersonally dubbed Alpha, Beta, Gamma, and so on, *Monocerotis,* as the Latin genitive has it. She doesn't give a damn about the myth either, the Ur-horse with the long forehead horn, upon which it lands after leaping from great heights when pursued, and which breaks its fall. "Wynd," she commands, so *wynd* I do, but not what she expects. I'm going to light up something other than those mediocre stars.

Cut from telescope catalogues that arrive in the mail, three-inch-wide photographs of nebulae get her purring, glued as they are over the bulb-holders bought in dozens by my landlord, Frank Etna, who a year ago picked up half a ton of stuff, cheap, on one of his forays into the city. Lucky the paper's thin enough to let the light come through. I show her, in turn, each photonic button: Hubble's Variable Nebula, like a flying saucer, half in shadow, sleek in black and white; then the Cone Nebula, a stuccoed pizza minus a thirty-degree slice and studded with garish infant stars, again in black and white; and third, the famed Rosette, a scarlet convolvulus of stellar frog spawn spotted white, which pleases her no end. "Up," she tells me, meaning: Drill the holes and screw them into holders fast. I do while she holds each nebula close to her eyes, peering through it at the basement sunlight and attempting a little unselfconscious jig on the matting floor. Heaven knows what she sees through these trumped-up crystals out of the light-years. I'm too busy with the power tool. In go the holders, touched with glue, then the nebulae. We light up right away, even before I have a chance to attach the studs denoting common-or-garden stars such as numbers 13 and 15, between which Hubble's Variable goes about its own peculiar business. The Rosette glows like a hot coal and the other two look just a bit wan and stark. She "Aahs" with glee, points across the Galaxy at the dark ground where Orion is going to be, and asks for more. First, though, I stand back to survey: in the black, Procyon burning margarine yellow, a bit lost-looking, and, camped across the silver, the linear apparatus of Monoceros, leaking light in two places, a tigerish hot eye in a third. More to come? More than she's dreamed; far beyond prosaic likeness to flashlight or antenna, she'll see more and more bizarre nebulae, the infra-structure of the

66

broadest magnesium ribbon ever to cross the sky.

Going out, with a clash of the screen door, she hauls up orange-yellow day lilies, a dozen or so, comes in demanding a vase, which I fetch, in my other hand a similar-colored popsicle, upon which she falls a-thirsting. Across the basement I see little glows coming from the board swung flush again, herself staring into them one by one as if mesmerized, with her body centered on the slow pulse of suck-suck-suck, an orally fixated gazer. I know I am doing something right. The mailman goes past again, I can't imagine why. She comes to see what I'm watching, chases a chipmunk, loses, pretends to swim across the unmown grass, seizes a fallen premature apple, green and wasp-drilled, mimes at me for permission. Not getting it, she whangs apple high up into the tree, whence it falls to start all over again on its rounds. As we on ours, ready to install Orion with all its wonders just off the furry brink of the Way. A sudden thought comes late, for which I blame myself: paint the Way luminous for an extra dollar or two, and I resolve to buy a can of the right paint, apply it while she sleeps.

Consulting again my handy folder of outlines, in which the Way is pale blue, the stars are dried blobs of poster color, I rejoice at Orion, our first biggie, crammed with white and blue brilliants, one red one, and, sprawling all over the black hinterland, legs and arms and knees, with all the big stars named. This is the region of Uru-anna, the Light of Heaven, otherwise known as Jugula, Algebra, Giant (error for Al Jauzah, old Arabic for a black sheep with a white spot on it); region of the Golden Nuts. Triorchous superman indeed! Yet to tell her of this, or of Orion's club, sword, and shield amidst what Flammarion, the French astronomer, called the California of the sky, I may have to wait another twenty years, and more. Here blaze, I'd love to tell her, the Armpit of the Central One (Betelgeuse); the Female Warrior (Bellatrix);

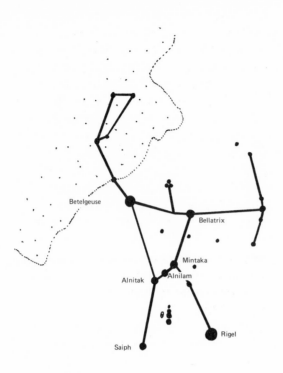

Betelgeuse

Bellatrix

Mintaka

Alnitak Alnilam

Saiph θ

Rigel

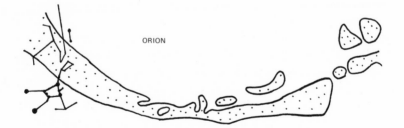

ORION

Peixie Boy, just a dark spot; Rigel the Foot, Saiph the Sword, Alnitak and Alnilam and Mintaka, the girdle and the belt of pearls and the belt. Yet, to her, talk of a blind giant whose sight returned as he faced the rising sun is fraught with semantic whiplash; deaf, she doesn't grasp what blindness is, any more than, barely verbal, she'd relish extra names. All the same, some things we can manage, with clippings from cards and catalogues. It is just going to have to be enough for *me* to know that sailors used to dread this constellation, six hundred light-years distant, receding from us at almost eleven miles a second, source—just after her mid-October birthday—of the Orionid meteor showers, fireworks on her behalf. For orange-red Betelgeuse, at times called the Roarer and 215 million miles across, a big orange-red bulb, and for all the others blue or white: seven in all, which I set in place, standard fashion, while she counts them with gracious correctness, summing up thus: "one red, zix why," which covers it pretty well. For the star called *theta,* really four in trapezium form, but veiled in a nebulosity several light-years wide, I have a quartet of narrow bulbs brushed white and all mounted together in one holder. As fast as I can, and not without some trembling of hands, I install the main orbs, test them, which is when she utters the one word "Blackpool," no celestial coal sack but the British coast resort famous for its Illuminations Week, as if not just she but Arthur Rimbaud too were in temporary residence each year. I've even heard it pronounced as going to the Eliminations.

Giant? I wonder as Orion's outline forms, connected up point-by-point like a child's puzzle. I see the club upheld, the lion skin brandished (or the shield if shield it be) at arm's length, while the knees come close together without unheroically knocking. At once, however, she sees her own thing, queen of Rorschach that she is, and shows me through motion, in fact serving at tennis with elongated, stealthy stretch, once, twice, thirty love, then smash. I can see it, as might a cubist at Wimbledon: the white bulbs of the balls, two on the ground, others whizzing through space or frozen fast, the racket swung back high into the Way behind the colossal ruddy ball of Betelgeuse, the other arm somewhat thrown forward as if the gathering action's already spent itself while the knees inflex to a fulcrum pivot. All actions in one view pre-empt my telling her this is Orion, Men's Singles Champion, the White Tiger of the frost-bitten toe. Instead, as she mock-serves to the four-inch manikin in lights, I ready our two nebulae, near-clichés of astronomical coffee-table books: the Horsehead and the Great, both in color, the one magenta and rose madder with spike-haloed stars adjoining a sharply distinct head of a seahorse, brownish purple as it juts up into an ultra-distant dawn, the other, unimaginably vast whirlpool of gas, a nacreous pink-white-cobalt speed-stunted firebird flaming northwestward, small beak and head for such enormous wing area. Total mysteries, these get her gazing hard and long as if at the faces of absent playmates. "Horse" and "bird," she says quietly to herself, peering through them, one to each eye, then calling for light. The full complement of Orion, tennis ace with exotic belly badges, blurts gloriously out, and she pats the whole thing as if saying goodbye, a bit like Sir William Herschel on January 19, 1811, when he laid his glass aside forever, looking last on the Great Nebula, as on it he had chosen to look first in 1774. Her entranced pout resembles the fish-mouth *theta* θ within the nebula itself, and I remember how Thomas De Quincey extolled it in an essay, how Galileo never even mentioned it, how a million globes, each equal in diameter to Earth's orbit round the Sun, would not equal the Great Nebula's extent.

Unstrung by that grid of fire, its threads of nebulosity older than mankind itself, and by the beauty of watching her watch whatever she sees (bird, horse, tennis, her giant self), I walk stiffly upstairs, unflip a can of beer, light a cigarillo, hear her following, give her a swig, mention food, hand her a chicken leg glazed with cold, help myself to another, prepare to go back downstairs. She wants to do another, like Goethe asking for more light. "More ly, Yah, pliz." Who of any god-like pretensions could refuse?

Gobbling chicken-salad sandwiches made from a canned paste (repetitious menu of my own lazy devising), we have little to say, are no doubt full of Galactic or prosaic thoughts. Two evening doves toot away, *the* two. The Pekinese next door yaps for twenty minutes at its own shadow, as usual. Cooling down, the house fidgets. Big swaths of cumulus arrive. The TV shuffles images like enameled playing cards. With a dish of butter-pecan ice cream, she settles down to watch a woman who talks to children with a macaw on her shoulder. Idly I scan a pocket book of astronomy, relishing white-lined constellations on dark blue as if they were coats of arms, souvenirs of the big system that abides in the basement. Trying to think of something intimate to do, something to remember each other by, I come up with nothing, realize how impersonal life with her can be. I end up being grateful she's almost at peace, not at risk or under the weather, less a person than a beguiling process, which only I and a few others are privileged to watch, instruct us as it may.

Ghastly thoughts have come and gone, of decompression and air crash, of her running riot through a customs shed, of a twelve-hour scream. Do I bathe her, I wonder, or she herself? I soon learn how out of date I am, banished from the bathroom with a loud "bye-bye." Now she begins to sing one of her blurred arias, not in English, and I marvel at the mellow agility of a voice whose owner hardly knows its power except through vibration. No guess plumbs her theme, and I soon give up trying to decipher the sounds, though not before inferring for my own satisfaction a lyric that goes: "raisin tree, shaved lung, dendrite and suet boas," as much sense as usual. Balked, my mind slips away to raucous newborn stars in Orion's sword or the Cone in Monoceros, those maternity wards of Creation. Can it be that no star fails, is unsuccessful? All stars achieve an adequate stardom, just as all galaxies achieve some kind of iridescence. And that includes even those stars that never quite fit the mainstream pattern, even those galaxies that never make it all the way along the normative line from irregular to spiral to elliptical (although the theory concerning that is changing; one type of galaxy's no older than another, I have read somewhere). To an extent, as now, taking her own bath, she runs her own show, but is never as self-sustaining as any of those clumps of gas and fire we pinpoint in the basement.

A bathroom awash has to be mopped up. She observes, hand on pink-chiffon-vested hip, while I unroll yards of paper toweling on the pools. It has snowed talc in here as well. Half her bottle of toilet water has gone. Her watch has stopped. Immersed? Unwound, perhaps. She wants action, so I begin to jog in place right there in the bathroom, and she laughingly joins in, as if finding a corporeal metaphor for prolonged infancy. Out of puff about fifteen minutes later, we're fit only for ginger ale in lidded steins, dwindling into inertia while the *agōn* of a framed cop frames itself in the wronged colors of Channel 10. The day runs down, but the light still has that above-the-ocean cleansedness of space on top of space. Waxing fanciful, I curb myself with minor chores: take my pulse, eighty and coming down; hers, sixty and steady, as befits a girl with the metabolism of a cheetah and all the short-dash prizes at the school sports. I watch her eyelids begin to close me out, then flutter up again as she hauls a leg aboard and lies full length on the couch. Two sips of warm milk are all she has energy for before removing herself, unbidden, heavy-footed, and without so much as a signal, to bed. Time was when two hours of soothing cajolery wouldn't get her to sleep, when midnight stimulated her to ask for breakfast or propose a dawn patrol with dog, even a bout of carpentry or the making of bread. Now she does this easy glide into depth. Who will ever know if she dreams, or what? She lacks the concept; but, clearly, phantoms have assignations with her at her most private. Sleep makes her a full member of the race, even if her daytime self still peers affably at ceiling corners and smiles back at jocose presences therein. I know nothing of them, hope against hope they are not ghouls, and keep telling myself she is not Hegel, after all, has no Beatles albums, cannot read *Little Women*, and knows next to nothing of her birthday, weight, height, home address, progress at school, or her prospects. Exceptional all round the clock, she fails only in the light. Waiting for the phone to ring, then wondering if it was I to phone, I think of how the Way too, formating invisibly overhead, comes into its own in the dark.

"Can you cope?" asks Pi, around midnight, when I call. I tell her I'm still waiting for something to go wrong, that we've built Orion, will do Gemini tomorrow. "She was like a gazelle all day," I report. Even as I talk, I hear the air-conditioner in Milk's room, and smile as if it's keeping her alive.

"Good. Have you written to her mother?" I haven't, I will, on an index card. "Don't stay up all night at the telescope. You'll have to get up before she does." I promise to set the alarm. A couple of tension-shedding puns later, I say good night, call Chad, who'll stroll over in a few days' time with his own daughter, six years old. Then out onto the balcony to appraise the chances of clear viewing. The bit of cloud will not impede, so I prepare, lug out the scope, plug in the drive to see the red bulb light up, unplug it, and look straight up at Cygnus, where the black rift in the Way begins. I am looking at the real thing. It has no competitors, not locally at any rate. There are so few days left, even after so few gone.

73

Will she want to take the Way with her? Not want to leave it? Or will she become bored with the whole thing tomorrow? Again and again I lift my head to stare at the long fume across the sky, realizing it isn't the silence of those vast spaces that bothers me, it's their longevity. After she and I burn out, there will never be anything again, a never of nevers, never a reprieve reconnaissance in say a million years, just to see how the world is faring. You happen once and then are extinguished, with no more communication. Not even a hiccup, a yawn, a blink. Minus-ness of oneself, and of a few others, that's what chills the heart.

Gruesome beyond belief, I study Deneb.

Couching things thus, in the present tense, amounts to showing that what one shows no longer exists, whereas in the past tense one gives the reader no chance at all of making up his own mind. So the present, for me, is ambiguous, as if defying him/her to deny that what he/she reads about has already vanished, whatever the tense pretends. I almost have the feeling that these things were done before they came into being, already lived through but trying to live again through some simulacrum of the immediate. Essentially there is no tense appropriate to time: the past is never done with, the present is a myth, the future cannot have any identity and still be referred to by that name. I therefore dub this mode the ongoing hypothetical, reporting too late, hypothesizing too soon, leaning into the future as if against a wall that isn't there.

At best, it's similar to living before Volta discovered electric current in 1800 and yet having a hunch about some force that's it. At worst, it's knowing that history will end before 1800, so that I know that I will never know I was right. The whole thing, like sleep, is provisional: an old fixity may start to vary, an element may disperse into a coronet of isotopes, a force may turn into a mere aspect of space. I start out to say: "The night air is cool," and with luck will not have to cancel the statement halfway through; but I can't ever say: "I am saying" because the statement is forever unbegun or under way or complete even while I'm proffering the masquerade. What I can say, though, is: "I am in process, a process is in me." Unless I devise some Chinese of the fingertips, such as *night air cool* or *I in process*, which sounds like the pidgin of the hypocrite, and there I go again, flirting with Now, *which not*.

Casuistical stuff, no doubt, it must have come from living all day with her, my head full of thoughts that bubble into my mouth only to return indoors without an airing. If that is how she feels, and there's no reason why she shouldn't have just as many windmilling thoughts as any of us, she's entitled to pique, having no paper to commit it to, or, rather, barred from committing. I wish her prolix dreams.

Under arm, a toy tiger smelling of plastic cement: her tiger, my arm. "Good morning," I say to the nurse (Frau N. Hofer), "Deulius and daughter. I hope we're not late." Some mistake, she informs me: there is no appointment for any Deulius. The tiger stirs and growls. I feel as if my face is disappearing through a hole in my forehead. "No," she says, "there are no mistakes *here.* The mistakes happen beforehand, before people arrive." A petrified lull. Then: "Good morning, Dr. Jeans, there seems to be some sort of mix-up." He removes a red tomato from his armpit; Milk smiles grandly. "You requested an appointment?" No, I tell him, we were sent for (he rolls his tomato into the far corner of the room in one movement). "For blood tests," I insist. He frowns: "But it was established months ago that you have no blood." Then what about Milk, I ask him. *"Who?"* Milk, I say. This lovely child here. "I see no one else," he remarks. "Nurse Hofer, do you?" The tiger leaps, rips off her watch fob. "Only one person," she gasps, recoiling.

75

Ubiquitous alibi, the same as ever: somehow, when together, one of us is always invisible to everyone else. A pair of stars, the one occulting the other. Once I longed for awareness to become something concrete that wasn't just another form of awareness, and it happened: a girl arrived who is a work of art, like the mountain bluebird of the western U.S.A., a remarkably silent creature. Can it be I'm reincarnate Lazarus Colloredo, born 1716 in Genoa, who bore at the lower end of his breastbone a living child? Who was born thus appendaged and could not have it removed, to give it a life of its own.

"Good morning," we all say, thinking of better mornings, turn and turn about. It is time to go. Another consultation has failed. We go on as before, passing the toy tiger to and fro between us on buses, trains, across the steaming platefuls on tables in restaurants. Life is linear all right, but its line goes in a circle, as if around the globe itself. Nature's full of the impossible: black holes from which light cannot escape; Earth-sized suns made of diamond; atomic nuclei a mile in width that rotate thirty times a second. If one breath from a housefly were spread evenly throughout the Empire State Building, the resulting gas density would exceed that of interstellar space. Thirty baseballs roaming the entire interior of Earth have more chance of colliding with one another than stars do. Galaxies collide more often than stars. S. Doradûs, the most luminous sun in the sky, outshines our own yellow dwarf of a sun by a factor of one million, yet is so remote that the naked eye can't see it. There are stars called FU Orionis, Zubenelgenubi, Azelfafage, Dschubba, Alkaffaljidhina, Mastabbaturtur, and Phakt. I can feel the impossible overlapping with the outlandish, the so-called "done thing" yielding to solecism. The parent cuckoo abandons its chick, but other birds instinctively feed it. The lily-trotter's enormous thin feet let it seem to walk on water. A cabbage has been crossed with a radish, successfully. Sometimes I almost cheer. *Let* the imperfect be our paradise; our hell is flawless.

Combing her hair, then brushing it for ten minutes as she stands before me in the process of waking up, I vow to speak to her non-stop for a whole hour, the only trouble being I won't know where she finishes and I begin, in the steady beat of that address that rams the whole world into the vocative.

Untellable thoughts: I've heard that old people in sanatoria have been hosed down, instead of being bathed, by "orderlies" recruited from flophouses for forty dollars a week and a jug of wine. Granted such a degree of uncivilization, what's to prevent the hosing-down of flawed children as well?

Grievous analogies come in. A vertical cross-section of the human brain resembles a kneeling pygmy; I have seen this in wall charts in doctors' offices. The head dips low, awaiting the ax.

Untold conversations with my father flood back, in one of which he shows how to keep the glans clean, a laudable and tabooless object-lesson, in none of which, however, he says: "Son, once upon a time, one of a crowd, you chased down this pipe, out of this little slot, into your mama." Never showed me that or said. One of those mentally enacted interludes you expect a boy to stage on his mother's behalf. Yes, and his father's. Imagine having such a start! Not one in a thousand exposes himself to Junior, who has to guess a lot at eleven or twelve.

Conversations that never happened with him half-match those un-had with Milk, to whom, even if I wished, I couldn't explain something so simple as how a human child gets started. To her, love's mansion mostly *is* a place of excrement, of one kind or another. "Poo!" she huffs, and such a sound might grace a birth as well, a siege of herons, a pod of

77

seals. Trying to tell, even show, to her, who has no notion of *next* or *month* or *birth,* only gives you, as British soldiers say, the screaming ab-dabs.

Under-heard, then, rather than over-, she and I do our best. We mime the Little Dog, Monoceros, Orion, in some awkward improvised playlet about a wolf who looks with a nasal flashlight for a tennis player in a sky full of moons. And, as ever, we go further and further away from what looks vital, what matters, better equipped for tangents than for basics, for play than for work, dreadfully exempted, like lions that laugh but cannot hunt, streamlined hawks that cannot fly, gorgeous flowers that frighten bees.

Under the Way, we meddle while it burns, forked and shredded by every cosmic wind.

Arrested in time, we are not here at all, but at a guesswork distance, a bit like our own Sun, seen from Alpha Centauri, just an extra star showing up in Cassiopeia, next to the star named Epsilon.

Cain's palimpsest I call the mess on my brow, where so many signs have been made; they cancel out into a splotch, in which, if you look hard enough, you can see anything. Erase, erase, erase. The board shows black, or rather mid-Caribbean green; against it, according to taste, a sperm in the stocks, a fustigated ovum, a brave imp with the face of Spinoza and woeful, seal-like limbs with which it taps at a whole but everted brain resting on top of its cranium like a wig. On with the motley. I mustn't bog down now, no matter what comes next.

Unreal, today, to have so many simple things in mind, most of all the developing comic strip of the Way, with all those august personifications gone to pot. Anyone who reads the funnies comes upon nothing like this: a lost flashlight is retrieved by a wolf, or a unicorn, who takes it in his teeth to a tennis player, who then . . . Ah, the cliff-hangings of fiction, in which the next happening feels always like spring, another breath taken, a gag of black rancid fleece plucked out of the mouth! Only *she* will decide what happens next. I'll steer her to Gemini, and that is all. If one certain Hans Spemann can produce Siamese newts by constricting an egg in the two-cell stage with a loop of hair, who can tell what *she*'ll come up with under similar auspices? With just as free a hand.

Come the weekend, we'll have an epic on our hands. Now, though, with transistor radio rammed against her ear, the one with vestigial hearing, she samples the local coach talking about last week's game. Maximum volume, each word striking me like a basalt pillar. So what? I plod on, show her the sketch of Gemini, and have hardly lapsed into my rehearsal of the lore—Leda's Nest, the Two Peacocks, the two Sprouting Plants—when she honks in recognition. "Doo men," she carefully says, insisting on shaking hands with me. "Hello," she says, three times. "Ewoe. Ewoe. Ewoe." Only a dunce wouldn't get that: Castor is greeting Pollux, maybe after a tennis game. So we enact our closet drama from the beginning, all the way from the flashlight, which the wolf finds and takes to the man serving the tennis ball. She kneels to pick up the flashlight, mimes it into her wolf's mouth, then muzzles me to receive it, which I do, lowering my arm from the service, while she stays at the crouch. Now we shake hands all over again. She runs to the Way itself, taps the relevant designs, motions for me to switch on the stars, does a dance of glee. It isn't much, our masque, but it's mutuality, a clog dance in semi-heaven. Out go Jupiter and Leda both, parents of these twins. Out go all the mariners who honor Saint Elmo's Fire as the Ledean Lights. Gemini is handshake, the tennis-court vow. But she lets me insert the one gaseous nebula into the pattern, after first peering at a lightbulb

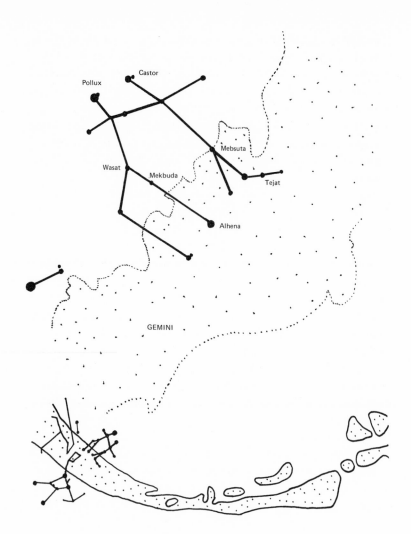

through it. I flick off the transistor she's slammed down, heedless of circuits, the whole thing to her just another damned big hearing aid.

Castor and Pollux linger in the mind, though, as Adam and Eve, two gazelles, two young men on horseback, with oval caps that represent the eggshell halves from which they came at birth. I remember reading pages of myth, but I forget the myths, grateful that Pollux is orange, Castor white: bright white and pale white mixed; or, rather, that the two of them aren't in the least alike, or even two. Castor is actually a multiple star, the chief components of which are hot and blue, a third being a small cool dwarf of reddish hue (how human it sounds!) whose period about the system's center of gravity is several tens of thousands of years, a slow-motion dwarf indeed. Just as I'm thinking: Yes, and when you find that Castor's twin components are in fact twin pairs only ten million kilometers apart, and thus have ellipsoid shapes, I realize that we can have some extra fun with these two hand-shaking tennis players. We can be anthropomorphic with the names of stars. I try, uttering "Wasat" as I point to the middle of Pollux's body. Spluttering with laughter, she hauls up her shirt and finger-stabs her navel. Next I try Mekbuda, which means a folded arm, but shows up in Pollux's knee, at which I point. A shrill reproof tells me I've blasphemed; knee, she shows and tells, is "knee," not "Mkbd," whether it's pale topaz or not. When I say Alhena and indicate Pollux's foot, she agrees, thinking I've said "ankle," a word she sometimes knows. Abandoning anatomy, I plug in the star cluster M 35, with its two streams running parallel northwest on either side, and light it up. Here *we* are, not adding up to sixty years between us, and there is old Castor, really a set of stellar sextuplets, forty-seven light-years distant, and there is Pollux, not quite so far off, but in fact a multiple star itself, with at least six very faint components. It used to be that Castor was brighter than Pollux, but no longer so, although whether the

81

one is increasing in brightness or the other is dwindling, we do not know. Were this October, *her* month, we'd see a meteor shower radiating from the feet of the Twins. Were it December, we'd spot fast meteors near the heads, leaving short trails. Puzzled, I check the handbook, and, while she holds colloquy between herself and our lit-up model of the Way, I find this for Castor: "Binary. Both greenish-white. A beautiful object." They never looked green to me, but I'm a peck color-blind, after all. It was a green or greenish star I was hunting a while back, wasn't it? Well, here are two. If we lived on a planet going around Castor, we'd see six suns all at once. I snap the book shut; she's demanding a popsicle, the phone is ringing, a siren is carving up the distance. I move to answer the phone, but she snatches it, quick as light, and booms a series of hellos. It's Asa, asking if we would like to go fly balloons, kites, streamers, whatever. There's wind. We do.

Grinning, he hands Milk a package, which she tears open with her big, fierce hands. A canary-yellow jumbo jet comes out, all floppy because this is an inflatable one. Half-expecting her to fling it at him, he catches it neatly when she does, whips a metal bottle out of his baggy pants, and inflates the plane in seconds. Helium, he tells me as it soars right out of her hands. I see the cord that makes it a kite, and only now remember his graffiti on the wings and fuselage: owls, infinity signs, pentagrams, many-eyed and many-mouthed faces. Milk takes the bracket that holds the plane, then makes her hand plunge to shift the thing aloft, giving out a husky gurgle of delight. Just ecstatic. This is Asa's technique, of course, as befits a man who lives in his own private DC-3, which he sometimes fits with streamers and ribbons; the only pink-and-white-striped Dakota in the world. He has designed a wind-sky fair for schoolchildren, reshaped hills in Hawaii, dumped confetti on factories. He sculpts with wind, makes poems with rubber and nylon. He is exuberant, just the kind of oddball to deal with Milk, who abhors the everyday, demands the gigantic, the outrageous, the wacky. Off we go to Asa's, a half-mile distant, in his London taxi, the helium jumbo five hundred feet above us, tethered to the windshield and touring in its bloat way above the streets we take. That high emblem lifts Milk's heart.

Grand big house left him by his father has turrets, cupola, numerous windsocks flying from poles. In a trice he has made Milk her own private flag, a humped rainbow on a black canvas ground. Eight feet long, it goes up the pole while she sings up to it, after it, almost seems to be flapping with it. Sun glints on his bald dome, roc's egg with vast smile-hiding black mustache beneath it. He lives on pasta, wears only sweaters and Dutch pantaloons, spends half his life (I think) in mid-air, sketching while the automatic pilot steers the plane. I all of a sudden lose the order in which things happen, recognizing that, even if only for a day or a week, he is her perfect father: coming at her with a trombone full of golden farts; throwing up a sculpture of rags on a wire frame; seating her in a giant eggcup right there on the groomed lawn; dashing out from the house with an entire pizza on a silver tray; handing her masks, noses, beards. We all play at being ghouls, run, chase, get out of breath, lie down while the wind flicks past us.

Going away yet again, he returns leading a taupe foal that walks with a bit of a reel. She goes mad over it, shoves pizza at his muzzle. "Ride?" "No!" So she leads it at the stoop, one arm over its neck, and makes two circuits of the garden before the foal twists free and stilt-walks again to Asa's side. I can't help feeling I've been trumped, scooped, but who cares? Here is a man who had a dimension waiting for her all this time: no Milky Way, but a true gala, a chromatic extravaganza. Then his housekeeper releases two rabbits, a black, a white, brings out the big parrot (which scares Milk), and, glory be, wheels out onto the lawn the biggest color TV I've ever seen, festooned with fake greenery made of sponges, with masks and flagstaffs. It works, it switches on, it even seems to breed when he erects a mirror in front of it, and she sites herself between the big screen and the equal mirror, seeming to bisect her view. Now the foal sits with her, in an awkward sprawl, and Asa says the one word: "Planning!" at which I shrug, astounded. He tells me he only just got back from Zürich. And I wonder if he doesn't perhaps want to borrow her for a year, install her in some organic sculpture set, plonk her down on red ice or a six-foot-high champagne cork. A wizard, that's what Asa is; a wizard is what she needs. We haul down the jumbo, attach a winking light to it, and send it up again. Milk watches in a dream, her senses swamped by foal, pizza, TV on the lawn, rabbits, and the mighty parrot. One final parade, with each of us bearing a clutch of balloons like a giant levitating molecule, and we go inside to eat. Milk is pink with fun.

Crisp-topped lasagna weighing us down, we go off again in the taxi to, of all things, the Middle Hall wine festival, where we all three tread grapes hilariously, and then with mired feet taxi off again to his house and rinse off in the goldfish pool. Sweet chaos, and she loves it. It's what she was born for. All that's lacking is an abacus, a coelacanth, and a gryphon, or so I think in my merriment as thousands of birds loop and pour across the afternoon sky like locusts. I no longer have any abstract ideas, just a blur of things. But I'm glad he's here, not in Zürich, where I'd thought he'd be for another three weeks. He swells the team; indeed, he swells the world, makes the Milky Way edge over for lack of room.

"Uncle" he gets to be called, like King Lear. He once had a wife, but he somehow lost her in (or to) the Philippines, and not during any war. He will take us aloft, in the DC-3 dubbed *Moby,* to trail streamers, inhale cloud, point a telescope at the daylight Moon. "Florida?" he inquires. "Too hot for her,"

84

I say. "Canada, then?" he follows up. "Maybe," I say, "it might be just right. But—not too much confusion, please, she's only just arrived." Gracious to the nth, he fishes out Polaroid cameras, and Milk actually takes a picture of herself watching the TV in the garden, by sheer good luck, at the fifth shot managing to get her face into the frame. We pat her on the shoulders, shake her hands, for hitting a home run, for breaking the record, for being herself.

Upset a bit as the sky darkens, Milk waves urgently at Asa, who switches on several arc lamps, ignites the barbecue. We toast marshmallows, swig beer and ginger ale, light two big phallic cigars that ought to explode but don't, give her a chocolate one, and lie there, in our chaise-longues, puffing smoke at the moon, lotos-eaters to the end. Even in the dusk I can see the dark rings under her eyes, in her a sign of exhaustive joy, and I reckon the day well spent. And spent is what I mean. We have nothing left, not even for the sky. Between us we lift her heavy, sleeping body and carry her inside to a daybed, after which he and I resume our cigars to a background of what he listens to: Mahler, Ives, and Crumb, in that order. It feels like being on stage during the last scene of a final act.

Generous people lap up the grotesque, don't they? I know only that one day soon I must fill the cracks between the bath and the tiled wall with cement or putty. Let Milk help, since her technique of bathing will soon wash out what of rotted filler holds.

Grinning at another foolish memory, I recoup a menu that said: "Tenderloin barbecued to your likeness." They serve up your face medium rare, which is why they photograph you on entering the restaurant. Then the chef kneads meat all day. Some tenderloins are even barbecued after the death masks of the famous. Eat George Washington's profile. Trough on Adam's chops.

Unseemly thoughts, whereas all I have in mind is a small, earthbound text, a souvenir in which tiniest meets vastest, or as nearly as makes no difference, while the pain floats in between them, sea-changing into measured delight or wooden-headed stoicism at least. On, on. I'm almost there.

Ungainly with fatigue, I ease her into Asa's taxi. "To the Charing Cross Hotel, sir." "Yes," he says with a bogus yawn.

Arriving at my house, we lift her out and in. All day the TV has been on. It reveals to me Boris Karloff, walking with atrocious gimp in an outsize surgical boot. Asa goes off to design something or other, nocturnal worker that he is, while I clean house, swobbing up dust with damp paper towels, and trying to follow the fate of Karloff as I move around. It sounds extreme: all gasp and saliva, a lurid wake for insomniac America. Then a beer, bad of me, and another cigar, which is worse. A day crossed off the calendar, out of our lives.

Uncle Asa has been a wizard, that I know.

Uncanny how the mind cavorts when tired. I lose the sense of time, at least as orthodoxly put, and see it as a mere shift from warm to cold, from tidy to untidy: an entropy there is no way to duck. An odd little calculation swims into mind, a bit of homemade, amateur's finding, not exactly news to the world of science, but news to me and my own. I worked out, from all the data in my star books, the favored speeds at which stars approach or recede from the Sun. Of forty-four, twenty-six approach and eighteen recede; and, as I figured it, at 1–2 miles per second as many approach as recede, whereas at 3–16 miles per second twice as many approach as recede, while of the few at 17–73 miles per second as many recede as approach. Tempted to call this Deulius' Law (or something vainglorious like that), I didn't, postponing self-glorification until the day I'd correlated the speeds with the distances, which still remains to do. Yet I drew the curve, happy to tell myself: This is how they go round the mulberry bush, and not otherwise, the only remaining question being why. At which I halt, not eager enough for explanation to commit hypothesis. Some perverse confidence in the universe, as in the human appetite for gossip and ice cream, keeps me going, helps my mind rest, as when I reassure myself that, no matter how many asteroids we find, we'll never run out of names for them, provided we're willing to dub them such things as Marilyn, Fanny, Crocus, China, Mussorgskia. *Homo sapiens* will never run out of names, no matter how many phenomena come his way.

Gently as a threatened bird, Milk eats breakfast, nibbling rather than troughing. Wide awake she does things handsomely grand, but heavy from sleep she tinkers, making half-irritable aloof gestures with minimum power. If we get back to the Way, we'll attempt Auriga, the so-called Charioteer, although for the life of me I never saw reins or driver in its clean steeple shape. Capella's ready, in the form of a big yellow bulb, and so is Menkarlina ("the shoulder of the driver"), white. The surprise, however, has to do with the thing aridly called Epsilon A *Aurigae,* which just happens to be the largest star we know, vast enough to accommodate the entire solar system out to Saturn inclusive. Over two and a quarter billion miles across, it's 2,700 times the size of our Sun, and yet transparent, emitting mostly invisible infra-red rays. In fact, it has a partner, a mere 190 times the Sun in size, which is the yellowish star we see and mark on charts. How slap-happy would I have to be to pass up such a chance? So I've devised something special that suggests the horrific vastness of the pair, the invisible one and the yellow one. As my Soviet textbook says, "Surely Nature did not skimp on wonders to startle the human imagination." Amen to that. I'll try to live up to it.

Coming round fast, she requests "sand," her version of a word that ends in *wich.* Receives corn beef, eats it, then a

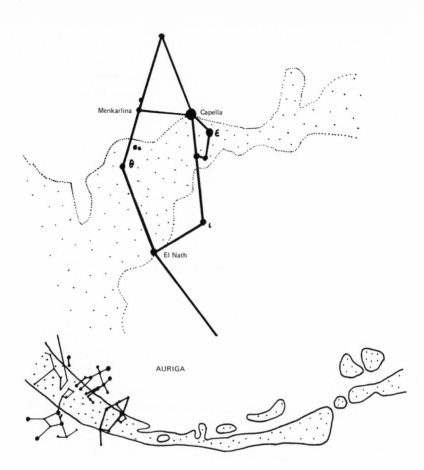

Menkarlina

Capella

ε

θ

ι

El Nath

AURIGA

second. No longer a finicky bird but a ravening furnace, she takes in milk, several rolls larded with strawberry preserve, and a boiled egg as well. She eats today as if she isn't coming back. I mean she eats, today, et cetera, but let it stand: she will devour the day as well, as the phrase implied. Remembering, she flashes down the stairs: no warning, no request, and when I arrive, cup in hand, she has switched on the Way, has begun to babble the comic-strip legend we fudged up. The flashlight. The wolf. The tennis server. The two players shaking hands. So we continue, my own mind as much on Asa's aerial feats as on Auriga. Now I remember something else: I forgot to call Pi, neglected to make arrangements with Chad to bring his daughter round. Arrange! Arrange! Arrange! Later, anyway. My young Vikingess demands the next scene, gets it, drawn small, and at once brandishes the template, informing me in elated yells what it is. Of course. "Kite." There even seems to be a string attached. After Asa, who can not think kites? Truly, though, it resembles a kite, and I no longer see the steeple or, a sibling image, the sentry box. Working fast, I line it out, planking Auriga slap across the Milky Way. Into its hole I plug Capella, the Little She-Goat, so-called, on whose actual color no one seems able to agree, red, gold, yellow, all the same forty-two light-years away and receding from us at nineteen miles per second. Then the white bulb for Menkarlina, another for El Nath, "the heel," even a blue one for *theta,* an orange one for *iota.* The entire pentagon lights up. No doubt I'm overdoing it, but, damn it all, this is the constellation of Erichthonius, fourth King of Athens, who was so deformed he couldn't walk and therefore invented the four-horse chariot supposed to be commemorated in this beautiful and conspicuous clutch of stars. While I think this, she is miming and motioning to me that the two players who shook hands have now come to fly a kite on what she calls a "yort ing," a short string. Indeed they have. Then she gapes in delighted bemusement as I affix

Epsilon A and its partner by cutting a big hole, over which I staple yellow plastic, behind which, after fifteen more minutes, a color disk begins to spin with a slight, almost nasal scrape. Irrationally, I've made A's partner a yellow spot on the disk itself. But we parted company with science long ago, so there's no need to insist on how the massive thing really behaves; in *our* Way, it spins wholesomely, almost white, like a blind vitreous body in an eye socket, dwarfing Capella and the rest. The unseen seen, the impossible scaled down. Strictly, according to the scale of Capella, my rotating Epsilon A ought to be six feet across. I ponder, for the few seconds she allows, the wild model that would embody the Way's third dimension, reaching miles beyond the last gas station in town!

Up and down she jumps, in explosive syllables reciting her tale of a kite; or so I presume, unable to follow a word. Some of it goes:

> "Men-drath, bugaboo.
> "Ban. Dry. Bane.
> "Ankela, Ankela. Bib.
> "More. No."

I say more or less the same to her, but she waves me imperiously off her verbal reservation. Some words belong to her alone, as code or gibberish. No trespassers allowed. And I once again feel confined in my own world of public signs, excluded (as of old) from the world in which she called a knife a *seven*, an escalator a *bo*. Once you learned her lingo, however, she dropped it and moved on to new misnomers, leaving you a-puff in her wake.

> "Brang, *brang*," she hoots.
> "Brang," I answer, to oblige. *Brang* indeed.
> "No," she insists. *"Milk."*

So, in tender retaliation, I spout our new constellation at her: "Capella, Menkarlina, El Nath, Epsilon A, *Auriga!*" At which she only collapses into laughter of the well-fed sort, as if a Hottentot had presumed to question Wittgenstein. Plainly, I am not to speak like that. It ruins her notion of my possible dignity. It fattens my daftness. In other words (literally too), I am to use neither her language nor mine, nor even standard English, but am to remain in dumb-struck astonishment while she mixes the sounds of aviary, stable, and black mass.

Granted, Your Majesty. I go upstairs to phone Pi, who is out; Chad, who is in, but busy, and who'll come tomorrow afternoon. Now Milk's upon me, leopard-like, wanting to tickle and be tickled, to roll and leap, on the bed. Hearty, clean-throated laughter comes from her for ten minutes. Then we jog. She does a handstand against the wall, transfers her weight to her head, talks madly at me from her upside-down position, but not a word can I grasp, can only think (record thus in inverted bafflement): *"Ehs si evif teef gnol. Or: Gnol teef evif si ehs.* I say it to her, in preposterous hope that today just happens to be back-to-front land: *"Gnol teef evif si ehs!"* Smirking feistily, she says, "Yes." (Can anyone wonder why I don't know if I'm coming or going?) One more try, and I end the game. "Olleh, Klim," I greet her, affably enough. *"Klim! Olleh."* It doesn't work; she just asks for "beebee": a carbonated beverage, I guess. I fetch. She takes it still upside down, tries to pour it into her mouth, all over the floor. I mop up, she pours some more, just so I won't feel I've nothing to do. Told no, she drinks the rest. The phone rings, a wrong number, so I let her talk to whoever it is on the other end, the careless dialer who will think he's got through to the Kafka Enigma Factory: just a deaf child announcing her presence repeatedly, plus a few "jabba"s and "blawn"s, whatever they happen to mean.

At Auriga again, we rehearse the action. That kite won't stay up forever, although in the Way it will. What next?

91

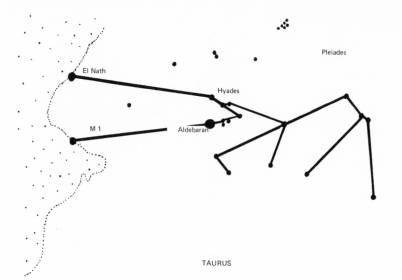

El Nath

Hyades

Pleiades

M 1

Aldebaran

TAURUS

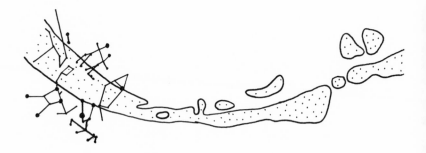

92

What's next is Taurus, on we go, moving along the Galaxy like two sleepwalkers hitching rides. When she scowls at the template, I wonder why, then get it: it's a disassembled kite, a kite that's crashed. No, she is saying "Yah," plus something else. Pointing at her legs, at mine, she raps out the one syllable: "long." Clear as day, what she means is *daddy longlegs,* an excellent likeness to fix on Taurus. Not what I had in mind, but I rarely do have in mind what she comes up with. Very well, I tell myself, as if telling her, that's what it's going to be. When the wolf takes the flashlight to the tennis players who end up flying a kite that just happens to include the biggest star we know, a daddy longlegs (otherwise known as harvestman or crane fly) will go aloft on its fabric. I'd almost expected her to think Taurus a broken kite string trailing untidily down, frozen in its last twirl, but not the charging bull with elongated horns that just touch the Way itself. Whether I can sustain our comic scenario, I'm not sure, but I'll give it the old Galactic try. Casually I flash at her a picture postcard of the Pleiades, white stars trapped in pale-blue brushstrokes done by a nervous hand, then one of the blue-green shell that is the Crab Nebula, with claws floating explosively away from the main body. Two astronomical golden oldies, these, at which she nods as if I've written out her name and she impatiently heeds it, wants to get on to something else. Working fast, almost by reflex, I install daddy-longlegs Taurus in the gloom off the Way, screw in the big bulb that's orange-red for gigantic Aldebaran, then the holders that will light up out-of-scale cut-outs of the Pleiades and the Crab Nebula. She "oo"s a little, even though I'm not ready to switch on. Weird thoughts accompany my swift but not deft hand motions. The Pleiades appear to be shivering, although their surface temperature is extremely high. And they are called young stars although two and a half million years old. My replica of Aldebaran is so big I haven't room for the Hyades cluster, in the middle of which the star appears to sit. A pity, because some of the Hyades are coolish and red, maybe a thousand million years old. Milk is in her middle teens. I switch on, wishing I could tell her just a little about Merope, seventh Pleiad, who was so careless as to marry a mortal, thus causing her light to fade, or about the rainy Hyades, grieving for their brother Hyas, by the wild boar slain, or even about how Charles Messier, in 1758, mistook the then unknown Crab Nebula for a comet and irritably began to compile his famous catalogue of nebulae, listing the Crab as "Interference Number 1." Why, the Pleiades are moving through space like a flock of birds; the Arabs called the Hyades the Little She Camels as they trekked toward a point somewhere just past Betelgeuse; and Aldebaran, thirty-seven million miles in diameter, is receding from us at thirty-four miles a second. To tell her wouldn't help her, no. It helps nobody, does it? Yet just to know, just to let curiosity, awe, and humility have a field day, that might not be so bad. As it is, she gets all the visuals; she wolfs color, she gorges herself on light. And all I can think of, when reviewing her progress, is what someone said about the chances of there being intelligent life in space: absence of evidence doesn't mean evidence of absence. Perhaps, from her point of view, I'm Interference Number 1; she's certainly not it, from mine. On the contrary, she's more like the faded Pleiad pouring out her light again: the young, hot star, sometimes blue, sometimes very pale, now on the premises again. Inane as it may be, to spend the days in a private amalgam of stars, kites, wordless horseplay, swims and guesses and haphazard meals, it's the only way I know, the only game in town. We could both be better employed, I'm sure, instead of doting on each other daylong during what's almost a clandestine "assignation" laced with incest, flawed by genes. It will soon be wise to fetch my mail from the office, call at the bank, make a sortie for groceries, et cetera. This kind of suspension, trance, can't last very long, no matter what the real or the fake Way is doing. I should trim the weeds from the front walk, the overgrowth from the rear one, collect up all the fallen apples, and mow the lawn. All right: we *will*.

Underhandedly I think: On your own behalf, Deulius, what is Taurus? What's it to you? And I answer that it resembles an insect with a prosthetic tuning fork upon its head. We're getting on, moving ahead, oh yes, but I don't see our model of the Milky Way ever being finished; I'll rather be completing the chore after she's gone. A plywood elegy complete with dwindling lights. We're not even keeping a straight course along the Way, backtracking a bit to take in Taurus, then lunging right to take in Perseus, as we no doubt will. There was a future, wasn't there? If only we could use it now.

Going into diary form, I make what sense I can of the hours, the days. Itemize. Itemize. Itemize. It has been busy. Pi arrives, without warning, but loaded with groceries bought on the way in, after that three-hour drive. So once again we have wheels, once again the zippy Datsun stands on the gravel glacis that slopes down to the house as if the house above, up the incline, were a fort. Milk and she regard each other for a moment, pondering tactics, then untidily hug, rivals in peace. Asa stops by, leaves a perpetual-motion toy with six balls that click to and fro. As he leaves, en route to the state capital, he vows to build a life-size one before she leaves. He goes. We all three swim. For once, we eat a proper meal, an enormous casserole followed by fresh fruit with ice cream. I, as ever, pass up the fruit but take the ice cream. At the drive-in movie, an eighth adventure of Sinbad, we suck popsicles and Milk utters a loud, acerbic commentary in a language unknown, from time to time grabbing at us as the action quickens, especially when Sinbad swims out to a ship on the rocks, buries himself in sand, and sets a bush over his head. At her level, we thrive on the crudeness of events, the colors, the non-stop causation of it all. As the ads say of actors, she *is* Sinbad, wild and slick on the poop of her own automotive bagala (word I learn from the movie, meaning a luxurious dhow or something such). Sipping a milkshake at the all-night diner, she behaves with impossible graciousness, a nun at an altar. No bellows, no muscle play, no snorts. I have rarely seen her so demure. Amiably she chats to us in a near-whisper in yet another of her private lingos, and no one even stares. She hasn't worn a hearing aid in days and doesn't intend to: out in society she leaves her crutches behind, just so much gear. Pi says the girl is amazing. "Yes," says Milk, who hasn't heard. Redundantly agreeing, I have to laugh, there being, between the two of them, enough hair for a small rug. Each has hair to well below the waist, Milk's mousy brown, Pi's carbon black. About the same height, though Milk has the fuller figure, they look as unalike as a Finn and a Turk, which they aren't. "Hi, Milk," says one, for something to begin with. " 'E'oe," comes the answer. A pause, and then: "Bye." How simple it all seems, a lingua franca of amnesty, an Esperanto of neighbor-numbness. I say nothing, but scratch the glue and the paint off my thumbs. Whatever happens, whatever gets said, slots into a stained-glass window that overlooks a charnel house I've too often looked into. A worsening view, past forty, past her twenty, slipping on blood into fifty and thirty, and there is over everything a bone-snapping pall of goodbyes that are going to be said, no matter what is in anyone's mouth: heart or gag, foot or food. I end that thought so fast it doubles back into the realm of also-ran. I never give the fates a hand to shake.

Grabbing at my mail, she slams and reslams the mailroom door, locking us in a giant oven. On the way home, we look in on Lee, in his dairyette, who recommends as almost always the frozen cod with a knob of butter on top, baked. Forcing on her a big bag of potato chips, he waves goodbye with dollars in his hand, affable gargoyle who cannot count, any more than can his Sunday deputy, a shriveled ancient whom we fondly nickname Malone Dies. Stumbling around in the dusk, we gather up the fallen apples, then sort them in the house, and a mighty joke follows: Pi will make a pie, and Milk envisions Pi in the oven, all three of us eating Pi with forks, what's left of Pi cooling in the refrigerator next to the milk. A breezy temperament the girl has; she laughs on this all the way to bedtime, and is still rehearsing it as she begins to drift, with that calmed-down curl of lip that tells you she's at peace. "It wasn't bad," we say. It could have been devilish. It may be yet. It could happen tomorrow. Let it not. I get a neck-rub. A weight lifts off the brainstem. I read Pi's new poem, by-product of insomnia at her parents' house. One of her A to A— poems, it still needs work, but she still sees (I tell her) finite infinities in all her grains of sand: a compliment, though sounding like a cavil. The Pi's-pie joke returns to haunt, even as we look up at Jupiter, that lolling gob-stopper of painless light. Out comes the telescope, the good one, and in fifteen minutes we have split Albireo into a yellow and a blue. The electric drive doesn't let it move, as if our eyes are standing still while the Earth moves round. Then, still in Cygnus, we aim at *psi*, find the lilac star, the white partner, and, in a reckless mood, shoot for Cygnus X-1, where the first-found of the black holes is supposed to be. When Cygnus goes out of range, behind the roof, we look at Andromeda and pick out the galaxy, a trembling blur most unlike its sumptuary portrait in our glossy picture books. The Way sprawls clear, high but not that high, blown into little tufts and smears or flowing thick. One sweep with the instrument sends thousands of astronomical billiard balls flashing past the eyepiece. The Pleiades become an outsize, scattered molecule. The Hyades blaze yellow and gold. Aldebaran batters away like a symphonic fireball, as if it knew of Wagner. Out of the blue, out of that uranian gray, a thought comes spinning at meteor speed, no trail. Our talking with Milk is uncannily like those conversations that, one gathers, will eventually happen: some intelligence over in Eridanus says, "Hello," and we answer, in our terrestrial way, "How are you?" And the entity in Eridanus responds, "Fine." Even at the speed of light, that little chat will take centuries. Heaven be thanked, then, that she answers almost at once (when she answers at all), and that we can see her face in all its detail. It may be daft to think she thinks us an immature civilization not worth communicating with, but I think it all the same. It certainly isn't the other way round, whatever several million *hoi polloi* might think as they squint at her in the street.

Upon a time, once: that's how I'll resume, I the only one awake, in front of cattle rustlers in Ochercolor on the Late Late Late Show. Both girls abed beneath the mouths of their respective air-conditioners. I bid the day come back. It won't. A saliva befitting Tantalus fills my mouth as I think how long everything takes, yet is done with in a mayfly's cough. We are all three of us too old to know what's out in the Galaxy, or even beyond it. When the aliens begin booming all their knowledge at us, and mankind races to fill all its copybooks with cures and miracles, we'll be long gone, smudged back into the flux as a dust. And all I can think of is: a century elapsed before anyone visited America, after it had been found. It is going to be at least that long before anything begins pouring into the recorders of the radio telescopes, which, so far, we haven't even readied on the proper scale. Including, oh what a vainglorious wish, the cure for brain damage, simple as clipping dry cuticle from your nail. Yet something I'm determined to find out, am hell-bent on it. What is the favored speed of stars? Is it, as I surmised, between three and sixteen miles per second? Knowing it helps nobody, but knowing it soothes me; I know the Sun travels at twelve, en route for Vega and Hercules, with a goodish chance of getting there, while we . . .

Gulliver at bay, with iris and pupil strained from the eye-piece, I pretend to know what's brewing in her flighty brain. As I tell Pi, it's a hell of a challenge for a fiction-writer to have to deal with someone whose inner life you hardly know at all. With characters, you can pretend to be omniscient, invent-ing your own verifications. In everyday life, you can always ask, or listen. But with Milk you're stymied into reporting a mighty live, impossibly attractive human from the outside non-stop. In her own way, she is more fictional than Beowulf, less given to explanations than Goya's Saturn. I guess, you guess, she guesses, we guess, they all guess. Ecstatic (or seem-ing so) in her frequent private trances, when her eyes almost cross or she peers up into the room's corners, she has to be invented *for.* As in the old saw: Silent woman maketh myth. From morning to night she sponsors rumor, the result being that, from time to time, I've had to settle my mind by fixing on the extent to which she fits the rubrics for hyperactive children—Doesn't Finish Projects, Fidgets, Can't Sit Still At Meals, Doesn't Stay With Games, Wears Out Furniture And Toys, Talks Too Much, ah!—or by devising impossible fugues that imply a world in which she belongs, one of these begin-ning: "Upon a time, once, when William Shakespeare was in Hawaii, he had to phone home for his coach-and-four, his microscope, and the first draft of his second novel, all left behind him with his third wife, Lady Hester Stanhope, who herself was fond of visiting Tibet and there encountered Lawrence of Arabia soon after the amputation of his right leg following a helicopter accident in November 1255. . . ." Off-the-cuff madness, of course, and such shifts work no longer, mainly because I have made up *my* mind about what goes on in Milk's, and she thus far hasn't provided any evidence to the contrary. She rolls with a whirlwind all her own, at which I've guessed, and now have canonized the guess. After all, as I tell Pi, when you're dealing with a girl whom am-phetamines quieten, whom sedatives turn on, your whole world gets topsy-turvy and you cling to certain facts: for example, that amphetamine stimulates the release of norepinephrine from nerve endings in the hypothalamus and brainstem, parts that have a lot to do with moods and awareness. Then you realize that a tense situation—at the doctor's office, or when strangers are in the house—produces an anxiety that creates just the same effect as the drug, and through the same mechanism. Holy cow: but you can't habituate a child to stimulants or anxiety, especially in her/his/its teens. What I'm doing, in fact, is something else, getting on with Perseus before our social life wipes out the Galaxy for good.

Uppity and a bit skittish, she informs me that this lovely outline, whose pointed tip I think a dog's unhooded penis, is a clown with three yellow pom-poms on his person, one on the hat, one at the back of his neck, one on his shoulder. Miming the whole thing with sardonic agility, she stabs her finger at the Way and demands results. Perseus, of course, shows up in the older star maps in warrior stance, in his right hand a sword, in his left the awful head of Medusa, just as if (I've thought it) he were the patron saint of the divorce court. But, looking at the outline, I detect the element of frolic, the wacky wide-legged splits, the left arm outreached to touch the audience. Reaching into my bag of tricks (an old cardboard liquor case in which, on the quiet, she's already been rummaging), I fish out the fluctuating Christmas-tree light that's going to be Algol, the demon star that is Medusa's eye twinkling, and sight through it at the ceiling. "More," she cries. "More lamp." To work I go, rushing through the early stages, hardly even pausing to smirk as I do the hole for Mirfak, the yellow star that is the lowest of her three pom-poms. The joke, such as it is, concerns only Pi and me and the salt- and pepper-holders on the kitchen table, which for mildly lewd reasons we have named Mirfak and Ophiuchus: a star and a constellation reduced to humbler service. Suppressing levity, I recall that John Goodricke, the deaf and

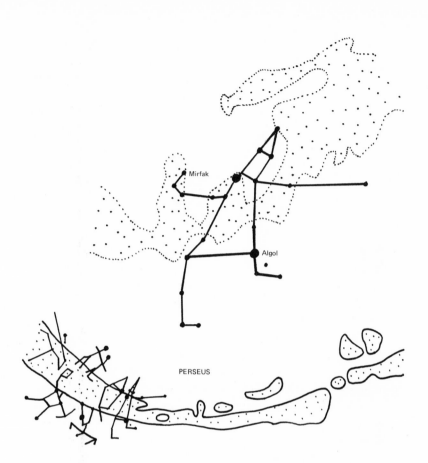

Mirfak

Algol

PERSEUS

dumb astronomer, was the one who identified Algol as a spectral binary, or at least said the star was twin. As it is, which is why I've installed this shuntling blue-and-yellow bulb. "Algol," I tell her, just to see what she'll do; but she thinks I've said, "All gone," and scowls. "Al Gol," tries Pi, knowing she has said the Arabic for *ghoul*, but Milk just mimics the clown's pose, hooks one arm behind her, the other outstretched, mouthing the word "clown." There is nothing clownish about her, though. She looks both dignified and august, a tall blond athlete who has just accomplished the long jump with ballerina precision. So Pi and I applaud her stance, clapping as loud as we can, and I observe that my daughter is flighty with another woman around, has become just that bit more of a ham, more prima-donna-ish, and more verbal. Shaking her head, Pi hands me an open book in which a photograph with superimposed arrows reveals how the star group called Perseus II will look in half a million years at over seven miles a second. Why, over a million years ago they were all at the same point, were born then, and even now rank as newborn infants. On the scale of a human span of seventy years, these twelve stars correspond to an infant on its first day. A nausea takes hold of me, something abstract and spiky in the gut, and I try to fend off all the human comparisons that leap to mind. Better, I tell myself, then Pi, to reiterate the fact that, thus far along the Way, we have added a clown to the flashlight-wolf-tennis-handshake-kite-flying-daddy-longlegs main sequence, with Cassiopeia next. Hopeless, though: the tiny progress those twelve stars will make in half a million years has made me physically ill, with an odd stitch just below the belt. Meanwhile, the mind is off again, this time adding insult to injury by remembering something brand new: the radio galaxy some Leyden astronomers found, after prolonged efforts, to be two thousand million light-years *away* from us, and, oh heavens, eighteen million light-years *wide*. Its name, 3C 236. And it has a little partner (how gregarious are the contents of space!) only six and a half million light-years wide. A saner person wouldn't try to figure against such an incomprehensible ground, would choose a hemisphere, a desert, a parking lot, happy to let like do duty for like: *similia similibus curantur,* as homeopaths have it. Yet here I go, aided and abetted by Pi (who rejoices more in planets than in galaxies, but still . . .), doing my best to dwarf us all, make of Man a midge. But only, I tell myself, to minimize Milk's flaw. 3C 236 just happens, I keep on telling myself, to be the largest known object in the universe. Big as it is, however, it shouldn't make any difference to me, to Milk; but it does, at least to me, fattening awe till every other emotion I feel becomes awe-struck too. And the sense of triumph I feel when peering at the photograph comes out in an unspoken ditty that runs: "Did whatever made 3C 236 make me?" End of song. I feel like a stoic, epistemological non-combatant, losing all emotions in a blanket reverence. Hating the universe just a little, I marvel at its lack of modesty. The brash big. The brash big unending. The brash big unending inhuman. The brash big unending inhuman self-centered. The brash big unending inhuman self-centered helpless. The brash big unending inhuman self-centered helpless to-do, with which our minds go on shadow-boxing to no point. Our perhaps unknowing sponsor. How anyone can *not* speak of it, I have no idea, though men have been only too ready to celebrate, say, Jupiter and Hercules, as if they were men, but not an enormous whirling sphere of methane and ammonia, and a vast drill-ground of gas in heat. Which is where Pi and her planetary poems come in: one woman addressing herself to the solar system, in neighborly esteem. Inhuman? Not in the least. It is the so-called human view that's inhuman when human means Man-centered and inhuman means unworthy of our brains. The least we can do is to muse on all that is not ourselves, the most is to see how accidental our presence is. From all accounts, it looks as if the teleology that says we occurred in order to link up with other forms of life outside the local system is wrong; the race is likely to perish without having made contact at all, while, at unthinkable distances from us, cleverer and saner forms of entity go about their business, even making *their* teleology come true. I can't discount the random in it all, as when, each year, to only one of two thousand radium atoms fate comes knocking, kills it off into lead and helium. Why that one, out of an identical two thousand, no one knows, or why even only one. But happen it does, and to our own cells too, whether or not the victim is able to think.

Under the influence of such outsize runes, I decide to go for Cassiopeia in the basement while Pi mixes a quiche. Paradoxes begin anew, with my mind limping back to the vain queen, wife of King Cepheus, who for conceit about her looks was transferred to the sky, seated in a starry chair that circles the Pole and sometimes stands her on her head. Waving me on, Milk arranges her face into acidulous forbearingness: I'm too slow, I haven't reduced my constellation-building to a sleight-of-hand. Perhaps that is how Andromeda, daughter of Cassiopeia, scowled while chained to the rocks, doing punishment for her mother's lack of tact. I maneuver fast with template, juggling the cardboard so that Cassiopeia's scintillant zigzag is now an M, now a W, as in the sky itself. Surely Milk will see the letter as what it is. But she says nothing, curves a long tongue down her chin, and begins to tap her foot. I can smell pastry baking upstairs as I make the hole for Schedar, the orange star, and Chaph, the yellow. "Bagdei," I say, intoning the mnemonic for the stars that make up Cassiopeia's chair: *beta, alpha, gamma,* et cetera, another bit of my mind on the supernova that Tycho Brahe spotted here in November 1572, when returning from Germany to his native Denmark and stopping over in the picturesque old monastery of Herrizwald. The new star had no tail, was not

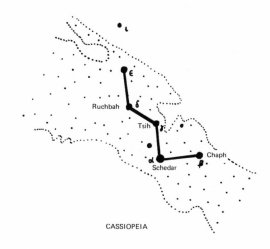

CASSIOPEIA

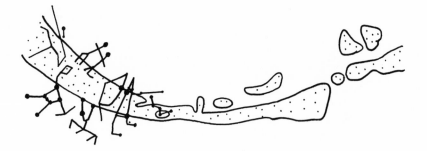

surrounded by any nebula, was almost as bright as Venus when that planet is nearest Earth. It could even be seen at noon, and at night through thick cloud cover. Then, in December 1572, it began to fade and in fact vanished in March 1574. Many people prepared for death, having decided that the new star was a signal, coming hard after the Massacre of Saint Bartholomew; but all that ensued was radio waves, faint ones detected in 1952, whereas another part of Cassiopeia, named A, is the most powerful source of radio waves anywhere in the sky. Mocking myself for parading information as I plant my pseudo-stars, I look quizzically at Milk, who takes one look and pronounces *M.* Child's play. She runs upstairs, led on by her nose. I finish the job, still musing on the constellation that was Leg to the Egyptians, Stone Lamp to Eskimos, Key to Greeks, Kneeling Camel to Arabs. There goes the Queen of Ethiopia, around the Pole head downward, like a tumbler, fair-complected and lightly clad (according to one account), and sometimes under an alias: Mary Magdalene, Bathsheba, or even Deborah, sitting under her palm tree on Mount Ephraim. Schedar, pale rose to some but not to me, has a smalt-blue companion I omit; *breast,* the word means, while Chaph is *hand* or *camel's hump,* and brilliant white Tsih is Chinese for *whip,* Ruchbah is Arabic for *knee.* I switch on as a drumming scuffle begins upstairs (a tickling contest it seems), and feel just as conceited as Cassiopeia: my one fourth of the Way is a dazzling vision, like a stained-glass window gone haywire, and festively so. Yet I suspect there will soon be only me to admire it, flick it on and off, swing it back and forth, perfect the nebulae and concoct some way of indicating radio sources and black holes: the father playing with his child's toy train set. All of a sudden I feel remarkably standard, whereas I usually feel freakish, and the feeling has little to do with memories of how Cassiopeia contained the star (Tycho's) that was supposed to herald the second coming, or with the tangerine tint of Schedar (only that hue to one as partly color-blind as I), or with thoughts of biting into quiche. No: it is the long-absent feeling of being with the girl on Christmas Day, when all the brand-new mechanical toys buzzed wild at the same time, and Milk looked right at home in God's shop. At such times I've felt that she, and even I, possessed whatever it is that qualifies you for humanhood: self-awareness, minimal intelligence, self-control, sense of time, sense of futurity, concern for others, balance of rationality and feeling, and so on. Unhappily, Christmas lasts a few days only; the suspended norms renew themselves, the access of vitality and honed awareness falls away; and some of the toys break. I go upstairs to eat quiche, summoned by two sets of feet tattooing on the floor above, and I leave the Way blazing with light, just for joy.

"Uh," Milk seems to say, but it's an imperative whose full text reads, *Big hug!*, said as "Bi' 'uh." It's the first time she has used it during her stay. That very thought reminds me that we are no longer nibbling into the first day, but working past the second or third. Preliminary is over, when you can use up a day without the sense of reducing the days; and the calendar has begun to count. Mouth full of hot and tangy pie, I go to the calendar on the wall and outline the remainder of her stay in squeaky black, my head on some old distinction between seasonal time and mere chronicity. Limned in black, our own short season has a lugubrious aspect I want to wish away, but, as I tell Pi, there *is* something terminal about the whole idea of visitation rights, a child on loan, a parent out of cold storage. Tactfully she asks if I left the lights on, while Milk gobbles or swigs. "Yes," I answer, saying something about leaving a beacon in the underworld, "sorry about the fatuous hyperbole." She mentions visitors, Asa first, as always, then Chad and his daughter, he to fidget non-stop with the books left out on tables and chairs (as if we had left underwear around for a fetishist to thumb), she to demand that I pull a monster face, make a monster noise, and pursue her gently. I agree there's all that to come, while Milk, like an inspector general, sniffs at their clothes and hands, peers into their eyes as if to decipher Linear B engraved on their frontal lobes, and prods them with her fingers, maybe to see if they have soft centers. I decide to draw up a list of things to do, then to transfer it to the calendar: a call at the nearby private school for the handicapped (children up to eight years); a dip in the Olympic pool on campus; a ride in Asa's plane; a game of tennis (of course!), and perhaps a look inside the nuclear-reactor building where the Cerenkov radiation is blue. Big-hugging while I chew my second slice of pie, I figure the pros and cons, but also the vast context that somehow enlarges everything we do, makes our fun acute. The big enchilada, 3C 236, the biggest thing in the universe, gets a hard run for its money from the dust-laden envelope surrounding the star cutely called RU Lupi, where stars have only recently condensed from gas and are making, so to speak, final adjustments to their format before becoming regular stars on the main sequence. Why, those opaque clouds move at planetary distances and RU Lupi might be surrounded by a system of protoplanets, a nascent solar system to which one might be able to transfer during one's next incarnation. For the present, we have to be amiable, busy, and familial. With all my force, I try: tonight we play scrabble, with Milk assembling (then upsetting) words the language might do well to have, a couple being *fnog* and *mubb*. Her own name she spells out first time, with ringmaster polish, and then mine, Pi's. In no time she sets all our names together as one word and then pronounces it at speed, with joking brio. Cued by me, Pi applauds. Then Milk, Russian-style, applauds herself, blinking heavily as she does. For half an hour she paints quietly, daubing a three-foot sheet of rough paper with red and yellow helixes which she then converts into tapered towers, whose tops she links with

108

green foliage. Telling her to let it dry, I point to the thumb-tacks; but she insists on my lifting them out and rolls up the wet paper into a cylinder that goes to bed with her, under her pillow, like a Dead-Sea Rorschach scroll. Never mind, we have paper, bedsheets, pillowcases galore. She will enjoy running the linens through the washing machine, having never outgrown hydraulic delight, whether of the dip, the plunge, the broad hand slapped deep into its face, or the even, al-most-hypnotized gaze from bank or shore. Next to that comes, I suspect, baking bread, an old favorite, especially when she kneads and tears, fits loaves with eyes, and rolls with pom-poms. Once she made a loaf that included poster color, sand, a lock of her own hair, and the head of a small doll. An oven mutant, this came out smelling of celluloid and burned paint. We then painted it blue (a hint from Man Ray) and hammered nails into its teaklike shell. Always, I tell my-self, I tell Pi, I tell all and sundry, you can cheer Milk up by deforming a bit of the present civilization: wash an electric motor in thick suds, file the nose off a doll, paint any window yellow or black (I don't know why other colors won't do). There will never come, I'm sure, a day when I run out of remedies.

"Upward of a hundred pages, bighand, longhand," I say to Pi when Milk has gone to sleep. "Of what?" she asks, puzzled. I explain about the verbal spoor I've been keeping, bits of scribble cached here and there during the day while Milk has been around, but begun before she arrived. The amount surprises her. Then I confess to my scheme, which, hardly noticeable to anyone not in the know, has consisted of three-paragraph groups assembled according to the genetic chain: sixty-four in all, with only G or C or A or U to begin the first word of each paragraph with. She shakes her head, thinks the whole thing maniacal, especially when I point out that not a single topic sentence, thus far, has begun with, say, *The*. This very paragraph I'm writing now, I tell her, is the last one in the chain, the sixty-fourth group, third paragraph, beginning with the final U of the group U-U-U. She bursts out laughing, but redeems herself by nodding at the need to provide a stair rail, as it were, an obstacle, a matrix, a curb. "A *handicap!* Out of mother nature by necessity, nothing as tough as *terza rima* or the sonnet, but a virtuosity-provoking nuisance at least." I stop explaining, tell her I've reached the point of no return now I've used up the permutations of the code. What now? Start again with the same three (a C, an A, an A), or cull triplets at random? "Hell," she says, "maybe the code isn't exhaustive; maybe there are combinations of three that aren't there. Really dysgenic ones." There and then we try, with pads and pencils, to combine G, A, C, U in ways that nature lacks, so that, having come full circle with my balked child only half a week on the premises, I can go off at a tangent, implying combinations of sugar and phosphorus and acids that slipped the First Cause's mind. With the following result. There isn't one. So: I re-count. I have used, of all the words available, *Going,* to begin twelve paragraphs, and *A, As, At,* five or six times apiece. Four *Good*s, three *Can*s, two *Under*s, if I've counted right. Watching me write this down, Pi tells me to repeat the same random procedure, if I *must* go on. I will. Use every moment. Waste not, runs the adage, want not. I'll always want. Want means lack. More soon. After refreshment, of whatever kind. When I'll once more snail-track my gabble up the spiral alphabet that lords it over us, whatever else we think we are.

TWO

Andromeda to Scorpius

Underhandedly, after all that, I change my mind, decide to paragraph not at random as before but observing triplet order as it is in my table of the code. Thus, I begin UUU and end GGG. Failure of nerve, access of self-control: call it what I will, it's a system of sorts, reasserting what's inexorable as our two-week gala flops down the watershed of its halfway mark. I can still make the paragraphs as long or as short as I fancy, but I'll distribute the subject matter exactly as the twenty amino acids are distributed over the grid of the sixty-four triplets. So: UUU and UUC, both phenylalinine, could be this or that subject (balloons perhaps) while UUA and UUG, which follow, are leucine and could be, oh, Milk's departure anticipated. *Could* be, I say; it's likely they won't, not if things keep on going the way they are. Rat in the maze, I brood on being rat instead of making the maze sustain me. In any event, since phenylalinine doesn't occur again, whereas leucine does, I'd better work out which subjects I've most to say about and which I'll skimp. Thus leading to another problem, by which I mean spreading myself on evasions and minifying the pain. No: I'll handle, as long as required, the acids that burn, be glad of those that don't. If any of these acids burns at all. There are six leucines, serines, arginines, but only one methionine, one tryptophan, while others add to two, three, or four. Nature favors some over others, as we know. This fact we call degeneracy of the code. And how do you reform that? Helplessly, I start out by favoring the minority acids, even though there's nothing wrong with them—unless, as the textbook has it, "in its *exceptional* state, C pairs with A rather than with G, and so on," and the result is various "deletions" or "garblings." The chemistry behind some mutations is today fairly well understood, or so I'm told. I'm glad. I hear of mutagens, which augment the probability of "illicit" pairings, which puts me in mind of the forbidden degrees of consanguinity. I call that tightening the Bible's belt.

UAA, UAG, and UGA, however, stand for no acid at all, are designated "Nonsense" or "Stop" in the tables. Perfectly all right by me. Punctuation or funk, they'll come in useful. Kiss and be off. Luckily, this isn't DNA I'm dabbling in, but messenger RNA and therefore single-stranded (even though I'm doubling up in the written text, with two successive onslaughts on the code). Doubled up with anxiety, or even pain (an ulcer or despair?), I feel hysteria gather each time I check the calendar. No wonder I need the grid to keep me calm, or this time stick to the letter of the law.

Useful reference material follows: book's template. Or bookplate, indicating rightful owner. Garbled hitherto, honored from now on: see p. 115, and reel.

Unlike, isn't it, a plot of Sir Walter Scott's, or of Dostoevsky's? It evokes the hymn board on the church pillar, or baseball scoreboards, timetables of trains, the stock-market report unrolling on TV. It (I propel the next word downward into the place it belongs in)

usurps natural flow, of course, but can be regarded as an

1	UUU p	3	AUU i	5	UCU s	7	ACU t
	UUC p		AUC i		UCC s		ACC t
	UUA l		AUA i		UCA s		ACA t
	UUG l		AUG m		UCG s		ACG t
2	CUU l	4	GUU v	6	CCU pr	8	GCU a
	CUC l		GUC v		CCC pr		GCC a
	CUA l		GUA v		CCA pr		GCA a
	CUG l		GUG v		CCG pr		GCG a

9	UAU ty	11	AAU as	13	UGU c
	UAC ty		AAC as		UGC c
	UAA STOP		AAA ly		UGA STOP
	UAG STOP		AAG ly		UGG tr
10	CAU h	12	GAU asp		
	CAC h		GAC asp		
	CAA g		GAA gl		
	CAG g		GAG gl		

14	CGU ar	16	GGU gly
	CGC ar		GGC gly
	CGA ar		GGA gly
	CGG ar		GGG gly
15	AGU s		
	AGC s		
	AGA ar		
	AGG ar		

(A: Adenine
C: Cytosine
G: Guanine
U: Uracil

a: alanine
ar: arginine
as: asparagine
asp: aspartic acid
c: cysteine
g: glutamine
gl: glutamic acid
gly: glycine
h: histidine
i: isoleucine
l: leucine
ly: lysine
m: methionine
p: phenylalanine
pr: proline
s: serine
t: threonine
tr: tryptophan
ty: tyrosine
v: valine)

obstacle course, a systemics, challenging the virtuoso. Most of all by an optimist. Who might recite the Geneva Convention during a bombardment, or spout logarithms while having a locally anesthetized limb amputated. That kind of starched upper lip. I think of the stanza named after Edmund Spenser, or of how, according to William Wordsworth, nuns fret not when confined in a sonnet's narrow room.

And so it's much easier when an A shows up (or a C or a G), like an oasis or the face of a long-missed friend. What a nervous rebeginning this is, and with a vengeance not mine.

Under such auspices, I become a mere example of someone clinging to shibboleth: the password that keeps other words out. Where, just now, it was *under,* it might have been *untold* or *urn.* I cling as best I can. See what comes to fit next, what next fit comes.

U-turn it is, permitting me to reverse my direction of travel, recheck the grid over which I move like an analphabetical ant, or an insane checkers addict, trying to match theme to acid, yet squandering the vacant space on thoughts about, or previous to, the thought that ought to be. I use my means against my end, my end against my means. Was ever human so divided? Was ever code so bleak?

Giddey-up, I tell myself. Back to the action, the girls, Asa, and Co.

Chad's daughter and Milk embrace on meeting, no reason at all, the petite prodigy who at six years could classify dinosaurs without putting a syllable wrong and the long Viking who still hasn't made it through her first reading primer. The one chatters at the other's grin. They stand back and survey each other, sharing some secret giggle they might have been building for years by transatlantic telephone, and then join up again. The helpless one lets the helpful one help her, mirrors the diamond kindness. Off they go downstairs with ice-cream cones. At least a piece of the Milky Way awaits them. All the way from Canis Minor to Cassiopeia. I wonder if we'll ever get to Cygnus and the rest; the social pace has hotted up.

Unruly laughter from below. Is it at or with? Has it an object at all? Is it something that just spilled over out of their systems? Pi says yes, it's alchemy, their glottal shivers. Chad says it's the obbligato that being unmarried yields. I go down to see. They are pointing at, laughing at, the two tennis players in Gemini, and have been having a duet of mimed expostulations, unless it was wit rammed into numbness, an agitated hand-sweep from Milk that fanned Meg's glowing coal. Two girls have found each other, that's for sure. Two only children are being childlike together. So who cares about symmetry when there's fusion?

Umpire not needed, they'll make rules of their own, a truce where no war was.

Creeping down to see, we all marvel at their engrossed-ness. Milk points at the Way, then they mime something or other, gurgling their mirth, both their ice-cream cones eaten. One of them has switched on the stars. I wonder which. The one who thinks she is a *Tyrannosaurus rex?* Or the one who babbles on behalf of a brain whose cells have the wrong kinds of spikes? Now they chase through and find us, instruct us, in various ways, to leave them to it. We do. Samarkand was never so special as this basement is, with an Alice and a Snow White together.

Unbuttoning his shirt after slackening his tie, Chad gives his best avuncular-patrician nod. They'll find a language, he says. We all three concur. They have. We eat the late lunch of soup, tuna sandwiches, and cheese. Beer and coffee. Above the house, azure light fills curving space and a hot wind all the way from the Gulf, or the Islands, rattles the screens. I put on some Elgar, the First Symphony, all heart and luscious

117

nobility. Hardly any pomp at all. The girls come upstairs, munch sandwiches at refugee speed, then go down again with a cold can each. Pi and Chad sit outside on the balcony, call in to tell me they can hear the doves, which I then drown with Bruckner's Seventh, more massive, more plangent, than Elgar, and less urbane. In Elgar there are just people; you feel that Bruckner is guessing at God. Boa-constricting his own hubris, he takes his time, knows it's a loan only.

Conversation sparkles awhile, then flags. Pi asks what the Virgin Mary would be wearing if coming toward us. We don't know. "An inviolet shift," she says. Russian psychiatrists, Chad reports, are being ordered to report anyone claiming to be normal, since normality has now become a front for deviants. All I can offer is the TV commercial that, peddling a record album, said: So you don't forget, send before midnight tomorrow. "Gra-tuit-ous," Pi says. "We live in a big catalogue," says he. *"And,"* I add, *"what bargains we are."*

Calmly, Milk and Meg get across the pool. Neither swims, but the tall one ferries the short. Lounging in chairs at the poolside, we plan the week (though it might be better to plan for *after* the week, when anti-climax and deprivation will be working their worst on me at least). Now the girls go back across the pool, making exaggerated birdcalls and turning round to look at us. I seem to see a vulture planing low, its copyright infringed. An ostrich raises a haughty, bedraggled head, but it's only Milk after dunking herself. It must be ninety today, whatever day it is.

Unexpected, my landlord arrives, runs off ten minutes of ciné film as the girls romp in the pool, and leaves, promising to let me see the results. Another spoor! And all this time, or most of it, I am writing my own, a paragraph or even a page, scratched into a thin examination answer-book with a 2-B pencil. That does it. I'll tape-record Milk as well, must above all have a synesthetic portrait to relive her by.

(At some point, perhaps this, chronology became a mosaic, with everything separate from everything else, but also seen in sharper detail. Cameos. Etchings.) I insert this, looking back, which I suppose means I survived. There are stills that begin to move, then freeze, which don't connect with other stills. And won't. The aural equivalent I see when listening to electronic music such as Morton Subotnick's *Silver Apples of the Moon*. Arranged in ranks on a forty-five-degree slope, like players in an old-style swing band, fat foot-high goblins with innocent, impassive faces are flailing at tiny drums on their knees with brushes while playing jew's-harps at top speed with their mouths, the resultant meld of jittery cross-rhythms being too fast to tap to and so crammed with blurp, twang, tsk-tsk, fglizz, and klontch that, while I know each goblin is playing a separate part, I can't separate it from any of the others. What precedes what, I have no idea, but the demented side-of-the-mouth acceleration of this jellybean music "for syntheziser" seems fraught with uniqueness. Like several short-wave radio stations coming in all at once, distorted and overlapping, alike but not. It's the speed does it. Remembering, I smother Milk in sun-screen cream, Meg too. The sun is still high enough to burn. Then Milk, rolling her eyes, asks for Asa: "Ay-a," and I know she is taking root.

Curious what happened next. See how I have changed to the past tense. Perhaps it was the smart of looking forward to Milk's departure. I was living in the future so much that I left the narrative alone, to be related in the past. Safer. Cooler. Harder. Notes, I kept on making those, but I gave up writing out paragraphs according to the genetic code. And that is the chore that now confronts me. I have to make up all the missed work; with, to fortify me, the famous compensation of hindsight. "A good idea," Pi told me: "you'll be more collected afterwards" (as if I were a *Works*). I explained to her the problem of writing in the present: "It's only the

119

words that are in the present, never what they mention." The whole thing's a cheat, I told myself. What's to choose between writing in the belated present and the immediate past? What a tricky thing to say! I mean: both tenses are an illusion, both are modes of the past. Indeed, events are just as much alive in the past tense as in the present. The difference is one of sounds only. The time lapse is literal, which is to say it takes place in the words' letters only. At any rate, I left it all for later, meaning now. A real then instead of a fake now. That's why I just now stuck in that section in parentheses, beginning with *At some point* and ending with *Etchings.* I was getting into trim, I suppose, sneaking it in as an earnest of future endeavor. But while Milk was still here, it was too much to bear: all my thoughts were of foreboding, no joy in the here-at-hand at all. So I quit.

Unless it was an ulcer coming on. The crisis, the commotion, the treatment. And the diet that is slops, and, insult after injury, is a weight-loss diet made bland as well. Enough of that. For a mere necrosis of tissue you don't write an elegy.

Going back over it all, I know that as soon as events began to feel simultaneous, there was no point in using any tense at all. After later, I told myself. That's when to do it. So long as you let stand what's already done in the so-called present. I hope that's clear. What's the point in writing *now* if you no longer have any sense of *when?*

As it is, I feed on things that might be thought to hurt, like the bacterium *Pseudomonas radiodurans* that thrives in the large neutron flux at the cores of nuclear reactors. A perverse entity, for sure. Or am I even worse? Like the so-called obligate aerobe that oxygen poisons. Freaks. Yet there are plenty of us. There is an enzyme that's more active in ice than in water. Don Juan Pond, in Antarctica, contains a possibly unique microflora that metabolizes in extreme cold, at least down to $-23°$ Centigrade. All very well to cite these, if only comparisons could get me off the hook. They won't. They only bait the hook better. Therefore, back to the mainstream which has flowed down past me. Into some irrefragable distance, middle or far.

Up early one day, Milk and I larded patching paste into the cracks between wall and bath, using ordinary table knives. First a big blob, then a long horizontal motion that left a six-inch-long fairing behind it. We might have been filling in a space between wing and fuselage to reduce drag. Carried away, she also smoothed in the drainhole and invented the game of raising the white patch by flipping the plug lever to and fro. Pi was typing away at a new poem in the basement, the sounds those of a small factory that makes badges or buckles. Hers had been the invention of a domestic custom known as tokens, by which each partner caches small gifts for the other in obscure parts of the house. In a book not often consulted. Between wads of Kleenex in their box. Behind a can of shaving foam. In this way we had regaled each other with sticks of gum, new pens, bizarre clippings from the local papers. Catching on fast, Milk thus acquired a kaleidoscope, a plastic spider that walked when she squeezed a rubber ball, and various rolls of ribbon. Unselfish to the core, but unable to do shopping, she gave us things of our own. I found one of my neckties rolled up in a plastic bag in the flour canister. Pi received a fancy ring in her face cloth. If I took the time, I'd tell of the Tampon in the typewriter, the typewriter in the oven, the toilet seat Scotch-taped down. All these were offerings. Once Milk saw that we allowed odd things, she responded with all her heart. We crawled on the floors, we had pillow fights. We droned, we went blindfold, we handstood, we linked arms when out walking, we watched TV through cupped hands, we played chase all through the house, we pounded garbage-can lids together for cymbals, we rode one another piggy-back and even tried to play leapfrog. When Meg came, she and Milk painted liquor boxes

121

with poster colors. Milk's was usually black or red, whereas Meg stippled hers with colors worthy of temples at Isfahan. They are still there, in the basement, dried and a bit warped, ready to hold books and papers on the next trip. Urns? Oubliettes? Jackless boxes? No, building blocks, I think. Or treasure chests. Even if the spiders have set up house inside.

Uncanny with children, one day Asa fetched us to his lawn to see a small tree decorated with what seemed catkins or tissue-paper tassels. Then one peeled open, all by itself, and we saw a red Monarch butterfly emerge, then another, within a half-hour ten. He had attached several dozen pupas to the branches. At the spectacle of all those Monarchs unfolding, drying out, and preening themselves, Milk spun with glee, and ever after kept asking for the "bu-fla dree." And got it most days, even being so bold as to go off alone with him in his car. I think she spent hours there on the grass, watching what dangled come to life, at least until she tried to pick a few and by accident pulped a couple. Of the dozen crucial memories, the ones that biting heal, this is one. Something heraldic about it, something chromatically sumptuous, haunts me each time I pass a shrub or see a butterfly. The shrub erupts into scarlet flame, the tassels give birth.

About this time Asa confided to us why he'd given up beekeeping. One more bee sting might be fatal, he said. Yet that weird bit of information fell back into the rest of his bristling talk, about how skulls found in Jericho have cowries over the eyes, how the seventeen-year cicada lives for one day only, how a certain silkworm moth need release only 10^{-8} grams of sex attractant per second to draw to her every male within an area miles wide. Or so he said. One day he came with us to see the reactor building on campus, when Milk shrieked "boo warbar!" non-stop, in some radioactive frenzy. Another, more signal day, he had us all up to his laboratory, where, with a few simple pieces of apparatus, he combined methane, ammonia, hydrogen, and water vapor, sent them again and again through a liquid-water solution, and then sparked the mixture with a corona discharge. Come back in a few days, he said. We did, to find new colors. "Pretty," Milk whispered, using one of her best words (it came out "pre'y"), little realizing she was looking at amino acids new-created. Asa's genesis, that of us all. Yet I think we all, even he, preferred the Monarch tree, out in the air, blooming with wings even as we bibbed our sodas and beer, puffed our cigars, nibbled on pretzels.

Upstairs, Milk played his piano, first of all by pounding on the keys, even using her elbows *à la* Charles Ives, then by going inside with a light chain she trailed across the strings. She plucked, she twanged. Then she played on the keys again, but with thimbles capping her fingers. Thanks to Asa, she went right beyond the sound barrier, watching the sound on a motiondizer screen. The air in the cone moved the membrane's mirrors and her loud piano twirled through in plastic, swift helixes of naked light. Only a day later, he had a color wheel set up for her, as well as a projection set that blazoned the wall with starbursts, multi-colored clouds, and colliding planets, at which she crooned and waved. When he started up a slowly rotating mirrored ball a foot in diameter, she leaped toward it, trying to touch, but fell six inches short. By then it was almost redundant to let her look through a stereo viewer at infra-red aerial photos, but he did it, only to have her administer a swift nod and return her gaze to the the wall, asking for stars and clouds all over again. These Asa provided, and Milk looked away only when a startlingly tall black woman walked in, exotically named Kashmiri, and stroked Milk's long hair with creased pink palms. Milk shook hands left-handedly and peered right into the girl's eyes, the pale blue-green into the black. Then we all went downstairs, Milk looking at us all through a distorting pliable plastic lens which, as I found, having my turn, gave anyone two heads if you held it right. "One more face!" ordered Milk, eager for grimaces to transform into something even worse, and thus we descended, leering and twitching. It was a wonder we didn't fall on the stairs.

"Come," said Asa, and we went into what he jokingly called his Living Room. Rabbits running loose (and an aroma to suit), an ant farm which Milk looked disdainfully at for half a minute, and a white mouse in a treadmill, certainly earned the adjective. But Asa had other wares to show today. First he gave Milk two magnets, which either sprang together or stayed neutrally apart while she marveled at the pull that waxed and waned, sighting along her arms for the motive force: the tiny engineer in the armpit, the gremlin inside the ulna who pushed. Bored with this, she gladly watched Asa make a Cartesian diver rise and descend in its bottle by simple hand-pressure. Trying it, she addressed the miniature plastic man inside in a language she thought right ("bond, bond," it sounded like, flanked by "ebba boe"). A low-friction Air Puck, powered by a balloon, skimmed above the fitted carpet like a peregrinating flash, and rather frightened her. Perhaps she thought it an animal that would bite. Next he balanced a small gyroscope on her finger while she froze and he told us about the rotor, weighted with so-called fluid sand, and the micro-bearings so tiny that a thimble would hold hundreds of them. Ten minutes she stood while the gyro-scope spun and leaned, after which she eyed the dent in her finger, mock-woundedly whispering "sore, sore," while Asa, a Marx Brothers Leonardo, tried to distract her with conjur-ing tricks: eggs that came and went, puffs of smoke from his fingertips, dimes that turned into pennies and back, an al-ways-full water jug, and a cigarette that went right through a handkerchief. Pensively handling a prism, Asa changed his mind as she grinned mad-wide and let out a plangent "More!" "Hold on honey," said the black girl, signing with her astonishing hands, and Milk promptly signed back, which is to say she rubbed her tummy, a school gesture for "I'm sorry." They gave her a pair of diffraction-grating glasses that spellbound her from the outset. I tried a pair myself, sharing the spectrum with her. Weird how the split light seemed to enfilade. Even more so outside, where, in no time, Asa had a menagerie going. Rabbits and the foal. A nine-foot hot-air balloon whose red and white gores lofted up to two hundred feet. Like a fisherman's float in the wrong element. I say red and white, but it was a color total. Asa left it up while he busied himself with a giant flying saucer he'd built from a kit. Tethered, it went up to join the balloon. Whooping, Milk almost trod on a rabbit. In the act of trying to leap skyward, glasses on, she launched herself sideways into the group of us. Asa readied a balloon copter powered by three little jet streams. It circled the yard and landed in a tree, panicking cardinals and grackles. Now he took Milk off to the redwood geodesic greenhouse, out of which she peered, grinning allusively. When she came back, she had left her glasses in it, so she sprinted back and spent the next half-hour touring the garden. All of us wore glasses to look at the roses. The hues of everything reeled in echelon away from us. "Richard Of York Gave Battle," I murmured, as tectonic plates of Richard's colors moved right and left in that order. Indigo. Violet. In. Vain. The ghost of Aldous Huxley stalked tall among us, approving. The garden swelled like the hot-air balloon, soared like the tethered saucer. A high jet exploded. On my hand a ladybug bulged like an awning. The little rock in the goldfish pond opened up into a Bermuda of the eye. Kashmiri brought tea and coffee on a tray scarred vermilion and green. Even the rattle of cups and saucers took on a slapdash atonality denied to Milk. We grouped for ring-a-ring-of-roses, laughing zanily, then (as the song has it) all sat down. Flopped. "Nobody take your glasses off," called Asa. "No scabs here!" Nobody did. "Let there be light," I quoted aloud, and there *was.* "Rosetta Stone!" cried Pi, in high-altitude spirits. "Anoxia!" yelled Asa. "The Wars of the Roses!" Kashmiri said nothing, but poured. Milk jabbered, pointing at this or that, shrieking hugely as a bee zoomed past. The firmament twirled. A grand way of putting it. But what they say about rose-colored glasses is true: you see the air, and like it. You are inhaling color. Come into our parlor, say the tiny macrophages in the lung to the well-dressed molecules as they enter all dolled up. Someone, perhaps Pi, said how stunning it would be to be underwater with such glasses on, or even a mask whose entire disk did this with light. We'll do it, I elatedly called out. We'll take her to the Bahamas. Asa will make us special masks, won't you? Asa can make anything. Right? Maybe so, he said, but Africa would take him longer than usual; a spiral nebula here and there would take him even longer. But, Pi told him, while Kashmiri laughed in a proprietorial way, wizards don't apologize. Milk didn't care. She was already underwater. She swam. She looped her body as if at the end of a pool length, and swam off again, at the crawl. Already my own mind had gone truant, prompted by Asa's talk of a spiral nebula. I wanted to finish the Way, at least the northern part of it, such as you see if you stay north of the Florida keys. The big wheel of M 51, partnered by a little one, soared at me out of the constellation called the Hunting Dogs, an independent Milky Way system itself holding many billions of stars. I felt a knot of pain, not that ulcer, but the core of an ill-formed metaphor for Milk, who, universe-like, receded faster from us the farther away she was. And, oh, she was far enough. In some ways, out at the beginning of the universe which forever zoomed out of sight the farther we saw. Heavens, indeed. A universe only months ago thought to be ten or twelve billion years old was already sixteen, with a promise of more. Hopeless. What a game, when the better the instrument the more inaccessible the answer becomes. So we settle for M 51, say, glad that it resembles a whirlpool or a Scotch-tape dispenser with tiny delivery platform, or for its neighbors, the stars named Cor Caroli (after Charles I of England) and La Superba, gaudy tumbling red. Meanwhile, back here, the wild goings-on got wilder. Asa walked right up a tree and started to munch a balloon. Kashmiri, real name Eloise Robinson, stripped naked and dowsed herself with warm tea. Milk, for reasons known only to her, burst out with words filched from *The Damnation of Faust* by Berlioz: "Irimiru! Hass! Hass! Karabrao!" Whiplash, death-knell words, they frappéd my blood. All I could do was to haul down the hot-air balloon. When we took off our glasses, we had no eyes. Pi had gone inside, no doubt to meditate a poem on our preposterous doings, although doubtless something more ambitious than the maxim of hers that I was remembering: *"Mrok* and the world *mroks* with you; *grenkle,* and you *grenkle* alone."* Then, as now, *mrok* meant to be be persistently affable, *grenkle* its opposite. The upshot of this policy, it seemed to me, was that one would be either dishonest but with companions, or honest and alone. Such was my mood, one of apodictic gloom. All of a sudden. Out of that fleecy sky. Sometimes it no more pays to get up than to go to bed. I heard more synthesizer music, each wobble and squiggle and squelch an ad-lib scoff from the cosmic joker.

Actually, Milk was sitting peacefully in the geodesic greenhouse with a thermometer in her mouth, self-condemned to silence. A mighty being, like Wordsworth's, not so much awake as insomniac. Asa was lying flat on the grass, shirt off, hairless chest upward. Kashmiri was in the act of conducting the skittish foal round the back. Pi was scribbling on a little ruled yellow pad. The aerial objects were floating high, bucking and tilting in a minor breeze. Over on the far side of the garden, someone in dungarees was hosing a shrub. One big bucolic halt. Best expressed in an unending paragraph dedicated to Samuel Beckett, an underdone offering on the altar of the comma. Or in a flurry of short ones, like neutrinos cutting through the afternoon without disturbing it at all.

Ugli: a Jamaican citrus fruit produced by crossing a grapefruit with a tangerine.

A word that Milk won't ever have, or need. On the other hand, since she is not expected to become competent, she can be whimsical, garner a few luxury words such as communicative folk don't want. On that day, or in that year, at thirteen past Wednesday on the 77th of October, I'll regale her with *lemma, hoplite,* and *chinquapin.* The day I was describing ran down peacefully to a shrimp dinner at an informal eatery called The Fireplace. Milk troughed as if it were all going not into her body but into a hopper outside. Pi was witty, as usual, conjuring diabolical riddles out of inoffensive words ("A brown bear having a heart attack is having?" "A Kodiak arrest"). Asa balanced forks and knives on tumblers, made a small and accurate mouse out of bread, which Milk devoured, and spoke of visiting New York City. Kashmiri, she hummed, she alluded briefly to Magritte, Stockhausen, and Heidegger, as if presenting cultural credentials; not that she needed to, since anyone capable of surviving Asa must be egregiously gifted at very least. She was. "Why 'Kashmiri'?" I asked. "Because," she said, "I'm woolly. Not straight. The money I might have used to fix my hair, I used to buy *Britannica Three.* The book that sounds like a cruise ship! I have read about one third, and will finish before I'm thirty, in two years' time. Then I'll test myself, or Asa will, to see if I'm fit to embark on *The New English Dictionary.* All umpteen volumes. No sense in just cooling your heels, in this civilization. A person should absorb."

Ado, much. So it seemed at the time to Pi, herself a woman so coordinated intellectually that she seems muscle-bound and all the little Golgi or Purkinje cells in her brain are asking to be set free. After Asa, that Golden Age polymath, that horn of plenty masquerading as a human, it was Pi, not I, who made the phenomenal world perform, quietly folding a cootie (paper beak that pecks if you squeeze and release it) or snipping away at several thicknesses of paper until she revealed between her hands a row of little people holding hands, who became a zigzag that would stand on its own. Her origami comes from the age of five, ten years before she went through a dark night of the cerebellum (or whatever) and began drawing herself tiny in the bottom corners of large sheets of paper. There, in those right-angles, the poet began, born not made. And now she writes about the solar system, sees little cows that sip the hoarfrost at the Martian poles. She has been mighty patient with this pup of a text, must surely have reasoned: After the bravura blather of impatient narcissism, he'll arrive at the runic contradictions of grandstand virtuosity, and then, before the convention he's flouting breaks down entirely, the dreamlike intermittences of resentful improvisation. The rest is silage.

Unkind attributions, these. I'll quit. I'll undertake another book altogether. *Six Characters, Seven Funerals.* If not one entitled *And/Or,* set in Andorra la Vella. I'll go away, disguised as my own baggage. I'll speak Indo-European to the hostess, Esperanto to the taxi men. I'll go out of the top of my head. No. I'll pay my bills, catch up on ten days' correspondence, defrost the refrigerator, trim the shrubs that block the walk, scour the toilet bowl, find a screw that fits the hole in the screen. That's it! Be practical, use our hands together so that Milk can say "Wynd, wynd," even while the angel of silence is flying over us. What I did was to go round the ceiling of the living room and mop up a new brood of spiders, pinhead small but fast. Omit that chore and you have scores of big ones in a week. Ours is a house of spiders, ours is, the cause the trees. I dabbed them to death with tissues while Pi and Milk clipped flowers in the garden, lucky to find white bottle gentians, otherwise known as closed. After a few days the tube splits open to form high-aspect-ratio petals. I'm told the brain is light-sensitive, but not as sensitive as those gentians, I'm stupidly sure. On, on, on.

Galloping about the tennis court, we lost balls and bruised our knees. Milk hit with shocking force when she did hit, maybe under the impression that the game's object was to knock your opponent down. Or maim. I blistered my thumb and forefinger, Pi turned an already tricky ankle. But (bonuses) Milk did an exquisite headstand against the net post, aligned like a plunging egret, her face serene and red, her breath insanely held. For half an hour, having got the patter, she scored in ecstatic disregard of the game, calling her favorite words: "Dirty" (Thirty), "Dew" (Deuce), and most of all "Lo'" (Love). Love-love, love-love, she cried up and down the court, whether playing or not, whether watching or not, even when she looked up at the far corner of the high side net and inexplicably, first, called "ice, ice." The ice, as usual, was in her eye, a refraction, an eyelash icicle. She had done it at five years, had no reason not to do it in her teens. Yet, when her warble brought ice and love together again and again, in the heat of another hot day, with only a couple of teenagers to gape at her, some wildly improbable purity suffused the afternoon, fixed it in mind as a victory over trash, glibness, cant, and pain. Her next-best trick was to stand on two tennis balls, doing something between a sway and a wobble, yet pliably elegant, the spirit of the molecule riding on twin atoms. On her return to the house, she spent an hour in the bath, running it cooler and cooler and testing the filled-in cracks with the tip of a nail brush's handle.

Good days, bad, there weren't that many left. An impossible urge to cram each minute, or not to share her with anyone save Pi, came and went. Hoarding only made things worse. So Milk and I made a morning excursion, all of fifty yards, to a neighboring house converted from fraternity use into a school for handicapped children up to the age of eight. Unlike most schools of this kind, it went on through the summer, although with a contingent reduced from fifteen to half a dozen. I'd seen the children returning from the nearby elementary school, lined up to cross the road, or crouched in refusal on the sidewalk, or expostulating in slurred language on the way home. A little bent, or incomplete, is how they looked, somehow frost-bitten in the marrow, but given to affable cries and jolly scooping motions with the hand. One said hello, when I saw him, by jutting his head up and forward, as if through some invisible screen. A girl, who usually had him by the hand, being a year or two his senior, greeted with spastic flaps of her free hand, making her thumb peck. (I say *making*, but no doubt the thumb pleased itself.) Our visit was all very casual. Milk leered a bit from her teenage altitude, being after all a prefect in her own school: a keeper of law and order, with awful power of imperative and tongue-tied rebuke. I had seen her harangue wrongdoers, with her fierce Nordic temperament, bellowing, "Walk, don't run!" ("War, done ru"). And few dared run after that. Minus her hearing aids, which she has always seemed to think obsolete, she always comes on strong, knowing her defect isn't visible, and on that day, again without them, she interviewed each child a bit like Gulliver among the Lilliputians, using few words but an arsenal of gestures, signs, and discreetly given prods. At first they shrank from her, asking her complex questions from a distance, maybe wondering what it was like on her planet, or deep in the ice from which she had been excavated after several thousand years. After a while, though, they relaxed, took her outside to the slide and the sandbox, where she paused for an interrogative look at me, then all five feet of her careened down the slide, filled a bucket with sand, chased them with bubbling laughs and caught them all, and then let them chase her. So agile at the twist, the double-back, the feint, she might have been a top-class soccer player rehearsing without ball. In the end they mobbed her, closing all ways out, and she let them haul her to the dried-out ground, tickle her to the point of ecstatic distraction, even tears that made her eye make-up run (some days she sneaked it on, on others she forgot or didn't bother). Never having had a friend when out of school, she befriended them all on a sub-verbal level, grabbing and patting and stroking hair both long and short. It seemed she was encouraging them from a great height, though with a touch of sternness in all she did-said, for all the world an indulgent parent. Inside again, she even steered a trio of them through a reading lesson. She said the words written on the blackboard not better, but more loudly, than they, then scrawled a few of her own without erasing. That palimpsest included a few old favorites such as *slide, water,* and *pretty,* ungainly in form but legible, and she seemed shocked when they identified what she'd chalked up. Lord God, I thought, the fact or the art of communication surprises her still. Always doubting it, she lives in a world more random than Planck's. For five minutes, inspired by that breakthrough, she talked to them all with nasal hauteur, pausing and using her hands like some practiced lecturer, say Jacob Bronowski warming to the subject of transhumance, although without his semi-conspiratorial whisper, his oracular sigh. Caught up in this gabfest, while the three young teachers grinned indulgently, I took the eraser, wiped the board clean, and drew the first thing that came to mind, M 51, the Whirlpool Nebula, a rooster's tail in white chalk. Milk pointed, proudly uttered "Milk Way," which was brilliant although wrong, it's not in or near the Way at all. Then she tested them, asking, only to be told it was a firework, a spring, a mother's face. Unthinkingly, since I'd not long ago been looking at it, I'd drawn in the lines of radio emission, which look like fibers or wires within the speckle of the star lanes. And I saw it too, the maternal profile that looked down, maybe with eyes closed,

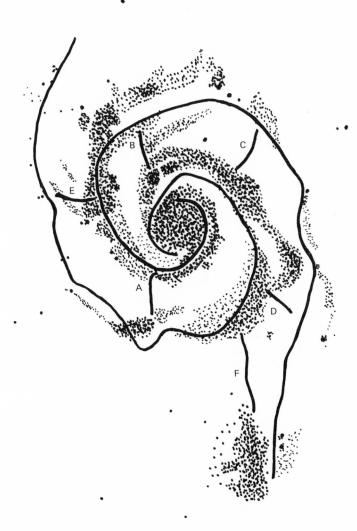

M 51 and Companion Galaxy NGC 5195.
Lines show radio emission. Lines ABCDE show
interarm links and F the link with NGC 5195.

133

the chin pressed into that slot at the bottom of the throat, the "heartspoon." A lovely analogy, a grand feat of simile, it nonetheless evoked for Milk the wrong image, of a woman several thousand miles away, or at least non-available. For whom she then asked, and our visit ended with repetitive demands from her, which on the walk homeward became an organized interrogation on her part: "Where? When? *Soon?*" Looking back, I saw two or three children waving at us, a goodbye or an invitation, a cheer or a salute, I'm not sure. She had moved among them like a flawed Amazon, leader, den mother, and premature aunt in one, heavy-handed in her ease, at once better and worse, farther along and therefore harder to handle, a vision for their teachers of those children's future, a portrait of the graduate walking tall. In spite of her big hat, she was pink and wet in the face, on the edge of being outright irritable, and she'd begun to walk with that minor limp which, when she was tired or put out, invaded her loose-legged quickstep shuffle. She went into the bath to soothe herself, and then she and Pi pored over the microscope at the kitchen table, examining hair and paper fiber while I made hamburgers, mixed a couple of Jellos for later on. Carried away, I nicked a finger with a scalded needle and gave them a spot of blood to view, the cells like tiny dinghies inflated, or azure doughnuts. "Blood," Milk said. "Blood," I agreed.

Us, after lunch, anti-climactic after my hamburgers. Only Milk is used to meat. I say so, aloud, and humid air swallows the words. Pi dreams. Milk has found a temporary land-of-heart's-desire in the flat plastic oval full of two powders, white and blue. Cut back to past tense; it's no use pretending she is still here. She tilted it this way and that, watching the blue pour into the white: powdered lapis lazuli into Bahamian sand. Blue-slate ice faces. Dune upon dune. Himalayas. Foreign strands. Then tilted it again. Blue galaxy invaded white. I saw teat-shaped rifts, animal-nosed snow zones. Peering through what of the plastic was empty, she examined the day's light, gave it an A minus, and resumed her slow maneuvering. The grains cascaded, merged, folded in. Twelve feet away, we saw the accidentality of shape at work. It was like looking through an oval porthole in a spacecraft. At, maybe, Earth, slithering about in Mary's colors. I saw a blackbird on the rail outside squirt white stuff backward and take flight. Milk was lost in a still-forming galaxy trapped inside an oval plastic plate. Not so much in two minds, I was in several, and the game plan grew of two states of mind for three people, or one for three, or even no state of mind at all but a few tiny parishes, grain-small, vanishing as soon as made. Thus the mind. "Time out," said Pi, walking right across the room and entering Milk's trance. Blue and white grains held them. This, I thought, might be the day when all things come together, meld: the empty tube from the toilet roll; Charlie Parker rippling through "Au Privave" and "Bloomdido" on a sax that had all the tones of talking languageless; a writer called Okot p'Bitek who is African; the hot gaseous spots on Betelgeuse; the use of the word *dynamic* as a noun; a baby hummingbird in a nest of fluff made from cinnamon fern; the Zonule of Zinn; Max Reger sitting on the toilet and writing to a critic that he had "your notice" before him and it would soon be behind him; humble copters ducking their noses; eisegesis; acupuncture; brain damage; giant turtles 250 years old; the airplane graveyard in New Mexico; the forever increasing age of the universe and therefore its size (or vice versa); the gaudy scarves of the Oxford and Cambridge colleges; the TV talk show as the death of the artifact (all's impromptu); the zinc-like jargon of literary critics who know what art is for without knowing what it is; the stamps my mother mails back to me to use again except that they are faintly flecked with ink; the limbic system; the solar system; the digestive system; chipmunks immobile on the front walk like pensive grandfathers; the woman who died at

109 after a lifetime in a mental home; Harvard Yard; Big Ben; the Eiffel Tower; eyes that can be made to grow on the limbs of frogs; the ten sexes available to paramecia; and, and, I am nothing if not imaginative, the sundance of the ego; the part of Paris called Montsartre; the habit called cogitus interruptus; a clam playing an accordion; all the symphonies of Beethoven recorded simultaneously on the same tape; the chance of head grafts by 1990; the first interviewed whale; the enormous fraternity house in the sky because of all the Greek letters fastened on stars; a story so baneful it kills all editors who receive it; the drinks tilting in the in-flight movie as the plane sways; a human's being 10^{14} cells; the non-existent end of this sentence which was going to sum up everything. As for the Many and the One, all I know is that I am few. The phone has not rung for days. I have paid no bills. I am living in the posthumous present, in which to write— if it's a tense as well—is to be like Buster Keaton underwater emptying out a sunken ship with a bucket.

Upanishad of a worrier. "Upanishad" means "secret session."

Glancing out, Milk saw the youth who mows the lawn arrive with his machine. She even heard the gruesome chatter as it neared the house. In a trice she had gone to help him with a pair of kitchen scissors, but I fetched her back, trusting neither her nor him. But, while he was out front, I let her clip bits of grass by the back door, and vice versa, which satisfied her just enough. Perhaps, I conjectured, this was a good time to urge her back to the Milky Way in the basement, so I fished out my drawings and plans, trying to figure out what came next. In my principal outline, Cepheus came after Cassiopeia; but, on this day of grace, there seemed no more reason to include Cepheus than to exclude Andromeda, neither being in the Way proper. Both were close, Cepheus pointing away toward the Pole Star and Andromeda straggling down

136

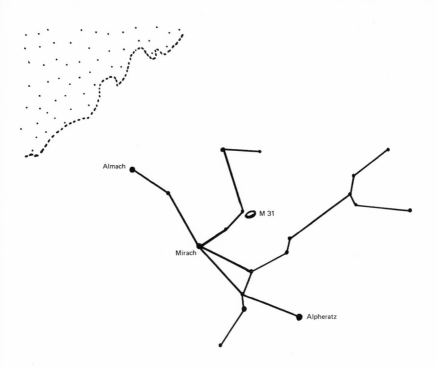

Almach

M 31

Mirach

Alpheratz

ANDROMEDA

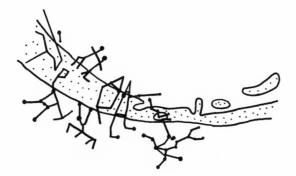

to Pegasus (with which it has a star in common: alpha of Andromeda, known as Alpheratz—"the head of the woman in chains"—is also Pegasus number two). Pi agreed to join in. The youth went, we all three went out and praised the shaved lawn, sat on and patted the stubble, spoke of picnics and ballgames. Coming in through the front door that led right into the basement, we saw the unlit Way. I pointed, said "wynd"; Milk said an almost sibilant "yes," and I got out the tools, the bits and pieces, ready to draw an outline straight from the pages of my *Field Book of the Skies*. It was no use trying to tell Milk how, because Queen Cassiopeia had boasted, Neptune had decreed that her cherished, beautiful daughter Andromeda should be chained to a rock by the seashore, where she would become the prey of a sea monster which Perseus, in the nick of time, changed to stone by flashing the Medusa's head at it. No, but I felt a kindred vibration, knowing a daughter that fitted the pattern, more or less, and angrily resisting while acknowledging the slang idiom about rocks plural and the head. I even felt a bit like Perseus, rescuing Milk by finding something for her to do, and with a private opinion as to where the Medusa's head really was: at a marvelous distance. I marked the holes, Milk drilled them, Pi chose the bulbs while I fitted the sockets. For Alpheratz, blue, doing duty for whitish purple which we didn't have; for others, yellow and green and orange. As soon as the connecting lines were clear, Milk made her interpretation, exclaiming "Fow, fow!" which neither of us understood. It was only while I was upstairs, hunting out a postcard of Messier 31, The Great Spiral Galaxy, that I realized what she'd said. Downstairs, I checked. She was right. Andromeda, drawn as I'd drawn it, resembled a fowl, strutting with a slight forward lean. Commended, Milk beamed, demanded light. Got it, fifteen minutes later, after I finished tinkering with my version of M 31, described by one early astronomer, Marius, as the diluted flame from a candle, seen through horn. Fire behind alabaster seemed nearer, and nothing to do with Keats's invocation: "Andromeda! Sweet woman! why delaying So timidly among the stars?" What we'd created, in our rough-and-ready way, was a visible fowl with an oval headlamp on its back, a headlamp that was a companion galaxy to our own. I thought of the metal-rich giants at its center, of its two companion galaxies (one of which I'd snipped off the postcard when making the cap for the bulb), and I remembered that the whole system was approaching us at about eight miles a second. Just about visible to the naked eye, at least as a fuzzy spot, it gleamed in the basement in lilac, purple, and cream, like elegant batter, crisp at the edges but viscous at center. Like all our other versions, it was hopelessly out of scale, at least as far as outlines and components went, but it seemed a Christmas tree just off the Way, a thing of beauty being a joy for now, most of all when Milk, asking as usual for a truth beyond truth, delivered herself of a long sentence that ran: "Drom'a, no, fow' two leg, one small lamp." A drum it was not, she was not having that; it was a fowl, pausing before it stuck a leg out into the celestial thoroughfare, in order to reach the other side, Cassiopeia, its mother, and then Polaris in the Little Bear.

Upbraiding me for slowness to answer, Milk tapped me on the hand. Quite right, I told her: those spiral arms aren't always as smooth as they look, wouldn't stand comparison with the hostess arms of the major international airlines. Often there are gaps and splits, fringes and loops, and professional astronomers have been heard expressing sympathy for their extra-galactic peers who, stuck inside one of the untidy sections of their galaxy, are trying to unravel the details of the spiral structure. We aren't so well fixed ourselves, knowing as we do only bits of about three arms of the Milky Way. Enjoy these pendant lamps of ours, it will be a long time before they vary or burn out. By the way, Andromeda, or "Fowl," is over two million light-years away, dangling like a charm. Still pondering, as I dubbed in dialogue that Milk deserved but couldn't have, I blotted a small spider with tissue as it scurried up the dark before the Way, and then, only minutes later, absent-mindedly wiped my mouth with the same ball of tissue, thus gaining my first taste of spider as I recoiled from a tart fusion of cocoa and wintergreen (if panic hasn't pitched me into using histrionically guessing likes). As in my name, which sometimes I half-think is not Deulius, but D'Alias, or even Delius, DuLiss, or Dooley. To D'Alias, perhaps, the spider tasted sweet, like a tangerine. But not as sweet as life, come what may; have come what has come, what had already come, namely another Andromeda chained, chained, chained, but in these paragraphs let loose.

Chaste lights prompting her, Alpheratz and M 31 above all, neither Almach nor Mirach much to write home about (said he, of those vast fireballs!), Milk talked to Pi, who couldn't follow, any more than I. Could she have been commenting on this sorry scheme of things entire, of which she'd never heard? "Gnang," she seemed to say. "Gnang," I helplessly replied, displeasing her a lot. "Gnong, gnung, gneng," Pi tried, resorting to blanket technique, but that failed as well. "Don't worry, it happens all the time," I told her: "abstract phonemes uttered for practice." In the end, it was Milk herself who sorted it out. She meant I should remove from Andromeda the small blue bulb I had stolen from the microscope upstairs. Her sense of order had erupted. Things belonged, could not be transplanted. Most of this she mimed, at last drawing a microscope in an exasperated hurry, waving me up the stairs even as she unscrewed the bulb. Behind me as I restored it to its place in the neat mirror under the scope's deck, she patted me on the rump for being good.

GET BULBS, I wrote on the kitchen memo board, by accident reminding myself of a fey ditty, bonus from one of my various childhoods:

Khyber, Khyber, Khyber Pass.
If you want a splendid Christlemas,
Get for your most secret self
That enigmatic Red Elf.

Red Elf, I supposed, was Santa Claus gone childish, while the Khyber Pass must have grown out of the old Empire, possibly via the nostalgic dream of a returned colonial administrator or of a child longing to blow bugle with Gunga Din. Get bulbs I would, that very minute. Back with two dozen, I vowed to install Cepheus before it grew dark, but Milk showed no interest, instead returned to the tilt-shaper upstairs, lying on her back and shuffling blue and white contrasts above her at arms' length. Busy preparing a big quiche, Pi murmured lines of her new poem, while I, half-suspecting an attack of migraine was on the way, the cause too many different kinds of light, made a cup of thin soup and in it drank the special salt that staves off the attack. It worked. I'd had no trouble in weeks, which was amazing in view of the pressures. Thank you for my luck, I said to the Caliph of cells, and went downstairs to switch off the Way. There it was, gaunt but sprawled, a touch of Las Vegas with a touch of the computer panel. One flick and a galaxy died, but I had never felt less like God. It wasn't me, yet it was none other.

Up and down the stairs Milk went, eager to exercise, and I suddenly thought how I used to lead a routine life which included a mile run each day. So I cleared the basement, ran the first of what would be fifty, sixty circuits, pursued by Milk, who wasn't even breathing hard when I halted at thirty, puffed and parched. One more run, she demanded, making the motions with arms and legs, but I switched the Way on instead, toured along it with her while my pulse eased up. To me it was a slow-motion haul from Canis Minor and Monoceros to Cassiopeia and Andromeda, but to Milk it was that same comic strip of flashlight, wolf, tennis, handshake, kite,

141

daddy longlegs, M, and fowl, though how fowl connected narratorially with M I wasn't yet sure, or through the M with the daddy longlegs. For each constellation she said her word, spelling out the names of the various colors, oo-ing at the fudged-up nebulae and then challenging, with an imperious hand-sweep, the blank of the remnant all the way to Sagittarius, and past it, into the southern heavens. Soon, I promised, answering myself as well. Before she went. Yet how? Unless we worked night and day. We had fallen badly behind the creator of all this, who held copyright not only of what but also how. Our second (or third?) quiche in a week wafted down from the oven. We switched off, went up. Followed by lots of odd thoughts while munching. "I've used the wrong cheese," Pi was saying, and there I was thinking, Milk won't eat cheese. But, of course, she already had, at least a couple of times before, deceived by the aroma of the ham and the pastry. Then it hit me: there was already a tradition of her stay, therefore much of her stay was over. And the heavy word *stay* jumped the track at that point, evoking lugubrious words about someone's being taken from this place to a lawful place of execution, et cetera. Cut off in one's prime. Gruesome, I thought, how many people, between their own first and second rattles (the baby's and the death), manage to kill off a few of their fellow humans. In the context of all that easy dispatch, then, why fuss about a mere deprivation? A parting? The sort of event Japanese women will emblematize by leaving behind a comb, a symbol with teeth. It was like sitting in a train, waiting to depart. Then the station vanishes as another train moves in. You seem to be moving, while it stays still, but it slides past and you haven't moved at all. Yes, I said in my head, compare with life and death. All your years, you think you have been on the go, but you've been stationary while death has rolled along, going about its never failing business while you've dawdled under the influence of hope. Eating three square meals a day for forty years, just to stave

142

off the inevitable. Drunk thousands of gallons merely to fend off the last parch. Washed and combed only to steer clear of the filth at the end, when the head in its box resembles a badly combed turnip. I came back to quiche with my relish a bit sapped, but ate twice as much as usual, just for ballast, just for spite. Two wonderful faces in front of me: Pi's, casually serious as if a new poem were docking between the cortices, Milk's flushed and prankish. It was like revisiting a country after it's been occupied by a foreign power and all the Czech names over the storefronts have been Germanized. Or as if, to change terms, Gdynia had become Danzig, or Antwerp Anvers. Something had gone, something come. Not the point of no return, which does not move; not that, but an ionization, in which a neutral configuration has altered slightly. As during any rainshower, an electrical uneasiness hung fire. Prickly. Faint. Stale.

Andromeda was done. I wanted to do Cepheus as soon as we could, Andromeda's father or a house with a steep roof, depending on how one saw. Instead of talking, I wandered up and down its outline, from Er Rai at the apex, aimed at Polaris, to *Delta,* the variable double star discovered in 1784 by the deaf astronomer Goodricke, and *Mu,* the so-called Garnet Star. Legend had it that Cepheus himself was one of the Argonauts whom Jason took on his expedition in quest of the Golden Fleece. Excusing myself, I went downstairs again, like some pattern-complex maniac, and drew lines, sawed bits of wood, drilled holes, installed a bulb or two (one white-blue, one garnet, so to speak), and installed the old boy in place just off the upper side of the Way. In the shape of one horizontally tumbling house. That done, I went up again for dessert, leaving a surprise behind. Yet was myself surprised. There on the table sat a vivid Jupiter done in jello, complete with colored bands and the Red Spot. Or, rather, a vertical cross-section through the poles, three inches thick, glistening and still. I clapped applause. Milk too. Then Pi,

143

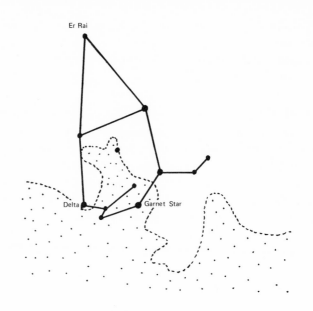

CEPHEUS

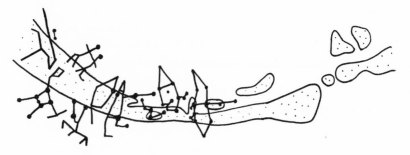

144

blushing a little, dug in a big spoon and served us outsize portions. Here we go, I murmured, slice-radius is over forty thousand miles. Milk ate the Red Spot, and I, before realizing, swallowed what Pi said was the shadow of the moon called Ganymede. Only one quarter of Big Jupe remained, vanished into Milk's unchewing maw. "Eating Jupiter," said Pi, giggling. How sexual, I thought. "Yes," said Pi, reading that near-illiterate thought, "that's really Ganymede's job, among others." It had taken her seven secret hours to prepare. "Let's," I suggested, "eat our way round the solar system. Saturn's the main problem: how?" "With meringue," she whispered. "Rings made of meringue." "Fine by me any time," I said, "but I'll settle for another Jupiter any time." In answer she quoted herself, an uncommon recourse for her, most modest of visionaries, and the amazed-amazing twinned lines clinched our feast:

> *"Vibrant as an African trade-bead with bone*
> *chips in orbit round it, Jupiter floods the night's*
>
> *black scullery, all those whirlpools and burbling*
> *aerosols little changed since the solar system began.*
>
> *The mind reels to berth so gelatinous a rainbow,*
> *suddenly pale salmon, then marbled blue."*

She patted her stomach. "Berthed, indeed," I said. Milk burped, heeded only the vibration, as unaware of breach in etiquette as of her being in the company of two space nuts, two characters who had never recovered from their amazement at being in the universe at all, at having so much of it to peer at. We were even devout, at least about the All's being a tribute to the subtlety of matter. Let's, at least, said our beating minds, look at literature *sub*, as the textbooks used to say, *specie aeternitatis.* Plant the merest thing in the mightiest context. Dwarf all that humans think is grand. And, both holist and reductionist, embarrass thought and style with star, with atom. Push everything to its uttermost, until the very joints of the brain's casing creak. That was us. It wouldn't, we thought, make dying easier, or suffering sweeter, but it would surely make life fuller, even at the cost of a lost hour of sleep each day. It wasn't eternity in a grain of sand so much as the grain in eternity, whose ready definition we found in telescopes that, bigger and better every year, got us nearer only to what would never be seen anyway, not while the speed of light was finite. There will always be something beyond the edge of the observable universe, but never mind: think of how much there is within it. First person plural, we roamed celestially, with, as often as not, a bizarre sense of how impersonal it was to be ourselves. "Hail, holy hydrogen," our prayers began, such as they were, and never have ended, but go on and on, in subjunctive salute.

Going at nothing like the speed even of sound (though in the prose it feels like light), we drove to Silver Hill in Maryland, a trip across the state border, to view the ghost squadron that belonged to the Smithsonian Institution. We were the Wright Brothers. We were Lindbergh. We were pilot, co-pilot, and stewardess aboard the Ford trimotor dubbed *Tin Goose*. Supervised by a lonely guard with a port-wine birthmark running from his ear to his mouth, we sat in seats and thumbed wheels, twanged wires, and peered into cockpits. "Off, off," cried Milk, wanting the frozen assembly to soar as one, taking us clear of grass and sheds. At the first German jet, the ME 262 I think, she leered, scorning its cold storage. At a biplane from World War One, she nodded, relishing the excess of wing area. At a neat little racer with a giant faired-in radial engine with blebs and an undercarriage with spats, she smiled as if recognizing a long-lost relative; something silver-beefy, something pyknic-eager, got her to caress the blebs, the spats, and clamp in her fist the tip of the two-bladed prop. For ten minutes, in that aeronautical

146

trance, she remained in position, linked to the ghost of thunder, while we breathed in the aroma of varnish and oil, flexed our shoulders at the shed's coolness, raised eyebrows when the rain began. Fingal's Cave, I thought; but we were not in the Hebrides, or the New Hebrides, or the newest Hebrides of all. This was the morgue of Icarus. The wax of his wings was the wax in her ears (I cleaned her out every two days with finicking care). I saw her then as a non-starter among contraptions frail, or unflown, or no longer airworthy, and found the analogies almost right. Her stilled soul was with, and of, those giant wings above and alongside her, their fabric dun and bronze as that of a dried-out tea bag, their angles of dihedral and attack a little out of true. She was talking to the engine, I knew not how, but maybe she was consoling it in its enforced idleness. Did I imagine or hear a purr, a cough, a lyrical splutter? What followed was audible beyond doubt: a bubbling flow from her throat. She had vomited on the spat.

Understandably, she recoiled, shaking her head in dismay. "Motion sickness," I told the port-wine guard. "Have you a cloth?" Mopping up, with breath held against the sharp tang of her bile, I told myself that this was really air-sickness after all. Spruced up again, thanks to Pi, who'd prudently got her away from the scene as fast as possible, to the ladies' room and then the open air, she embarked on a fit of guilty effusiveness, patting our backs, shaking our hands, exclaiming "Ah!" as she pointed to quite imaginary blemishes on our faces, arms, and shoes. Equipped with more than our fair share of postcards and leaflets, we drove away, only to stop en route and have Cokes. Once over the Pennsylvania line, we stopped again and had dinner, which Milk ate with benighted confidence, wincing at nothing, not even the big ice cream she hooted for. It all went down, and stayed.

Grinning at Cepheus, hours later, in her pajamas, Milk gave me the most exhausted version of what I call her Borgia nod. Criminals together, we held hands in yet another air

space, plotted yet another raid on the Way. "House," she said
baldly, meaning the constellation, and plunged both hands at
the empty space beyond, asking for more. Would that I
could, I'd turn hydrogen into helium, for her, like a well-
behaving star. We tucked her in, planted our kisses, waved
elaborate farewells. After which there was music, some
Nielsen (loud) and some Holst (louder) and some lush Bergsma written in and for Jamaica. Through the scope, we observed Jupiter for real, in between touring clouds, then sat
back on the balcony and rattled ice cubes in tumblers at the
night that was just as warm as the day had been. Asa was
away in New York. Chad had left for Boston. Even the neighbors who owned the pool weren't back. Only we and the stars
stayed put, could be counted on. Or so I joshed as, once more
inside, we half-watched Tyrone Power and Herbert Marshall
in *The Razor's Edge,* wishing only for a character called Oc-
cam to curtail the reel and send us to bed half an hour earlier.
As for the few days left, I didn't count. The reservations had
already been confirmed, for a stop in the country of origin.

Up early, but not bright, I scribbled notes on cards, for
inclusion in this. Jittery lines, awkward sketches, little bubbles of dialogue. A note on the prodding pain in my chest
went next to a sketch of the plane with spatted wheels and
bleb-faired engine. I jotted down the attendant's port-wine
nevus, adding: Why do characters with facial birthmarks appear almost mythic? Then I crossed out *characters* and wrote
in *people,* all the same remarking my writerly concern. The
man was cast before he opened mouth.
Coffee-sped, I slunk out of the house, bought groceries,
mailed cards, took out garbage, bellowed at the neighbor
dog. It was eleven when Pi got up, and ninety degrees; noon
when Milk arrived in a compensatory rush, and ninety-three.
A day of scorch, omelets, misquotations. Up to the Olympic

pool on campus we went, back to the air-conditioned cool of the bedrooms, to iced tea, and then, while Pi wrote (at a table dotted with Hawaiian rocks akin to what's on Mars), to the basement, where Milk and I made vital decisions about the next constellation. It was like doing a crossword during the bombardment of Pearl Harbor. Question: What's under the black squares? I showed Milk the *Field Guide*'s sketch of Lacerta, flighty little zigzag they call the Lizard, but she dismissed it with a hand-flash I'd seen rejecting food, people, weather, toys, dogs, and TV shows she'd seen before. Yet she made sense, she who'd seen Cassiopeia as an M for her. Lacerta was mere pastiche, whereas she (M) and I (Cepheus, perhaps?) were unique in our starry trespass, while she doubled as chained Andromeda as well, blamed for her mother's mouth. So we passed on, up the line, beyond the coal sack in Cepheus that I reckoned a blind spot in me, and on to Cygnus, one of the chief glories of the sky, headed by the raving white-blue of Deneb, tailed by Albireo, darling of astronomers, a double, gold and blue. This was better meat for her, not least because she called it "Abbala," for *plane*. Swan, I cautioned myself: don't say swan, whatever else you do, she says it's a plane. And it was almost wholly in the Milky Way, a cross planted right in the middle, like a lit-up airfield seen from fifteen thousand feet. We drew it fast, then chose the pegs and bulbs.

Uselessly thinking of Orpheus and Jupiter, both of whom Cygnus has been said to be, I mulled over the little bolt of piety that had soared out of the handbook, assuring us that Cygnus (the Cross) is seen best in winter, when it assumes an upright position, at nine P.M. on Christmas Eve, against the western sky, reminding us of Bethlehem: "a starry symbol of the Faith, a promise from the realm beyond." No, just a lovely clutch of stars, I told my saw as I rubbed it back and forth across the dowels. Here the Way splits into two big

he's an atheist; that was clear in WfgDDaughter

149

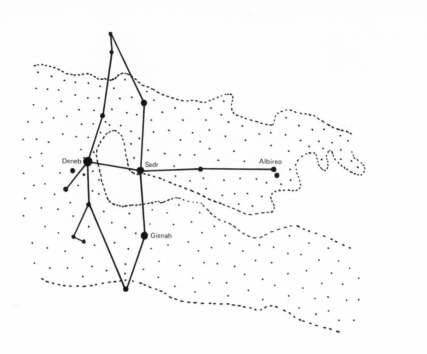

CYGNUS

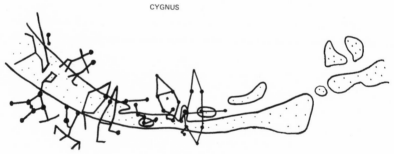

parallel streams that swarm with suns and sacks of stellar coal. Glued or screwed, in went the stars, the biggest bulb for Deneb, that approaches Earth at four miles per second from 1,630 light-years away. For Sadr, "the hen's breast," a yellow one; for Gienah, "the wing," a golden twin. According to the names, we were mixed up about Deneb and Albireo, since the former means *tail* and the latter *beak*, and that would make perfect sense if we were dealing with a swan's long neck. Fact was, however, we had on our hands a plane, which to Milk meant the wings were nearer to the nose than to the tail (certain ultra-sonic experimental models notwithstanding). So I let it stand, especially when she showed me which way the plane was going: eastward, back to Cassiopeia. Paint the mother could not dry fast enough, hands could not whirl at a brisk enough clip. "Wynd," she commanded, and then delivered a long voluntary in which she'd invested heart and soul. "Yah, Milk, out on abbala, zoon, up, znow, when moon i' ot, bye-bye, Pi!" A chunk of Paris plaster would have got the gist. What she followed up with was by no means as obvious. Not only would she and I be flying away from Pi (she *knew*), but we would be taking the Way with us. Hence her haste to fill in the blanks, stud it with other constellations. It was hers. To take away. To fold up, somehow, and stow in the hold of a jumbo jet. Like a shutter. Like a circus tent. Like—

Unselfishly I said "yes," meaning no.

Cosms, I thought: macro and micro. Without hyphens. All we need is a portable universe. It was no use offering her the long photograph from upstairs, of the Way from Cassiopeia to Sagittarius, put together from four separate takes. The balsa frame would snap. The picture didn't in the least resemble what we had down there. No bulbs, no silver paint, no lit-up nebulas. So I decided to make her a miniature as soon as she'd gone to sleep. Such a Milky Way as would fit into a girl's suitcase between her underwear and the raincoat she didn't need. A mini, of the micro, of the macro, that's what it would be, but unfortunately not electrical, nowhere near big enough to hide behind.

Clandestine, that night, I got to work with scissors, maps, and poster colors, tracing paper and a little box of colored paper stars found in a drawer, and made it all. By dawn I was blind, but it was done. I hid it in a storage closet, on top of discarded record albums, to let it dry. Doing it had not only brought departure closer, but given it a face of criss-crossed silver against Prussian blue. What little sleep I got was torn.

Up early, Pi went down and did the next constellation: Lyra, not far from the upper wing of Cygnus. In form, a small triangle attached to one corner of a parallelogram, Lyra just happens to be the direction in which the Sun is taking Earth at about twelve miles per second: our celestial goal, whose beacon is the blue-white Vega, once upon a time the Pole Star and, in twelve thousand years' time, destined to be it again. Taking in the work Pi had done, I thought of what Vega meant (the falling bird) and wondered at the manual skill with which she'd affixed the sapphire-blue bulb, the studs for Sulafat and Sheliak, the two tortoises, yellow and white.

Crazy people, I thought. We're not fit to be at any latitude. We interchangeably think of stars. We use our minds like sleds to get to the middle of nowhere. We eat a planet for dessert. I stay up all night to replicate a galaxy. She rises early and makes a copy of Lyra. And yet, this is a holy aberration, as extreme in attentiveness as in otherworldliness. We think big, neat, and often. We *like* the universe, *faute de mieux.* Solar she, galactic I, we're a team. That very fact was visible in what she'd done, not only installing Lyra (a poet putting the lyre into the universe), but also finding a postcard of the Ring Nebula to clip out and stick on. There it was, the famous

152

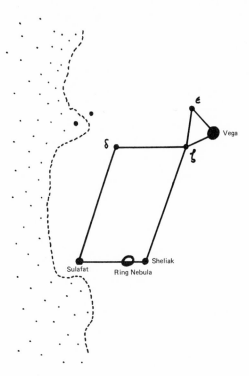

LYRA

chromatic smoke ring, in whose middle gleamed a fifteenth-magnitude blue star. Out of proportion, of course, but gloriously heraldic, it gave my vague, bloodshot eyes something to focus on. "It's beautiful," I yelled. "Thank you." I was very welcome, I heard, but she hadn't done it quite for me. Again I called upstairs, saying thank you, for Milk, for Orpheus' magic harp, for what in old Bohemia they called the Fiddle in the Sky. Odd how, in this geometrical figure of no great size, Earth's trajectory, the poetry of Orpheus and the vanished nymph Eurydice came together on behalf of an Earth-bound child going nowhere, at least by the standards of society, but imaginative to the roots of her teeth, and in a mighty hot region given to long sleeps. Something eerie skidded through my muddled brain; I groped after it, but lost it, summed it up as atavistic *déjà vu*, went up to breakfast, which only made me sleepier than ever, five cups of coffee or no. During the afternoon, I fell asleep while watching TV. When I woke, Pi and Milk had been out to collect mail from on campus, but not today's: this was Sunday. One letter was full of dithering legal palaver. Another came from my mother, who had been with a friend to a picnic in the grounds of the local manor house; how very English, I thought, and for a second I missed the click of ball on cricket bat, the chimes of that thirteenth-century church, the softly modulated tones of the BBC announcers. There was also a book to review, somebody's Life of Somebody, and I marveled at the phrase: it was as if the somebody were forcing back on the Somebody a Life the latter didn't have, at least not in that shape, not in words, not in chapters, nor with index. Only the photographs were true. I put the book away for after Milk had gone and I'd come back, full circle, my cut-rate gala done with. Confronted with only a few more days, and wondering feverishly what to cram into them, I could only think of the constellation that came next, as if that were the only thing that mattered. Longing, I'd learned, could become wholly disembodied. So I found myself insisting, with stupefied persistence, on Aquila, saying nothing about it, but centering my brain on it and building a myth which went: If you reach Aquila, all will be well. But it wouldn't; after Aquila I'd have to reach, oh, Sagittarius, that scalding fungus of white light wherein the center of the galaxy lay hidden. There was no end, just one halt after another. An old style of behaving had reasserted itself: with too much to do, or to envision doing, I'd do nothing, let everything slide as I sank into a far from pensive funk. Then the hands took over, as always. Paint. Repair. Build. Sweep. Sort out books. Rearrange shirts. Stack dishes into a pagoda tower. Yet I knew that, if time is short, doing nothing makes it longer. On that vapid level I stayed.

An hour later, though, Aquila tugged at my mind again. Leaving Milk and Pi to carry on with the oil painting they had in hand (a representational glimpse of the living room complete with rex begonia, standard lamp, and bookcase), I went downstairs and, with slow-motion relish, began to outline Aquila where Cygnus ended, faintly aware that the Way had taken on a compensatory aspect it hadn't had before, when it was celebratory. A star threnody it had come to be, all the lyricism sucked out. Yet it was some *thing* to do; in occupying the hands, it annulled the mind, gave a standard so vast that nothing mattered when shoved next it. Shrugging at my own brand of dark-brown romanticism, I thanked heaven for three stars in a line, the bright Altair flanked by two dimmer ones. This Eagle was the symbol of the noonday Sun, to the Sumerians at least, as well as the bird of Zeus. A close neighbor of ours, comparatively speaking, with Altair only eighteen light-years distant, it held an asterism called Sobieski's Shield on which I could splurge a cluster of little bulbs, if I felt inclined. No, I'd just mark it with some white-painted little studs, leave it at that, not being in the right mood for *all* things bright and beautiful. Perversely, I might

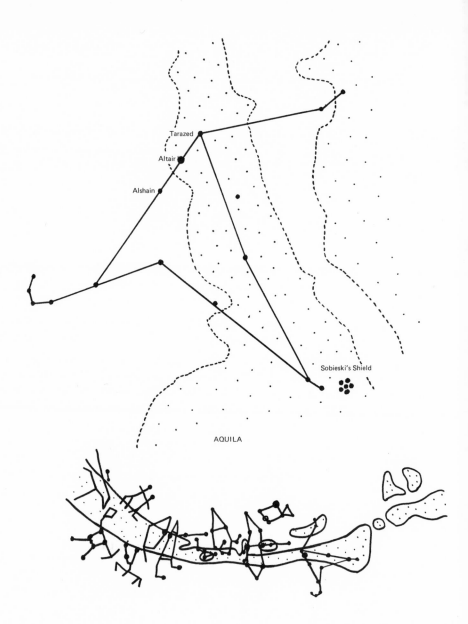

Tarazed

Altair

Alshain

Sobieski's Shield

AQUILA

even add a few stars of my own invention, company for Altair ("the flying eagle," a yellow), Alshain (just another Arabic name for the whole thing, an orange), and Tarazed ("the soaring falcon," a pale orange). I'd stick in, say, the new stars Funkair, Paralyx, Dumpnix, and Cafardalis, just for starters, all yellow, followed by a cluster all of smaller magnitude: Nadaz, Ditherium, Stallnar, and Slumpsych, not to mention the Panic Cluster, the Runaway Catatonia Star, and, of course, the famed Deulius Coal Sack. Poor Aquila! Drawn so differently in each reference book, all the way from a scarecrow to a kite, from a single line bearing three headlights to a chevron-like triangle. I would have to design an outline that Milk would enjoy, have some rapport with, and so I cheated a bit, in the end coming up with what resembled a tent pitched on steep ground, with a streamer flying from its top and a long guide rope that snaked out left. My three main stars, no, Aquila's three main stars (I jettisoned all my neo-stellar objects) came together in the upper half of the left-hand line, a pretty sight dominating the doubles which, quite pedantically, I filched from the most detailed reference book. So, for just about the first time, I had included objects visible only through instruments, not the unaided eye or the field glass. How flashy it looked, with one yellow-green, a white-lilac, a white-bluish, and a yellow-purple, all done with small bulbs, the result being that Aquila had a fairground look, agitated and festive. Cheered up just a little, I even included a version of Sobieski's Shield, capping a bulb with aluminum foil I'd riddled with tiny holes. Next stop, I thought, would be black light, luminous paint, an electronic-eye star that switched on the whole Way as soon as someone came in the door. Such devices I'd save for later, to come down to earth with, after she'd gone, after I'd eaten another seven thousand miles, like some demented runner trying to cross the Milky Way itself, whereas, of course, on this scale of distance my trip wouldn't even take me from one side of

157

a small bulb to the other. Less than a fourth of an inch. Yet
I lost that thought, just as well, in a small shock of remembering the so-called black hole, Cygnus X-1, most probably a pair
of stars that revolved around each other, one of them remaining invisible although perhaps ten times the mass of our Sun.
Moving back along the Way, I drilled two holes, implanted
one holder and one bulb, then painted the inside of the
second hole mat black and threaded a little black balloon
through it, tugging from the other side until the lips came
flush with the hole. This was my image of the star, or hole,
from which no light escaped. Cygnus was even richer than
before. I even thought of inflating the balloon, but decided
the effect would be wasted, as invisible as the black hole
itself. So I contented myself with bizarre, over-reaching
thoughts about the chance that our own universe is itself a
black hole as immune to investigation as a solipsist. We live
(I said), it all lives, all living is, inside a slot made by a cosmic
corpse. Then, recoiling from such hyperbole, I hunted
through a shelf of journals for the one in which a black hole
had appeared in vivid color. A double-page spread showed
Cygnus X-1 itself, a cerise whirlpool with a black spot at
center, sucking blue star-stuff into itself from its massive
companion. Scorning proportion, I tore out the two pages,
Scotch-taped them together, and stuck them in the dark off
the Way, just south of Cygnus. A cosmic drama happening
Off. I saw the red giant cook its planets as it bloated its
diameter to five hundred million miles, and then begin to
collapse as gravity squeezed the atoms closer and closer together until the former giant resembled an atomic nucleus
with elephantiasis, was only twenty miles across but tens of
millions of tons to each spoonful. As if in some gigantic thaw,
the neutron star fell down the black icicle of itself until,
invisible at the point, it sucked all after it, never to let it
return. Gratified by such a cosmic monster, I turned again to
twinkling Aquila. My bile was shed. My glooms, although not

gone, had moderated. Surely, I thought, at this point a voice should interrupt me, bring me back to the dear dimension of pretzels, eggs, tea, and toast. It is time for solidarity. Let's group again. I went to the foot of the stairs, could hear only faint grunts of concentration (Milk), murmurs of guidance from Pi. The painting went forward. All those pulpy tubes of Terra Verte, Titanium White, Shiva Scarlet, Shivastra Violet, and Cadmium Orange weren't going to waste. What a Hindu-planetary sound they had, even with the small found-poem doing its clinical counterpoint on the tube's back, something that ran: *Colloidal Co-precipitate of* PERMANENT *1. organo-inorganic pigment. 2. Ground in specially prepared non-yellowing drying oils.* The remainder I forgot, but it had something to do with freedom from lead. Of course. Nagged at by my own mind, I called up to them and had the following out-of-time non-conversation. "What are you doing?" "Painting in oils." "Have you finished?" "Nowhere near." "Aren't you hungry?" "I've no idea." "I've just done Aquila, aren't you glad?" "Yes: now do the next one, huh?"

Upset at feeling jealous, I went back to the Milky Way. Fatigue, I told it, is making me snappy. I should be glad, not cross.

Calm down, I told myself. Deulius, be still. Do Sagittarius. Clean up the mess. Be useful.

Going outside, through the screen door, I picked up a fallen apple, slung it high and away, heard the smash of glass from some house behind a row of trees. Inside again, flushed with small-boy naughtiness, I felt what the oil-paint tubes call permanent-opaque. From now on, I'd do the Way, seemly as a Boy Scout, aloof as an angel. Live on Jello. Run my daily mile. Do sit-ups by the score. Write my mother daily. Gladden everybody.

Child of five, when spoken to by strangers, I'd just say "Bugger Off."

Chastised for the next ten years for saying Bugger Off, I developed the habit of the silent scowl that issued the same command.

Ultimately, I learned to speak again, and in terms of mortifying acerbity; would say almost anything sharp, just for the exercise, and so gained a predictable number of friends. As cut off as that, you have to end up writing. After twenty years of that, you get to speak more mildly. Might even be called nice.

Called cruelly Wight, by my father, after the Isle I was conceived on, I wore that smart with honor in pain until the age of twenty, when it occurred to me that, unknowingly, he'd landed me with an old word that meant human being, or creature, as if folk needed to be reassured about my true status. I consoled myself with Blake's couplet ("What wailing wight / Calls the watchman of the night?") and finally got used to being written to as White. Things could have been worse. Had they gone to other islands for their inaugural fornication, I might have been dubbed with such grievous excerpts as these: Sark, from the Channel Islands; Uist, Tiree, Coll, Canna, Rhum, Elgg, or Muck, all from the Hebrides; Hoy, from the Orkneys. All in all, I am very glad they did not go to the Hebrides; had my name come thence, I'd not have lived to twenty. As things turned out, being Wight Deulius wasn't all that bad, for in imagination I joined the Wright Brothers, the White House, and the White Nile; and, when that mythos of mispronunciation didn't work, I enjoyed the frequent calls of *Wait, Wight!* that streamed after me as I ran away. Whitey, school called me, as if I were a pet rabbit, but I responded as bravely as I could, and now, fortune be praised, the name has a touch of erudite distinction, especially when displayed on the jackets of my books, and comes trippingly off the tongue of those who refer to me. It's also, as my father the engineer couldn't have known, beguilingly close to Wit. Perhaps, even, I am the only person in our whole civilization with this archaic name, evocative of our entire race, and in the old literature almost always prefaced with some such fol-de-rol as *Alas, poor.* My mother, I think, had no hand in it at all, so surprised to be pregnant that she almost lost the power of speech, certainly of innovative verbal reference. I think my father even told her some tale about a new law that would regularize society, entailing that children be named after the Eden in which they were conceived. I wonder how many walk this earth, to this day, called Dunfermline, Swansea, or Bath.

Call no man happy who is not dead, runs an old line of the Greeks. I'd alter that to: Call no man happy who hasn't chosen his own name. Call no wight . . .

Cheered by having gone into that, the joke being that you'd see it on the book's cover before you read it in the text, I go back to work, fired by the memory of my father's bewilderment that I didn't have to clock in at work, or keep to certain hours. "You get paid just for talking, just a few hours a week?" he'd say, wondering where he'd gone wrong all his life. The vacations left him speechless, who said little at the best of times. Yet, in his vaguely Neronic way, he was glad that, if I exerted myself, I could earn more in a day than he used to earn in a year. Or something just as preposterous, have more vacation in a year than he'd had hospital time, or sickness leave, in his entire life, before they gave him the gold watch that wouldn't tick, with his name on it. "A little tombstone," he said. "A foretaste. When they give you this, they're getting you ready." On that day, Retirement Day, my mother went into the best room and played Liszt for four hours straight, just to enclose her distress.

Cooking aromas came downstairs. Chicken, I decided, choosing not to find out. Still no sign of Milk, who for good reasons was declining to enter the underworld. All day I had left the two phones unplugged, almost as if the house were a deaf child who disdained appliances, didn't want to be reached. Things could go on like this for weeks, at which point I'd have written evidence from those folk desperate to get through. I liked, I think, the sense of power at being able to plug in a phone to call out, and then sever all communication until the next time. We were masters of our instruments, not they of us (as is more usual in the age of give-you-a-tinkle, give-us-a-call). Or was I just magnifying the fact that Asa and Chad were out of town? Did I not want to realize how little the phone would ring? Or was I shutting out Europe?

Casting around in the basement for something to do, I looked in the corners, found portly spiders at rest in their skeins, decided to exterminate them later, unless they were really gobbling ants and flies. The *Aviation and Space Sciences Encyclopedia* I put back into alphabetical order, then flipped my finger along the amassed spines, like a child with a stick along a fence. Petty doings, these; after Aquila and the revisit to Cygnus, I'd had enough, had a mind like a cross between a chanterelle and a patch of salted snow. Out again, I watched the loud birds, tried to hear the worms and beetles, got the sniff (I think) of the chipmunks and squirrels. And I scanned the local horizon for faces of people whose windows have been broken by party or parties unknown. Thrown by the same person who, in his day, had malingered, or seemed to, in front of the paperback display in the Elmira, N.Y., bus station. All of a sudden, there she was at his side, the ticket-seller-custodian who doubled as porter and Gorgon. Would he like to buy that book? "Which?" he asked, being profoundly startled, never in twenty years of browsing confronted by so intimate, so sportive, a question. "Which book?" he asked. "Any of those you've been reading for the last half-hour," she said. "Oh, I never buy them," he told her with his disingenuous grin of the traveler stranded. It wasn't a library, she announced. "What a shame," he said, "because if it were you'd have better books, and then, being tempted to buy, one wouldn't need to." At that, her officiousness deliquesced into what can only be called a raucous grimace, as if she had been offered a condom to blow her nose into. *Homo itinerans* is often subject to such accost, learns how to cope with the experience only after much standing and wondering. There are, he decided on that occasion, people who care about configurations that, seen from Williamsport or even Aquila, don't matter, are mere whorls in the texture of what only a shallow mind can term the big buzzing blooming confusion. It's not. It's the medium silent ananthous order. What star ever said hello?

As if that weren't bad enough, loitering with no intent to buy, he had also jaywalked on every street from Miami to Montreal, but was agile enough to keep alive. Only in Blackwell's Bookshop, after jaywalking across Broad Street, had he felt at peace, not only reading an entire book while crouched on the stairway, but taking notes from it, and returning months later to check his notes against the book's new edition, and then a year later rechecking his recheck against the third edition. Unless he imagined the whole thing, the punts, the champagne, the emancipated bluestockings who came to tea-and-crumpets but stayed for anatomy. In those days, when he didn't care, didn't have to care, he switched off and wrote poems thick with visionary sap. He hadn't even so much as looked up at the Milky Way, not even during the week-long crossing of the Atlantic that lodged him, like well-spoken jetsam, in 1314 John Jay Hall for an entire year. Manhattan wowed him; I loved it; didn't you? All his selves had a place there, all round the clock, as if the city were itself a sun. Filthy even then, bemerded, a-tremble, sky-high, the city, first seen pink with the sun behind it, had looked like a wedding cake of clay. It seemed a long time ago, almost in a different country. All was tonic, lush, optional. He could play his head as if it were a fish, saying to himself: I (?) am (?) in (?) two (?) minds (?). And get away with it, as little aware of minuend as of subtrahend. *Now* minus *then* equals twenty, years. What, I wonder, had been put into him (I who say he) to retard spoilage, as it says on food wrappers? Backbone, maybe, first installed in the town of Shanklin on the Isle of Wight, thereafter known as Wight's Isle. Or mother's milk, first administered not long after. Or country air, fresh grass, a swift dose of ultra-violet during one or two weeks of each fogbound, sopping year. At any rate, he survived immersion in Manhattan, felt slip away from him the image of an indri, big lemur so-called because the French naturalist Pierre Sonnerat, hearing the Madagascans cry out *Indry!* (Look!), took the imperative for a noun. Well, there were worse indignities by the million between 1943 and 1944. And there are things, even now, to be grateful for: I am not called Shanklin; I can spell; I have found a cigar that I enjoy. What more can I want?

Calmness.
Couthness, or couth (as the British say).
Guile.

An atamasco lily, with funnel-shaped pinkish flowers, to put under my pillow. Sweeten my dreams a bit.

"Come when I call, or tarry till I come. If you be deaf, I must prove dumb." I sure am. Now, where did I hear that?

Under the influence of—oh, an atomic novel I once composed, meaning a novel you cannot divide, at least not into meaningful subcombinations. Called nothing, it was composed wholly of two words, *a* and *the*, I having evacuated all else, as in wartime, from the danger zone. *The a, a the, the the*, it began. You can see the drift away from cliché. There are echoes. It is all action. The characterization is far from heavy-handed. It almost ends. The *the*'s win out over the *a*'s, inevitable when you think of our modern mania for precision.

As if it were winter, I see the lining of my mind out there on the balcony, pitted with the arrowhead tracks of birds. All that snow.

Choice of trees? Well, then, the redbud, known as the Judas tree.

Choice of shells? Make mine the wentletrap, with long ridges crossing its spiral taper. When one thinks one knows it all, one can always find something to add; therefore there's no all at all, at all. You never know.

"After all," then, means after some of it, after a bit of it, not even worth saying *after* in front of it. Nothing is ever said and done. Sagittarius next, and Scorpius to follow, thence to the southern heavens, round and back until the spiral is complete. Yet our Way's just a smattering. Who could count the stars in even it? Or those outside it. *Who counts?* That's what I mean. Something goes on, as behind closed blinds all over the world, has no need of us. As Inkwell, the Oxford sage, once remarked to me in Tom Quad, the sequence leading to man is tortuous and random; it is unlikely that, redone with the same quota of the random, the experiment would yield up man again. I envision, though, the thirty-foot butterfly whose lifetime's occupation (333 years) is to build puys of meringue-like sputum, miles high, visible from enormous altitudes. Conceivably, even, if one looks closely, the square eyes of the simoom bat; the double anus of the Caucasian flantellifer; the green rotary forceps of the Algerian swont. Or, failing these, there might be such novelties as the radioactive tail of the Arctic genferon (to be pronounced with a hard *g*); the navel tusk of the lesser rinderpoon; the rainbow eyes of the Himalayan gypsum roach; the transparent hooves of the Cuban swizzary; the fifth, retractable, foot of the Egyptian dune-fondler; the sonar cone in the muzzle of the Andean charcoal fox; the lethal septum of the banded Siberian frost veltanex.

Cave hybridam! Said: "Karvay," et cetera. Latin for beware of mongrel. I just wonder if there isn't some link between hybrid and hubris. No, that's too much to hope for. It's not so much that the etymology is dubious as that, for once, the dubiology is etymous.

And, and, and: the Andorran pith jaguar; the mint peccary that haunts the remains of nuclear reactors; and the Canberra hopping fecopod, self-propulsive on one perdurable turd. These, and a few others who have begun to stalk through what I genially call my dreams, will be my cell-soulmates when I come to a pretty pass, even the prettiest pass of all. I'll soon, yes, soon (there's a juicy word for you) begin to compose a little prayer, in other words a fit of subjunctive lust. "Please," you have to begin, "on December 25, if you can carry something as big, will you bring me a Junior Hydrogen Bomb? And . . ." Back to that later. What I am volunteering here, of facts as I understand them, must be suspect from the outset. It goes without saying that if someone is forcing something out of you, that person usually thinks it's the truth, whereas what's not extorted's not believed. Exit literature, enter confession.

At that moment Milk was bristling with delight as Pi clipped folded paper and produced a row of tiny creatures advancing hand-in-hand. Cloned in a minute. How describe that expression on Milk's face? Over the years I have tried, have never worded it right. It's a taut effervescence. No. It's a creamy evil-eye. No. It's fellow-conspiratorial élan. No. It has in it a highwayman, greedy but civil: Stand and deliver, ladies and gentlemen. It has also in it a high-honed intellect that should be peering into a cloud chamber as vapor condenses on the ions left in the trail of the speeding nuclear particles, and the cloud tracks form, comparable to the vapor trails of high-flying jets. As well as a touch of the diva who, somehow exults within the planes of her own face. Freebooting Greek *nous* made charismatic, then? No. But nearer. It's all in her face, not in her mind, whose mount (the brain) has too many long thin spines, too few short and fat. See the researches of Martin-Padilla and Dominick Purpura, as I think I mentioned before, perhaps not, what lovely names for research scientists, especially the latter. A Purple Master on the premises, visiting the cerebral cortex: "mental deficiency links with disrupted neuronal geometry, sets abnormalities of mental function alongside congenital heart abnormalities traceable to anatomical defects in the cardiac muscle and valves."

Charming epiphany, jargon-swelled.

Gruesome too, when you reflect that anyone who has prepared micro-slides of post-mortem brain samples from thirty retarded children has actually— I can't, I won't, finish the statement. Just that those thirty didn't make it, see. "OK. We know." "Do you? Good, I'm glad." Never mind the rage. Rage begets migraine, I'm told. Yet I had the migraine before the rage, long, long before.

Getting back to what I was saying, or was saying in order not to say something else, you can buy pristine blank forms, printed by the Oyez Publishers, which offer a small text for multiple-choice response. *"The said child is* [not] *suffering from serious disability or chronic illness."* Alter as appropriate, you're told, and if a child is so suffering, add "namely" and state. . . . Imagine that. It exists, like many thousands printed in 1972 with a 19_ _ on the back, which is only fair with a quarter of a century to go. I wonder who'll be here when they start printing them with a 20_ _. Convenient twin slots for the decade, et cetera. Cheering, when you come to think of it, they haven't printed any of the latter yet. Optimism like ice cream on the cavities.

Consonance, now, that's what's needed: a simultaneous combination of sounds conventionally regarded as pleasing and final in effect. *Ur. Ah. Ugh. Ow. Huh. Hm.* Aloha to all that, I am trying to get back to those days when we ran things down, I mean began the closure (there was no denigration). Roughly the plot runs as follows. The sun froze. The apples melted. The house flinched. Our eyeballs yellowed. We slept with our intestines in neat mounds on our midriffs. Witticisms were the fuel of the look that did not look, the mind that did not count the days. More than ever, with Milk at peace tilting blue and white powder to make estuaries and spurs, Pi and I went to superfine lengths to tie when playing Scrabble. Our scoring is bizarre anyway, so it was easy to make things come out: the last player, needing twenty-three to win, arranged combinations that scored twenty-two. Which is as it always was. We play out of inventive extravagance, to bend language, not to win. Or is it, backhandedly, not to yield? No, it has never been that. It's a case of level heads leveling, gentle fraud. I'd call it the happy version of what happened in Dresden during World War Two, when after the so-called firestorm couples were found melted together in what was left of each other's arms, and dreadfully shrunken. What is more human than that, I ask myself, than hugging together before you burn alive, neither able to help the other, but the arms doing some thing, some last thing, for both? It could never happen on the Isle of Wight, in Shanklin say, that's no target. At least, it hasn't happened yet. And the heat of indignation, or even the vaunted one of composition, is no match. An awful thing to say in the context. Or out. In our minor way we prevail, matching each other at Scrabble, fixing the scores. At one.

Uncommon thing, it took Milk ten days before she saw (or

remarked on, at any rate) the color photograph of herself taken years ago as, grinning smoothly, she prepared to launch herself down a slide. Over by the door to the balcony, it's nearest the sun of all the pictures on the walls. In the bottom left-hand corner there's a small snapshot of her at school, with three friends, all four of them in their hearing harnesses, hers white, theirs blue. Whereas the others look happy, she seems needled by something, holding her doll as if she means to sling it from her. They wear the school's uniform, maroon and blue, whereas she has on a red-white-and-blue dress, horizontally striped. When she finally saw herself behind the thumbprinted glass, she delivered a long-ish speech all to her image as it stood there, no doubt recovering time, and then chanted the girls' names. "Kool," she whirred, where she was now an officer of law and order. No more juicy anarchy for her, but stern waggings of the index finger. After a moment more of contemplation, she examined the other pictures, appearing to grade them privately. The more bizarre the better. She took to Dürer's engraving of a rhinoceros, to the photograph of a woman's head smeared all over with concrete to make a living statue with closed eyes, and seven Hungarian stamps mounted on black. Without a word, she stood before a busy, crowded drawing of spheres, cherubs, and astronomers, pointed with glee to the figure of Copernicus, whose body was covered with eyes and whose mouth was puffing skyward the words *Videbo Caelos tuos,* "I shall see your heavens," while a much relegated-looking Ptolemy leaned back against a shield on the ground, spouting *Erigor dum corrigor,* as well he might, the gist being: "I arise now I am straightened out." Or so I construe, rusty if not worse. At the Trifid and Ring Nebulae, recognizing them from the Way downstairs, she aimed her broad alabaster chin, maybe disdaining them for being no novelties at all, and she quite failed a chimpanzee, the printed plan of a small glider I'd designed at fourteen (a mere model), and, of all things, the composite photograph of the Way from Cassiopeia to Sagittarius. A nifty chiaroscuro picture of Pi playing pool, taking bare-armed aim, earned a passing grade, however, and a tight laugh. I think, of all, the rhino won, because she returned to it, and it only, trying to make her eyes bulge, going down on all fours in a pseudo-pachydermatous crouch, with her arms held up to be the ears. "What?" she asked. Told, she said "Rhine" perfectly, but not the second vowel. Next thing she'd cried "Biosh" and pinched my thigh. It was a rhino charge, of course. I should have known; "biosh" is how she says "pinch," always as a warning or a threat. In that same room, which is this, of course (I no longer being able to write in the basement), she later in the day squatted, thinking herself unobserved, and without a sound let the tears flood out, then slapped her knee in rebuke, being a big girl not entitled to cry. The saw-teeth of those five minutes are still sharp. I want to turn the rhino, Copernicus, all those images, to face the wall, as if to ban her reflected face; but no, I leave things be, as if she's dead. Go on using the room like an addict. Gape at the rhino, the rest, like a masochist. Find not many words that soothe. Or even tell. From time. To time. Like that. "Now then," says Pi, "it's on your face again. You're supposed to be celebrating the past, not mourning the present." I agree, but not without a memo to myself that part of the story of this book's story is the acid-on-the-nerves of writing it at all. Thank heavens, I say, for the strict wallbars of the RNA code called Messenger. It keeps me straight. After five more sets of three paragraphs, it will lead me to one of the three nonsense combinations. UAA, followed at once by UAG, later by UGA, which look no more like nonsense than the rest. At fourteen, an age that comes to mind too much, I lay in bed with a broken arm the doctor had splinted, an injury sustained in a football game and therefore slimy with honor. Why I hadn't been sent to the hospital there and then, I have no idea now; in the end, of course, I was. But, for one night, I slept in splints, or tried to sleep as the ache sharpened into a gnawing pain, and I perversely shoved at the wood that hemmed in the broken ulna. Again and again I made the red-hot flash that made the whole arm jump and a wet break out on the bridge of my nose, this at about three in the morning, a fine case of jubilant suffering. The hurt was mine, or so I reasoned, and worth getting to know while available. With each surge of pain, no one woke, neither my parents nor my sister. No one could tell. And now, with a new break to palp, I press the spot night and day, getting even more electrifying results. Yet, yet, the words haltingly move along. An ulna in the head I hadn't bargained for. Nonsense is quick, meaning is slow.

Goodness! the dawdling that goes on. It was easier, though, to do this with Milk on the premises. Had I not done any then, had the whole thing been retrospective, I'd never have started, no fear; I'd rather fry fish than do this, walking about the house, even the autumn garden, with yellow pad and felt pen in hand, trying to arouse the very echoes I want to go away.

"Calmly, that's how." Pi says this, with terse gentleness.

"Copy," I astronautically tell her. "Willco. If possible. But when you've given blood, you cannot lap it back. Therefore, give more, thus making of yourself an anemic beast." A what? One of Count Dracula's leavings. The one picture in the kitchen, gone unmentioned, reminds me; I see to my left, sneaking up on me from behind the shopwindow of their blood-curdling aquarium, the Count and, in a sturdy night-gown, his drained-dry bride, halted on some twisting steps while he stares away from her and partly through the giant cobweb that stops them live. He has heard something over there, out of sight, far in the dungeon's corner, where the light from his two-foot candle cannot reach. Perhaps it was a ghost moaning "Lugosi, Lugosi," or the outsize spider itself coming to monitor the vibration in its web. Meanwhile, with her long dark hair divided forward over her shoulders, the bride waits, her eyes glazed with destiny, the suck of her mouth compressed outward into a little raisin disk. How goes her choked ditty? Could she but croon.

> Apple, apple, on the tree,
> Have you heard of ecstasy?
> Be my pippin, bite my core;
> *I* don't suck *my* paramour.

Extremes, extremes; she still looks wholesome, whereas I, face all nicked with razor cuts, I look used. Did I nick from wanting not to look as the morning mirror burned with light?

Gluteus maximus, sterno-mastoid, masseter, old muscular friends, they'd leave me if they could. This here joint's done for, that's their creaking say. Backside, head, and jaw must move themselves from hereoninout. Bah, sez I, I'll not be put off, I'll fix them with some rubber bands. Whoa. Steady, girl. Gee-up, now we're off again, none the worse for being a bit awkward in the bandages. I hunch from room to room, hunting words in walls, but I have not even graffitoed my own house.

Collected now, I begin reporting all over again. The tide is in. An author, with a big herring lashed to the top of his skull, has been floated out to sea for the gulls to dive-bomb, his brain an open jar, and now he's back, none the worse for that experience. The trick, ever, is to see yourself as your own best raw material, be as impersonal as Dürer. Look again at his "Rhinocerus 1515." Minus the horn that's partly cut off by the frame, it's only an armor-plated rat. I think he knew. What's frightening isn't there in the so-called animal kingdom; it is cellular. So children may as well play as not, and sheep may as well graze as not, and swallows time the year. The ogre will come in any case.

Aimless, Milk and I wandered outside, played soccer with a big apple, kicked at a bush or two, chased one striped and one black cat, found and picked another bottle-nose gentian aromatic as Persia, gathered up withered pine cones into a paper bag, flew planes shaped from our hands with one thumb representing an entire wing, sprinted a hundred yards down the road, fenced with twigs, walked back pigeon-toed and giggling, sat on the grass and watched beetles, picked some wild scallions, came in with the flower and filled a vase with water. Then we joined Pi in the air-conditioned bedroom where she was reading Merezhkovski's Life of Leonardo, and then left her in peace, wandered downstairs to check the Way, make it blaze. "Our position," I told her, in the vein of the mock-heroic inaudible, "is not favorable to a correct survey; but, as we see it, it is marked by strange cavities and excrescences, with branches in all directions, and is interrupted in its course, especially at Ophiuchus and Argo, by the operation of some force as yet unknown. This is true of width as well as course. Curdled or flaky, it mingles bright patches with almost absolute vacancies." I talked as if quoting some ancient book, and no doubt was, but the only bit of what I mouthed that had a source was this: "It is a large part of a larger scheme exceeding the compass of finite minds to grasp in its entirety." Courtesy of Miss Agnes Clerke, in *System of the Stars.* We now call it the super-galaxy, its headquarters in Virgo; as for its hind ones, we'll forever have to guess.

Greedy for more of her mind, I outlined Sagittarius with bumbling speed, stood back, breathing hard, and asked. Both my hands flew apart as if a large bird had taken off from between them. "What?" I mimed. One look and she knew, riding a bicycle with both legs and steering with both arms. She'd seen a bicycle for the Moon, or for Mars, a sketchy grid that had not wheels but ball bearings, like a tripod recover-

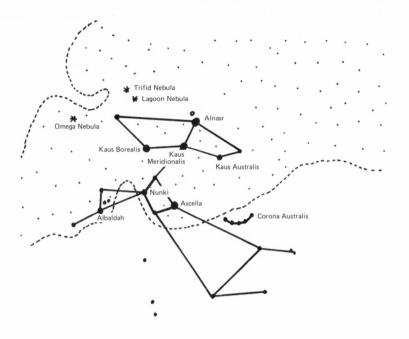

SAGITTARIUS

174

ing from the splits. Perfect vehicle for a weightless one, it floated lunar-lander-like, with that lovely small crescent of Corona Australis just a token seat. Mobilized in the abstract, she rode across the Way, turned and came back, eyes brimming with silver mirth, commanding me to watch. I did. I still do, still see that airy locomotion on the basement floor. Deep in the Galactic center without knowing it, she trod stardust as abler mortals water, and the little pluck of pain in my insides went numb, annulled. Calling to Pi to come and see, I remembered how this girl had never learned to balance on two wheels, had even been frightened to trust herself to a machine that had small side wheels that wouldn't let it tip. Unabashed, even with two observers, Milk toured the up-there neighborhood, all the way from the three famous nebulae—Trifid, Omega, Lagoon—to the Corona, flicking a heel at Alnasr, cocking a snoot at Albaldah, without coming off. Dilated in my trance, I could hardly believe what Pi told me, she having forgotten to do so yesterday. Milk, no child but woman, was having her period and, like a modern woman, was going ahead, pressing on with what mattered.

Cowed, I thankyoued, was okayed. Those who quietly get on with Merezhkovski's Life of Leonardo can see to those who cycle over Sagittarius. And with no fuss at all. You couldn't say that of the Grenadier Guards, the Strategic Air Command, or even the Red Cross. I took deep breaths to sap the shock.

Going back upstairs, after she'd applauded the ride, Pi shot a good word backward about Leonardo, firing me to start with what I suddenly thought of as the illumination of Sagittarius, done monklike, but with bulbs and bits of gaudy card. Down there, staring at the hub of the galaxy, at Archer's Bicycle, I felt moved in the same way as when I watched the Sun ease its way westward above the ridge of the long mountain at which the house points. Not ours, but loaned, the Sun. Old reliable, at least for as many more million years as doesn't matter. I gladdened at its steady tour above us while we tinkered with the apparatus of light: yellow for Alnasr, "the Point," and Kaus Borealis, the northern part of the Bow; then, splurging with two bulbs apiece for Kaus Meridionalis (orange and blue) and Kaus Australis (the same orange, the same blue). "This," I told her, "is the Milk Dipper," but she was more intent on having bulbs in place for Albaldah, Nunki, and Ascella. *Yes,* I mouthed: "yellow, blue, and white." She grinned, a celestial henchwoman. The wiring seemed to take hours. I cut my finger on the sharp rim of a socket. A length of perfectly good-looking wire snapped, and that almost moved her into a rage. My hands flew, planting five little bulbs into the Corona, shape of a nail clipping. Then our bicycle lit up, a riot of tones that made her hop, clap her hands above her head, and with shocking brilliance ask for nebulae by screwing her index finger into her other fist. Up I trotted for my wad of postcards, in which I accidentally put my hand on the Prometheus of Paul Manship, golden ephebe who lolls in the Sunken Gardens of Rockefeller Center with fire in his hand. In that second, I saw Milk, short-haired for once, traipsing across Sagittarius, but stealing the gift of fire from me, at any rate damping me down. She'd made me mellower. You wouldn't think a small bulb could shine through glossy card, but it can. We clipped and trimmed, then rolled narrow tubes of stiff paper, nicked triple flanges to stick to the card, and plugged them over the bulbs to make our three nebulae. A rose-and-white pucker with a white-hot bleb at center, the Trifid cried out for underwear even as my child exclaimed an histrionic "Poo!" See it and die laughing. Less suggestive, the Lagoon has a rift and not much blue, but a positive eczema of stars on one side and a blazing cluster on the other. The Omega is scarlet, shapeless, but studded with blues, an orange, a pure yellow, and has a baffling dark rectangular cloud cutting into its foot, a vortex box. On they glowed, as no telescope can produce them, but only cameras,

176

picking up colors which, when Rome was founded, say, had already been on the way for three hundred years. A far cry, even if you never come to think of it, like Milk, whose bike lamps bloom. Staring bemused at Nunki, so-called Star of the Proclamation of the Sea, I found my mind playing truant, occupied with nothing serene or noble, but caught up in the jargon of medical insurers: small bowel studies, price $30; treatment by radioactive phosphorus for polycythemia vera, $140 for four sessions; prostatectomy, suprapubic (one or two stages), $250. They get you coming and going; but, at least, you can get a platelet count for three dollars, a tubeless gastric diagnex for five. "Nunki," I said, "that would make a lovely nickname"; its sound is informal, biddable, tender, whereas Ascella ("the armpit") sounds like a cold droplet, as no doubt befits a star that's heading off, out of Sagittarius, to some destination of its own. As is the star called *fi*. After thousands of years, with these two runaways at a distance from where they are now, the Sagittarian Milk Dipper will look out of whack, in fact unrecognizable. As if that mattered. One thing about stars, they tend to give the mapmaker time to catch up. And constellations most of all.

Unwinding with a beer which Milk had sampled but didn't like ("sore," she said, getting not quite the exact word), I made her a tiny catapult from a rubber band, amazed to hear electronic sounds at certain tensions. She aimed a spit-heavy paper plug at the TV local newscaster, but, with a wild shot, struck Ptolemy where he sat, high and to the right of the set. "Some game to teach her," said Pi. "She was born to it," I answered. "You can't teach this girl anything; all she needs is practice." I said nothing else, gave over the room to news of area high-school sports, my mind on another of those dark, rotten images that had begun to rise in it like bubbles of mud. Such a lost-property office my head had become that I didn't mind most of its irrelevant fits, but this one wouldn't go away.

177

Long before the Milk Dipper lost its present shape, there would have been goodness knew how many purges, if not here then somewhere else, all in the interests of a thing variously dubbed Nation, Aryanism, Involvement. Goons with armbands or shiny-peaked hats would round up the undesirables all over again, first taking them to deserted schoolrooms, then to trains that would grind a slow one-way trip to some resettlement camp in, oh, Omaha, comparable to those already going full blast in the pampas, Hokkaido, the Baltic coast. And Milk would stand twice condemned, for fraternizing with Jews (Pi's renegade status notwithstanding) and for being unfit. Some summer evening, when the light persisted as if it might never come again, after the last uproarious bout of tennis, and while we were all sipping lemonade with even, blithe *Nachtmusik* drifting out from the house over the terrace to the lawns, the black car would draw up. Or horse box. Or van. I would not go quietly, I would have a gun, use it somehow, however much a mess I'd make. I heard the charge against her: a fraternizing, mentally incompetent Leftist, for whom the state had no use. God help us, I thought, one joins the state only when there is nothing left worth joining; that is the *last* membership short of death. Indeed, the latter had more savvy, knowing how to make the cells make errors after they've divided about fifty times, as well as better manners, oftener than not, and a longer tradition. Yes. Hoping hard, I foresaw how the next purge would bring total victory for the forces of defeat, meaning, I think, that we would all three somehow elude the fate worse than death. Rape scenes from Russian newsreels honed the edge of a certain resolution not to get caught with our drawers down. A ripped-open woman, long dead, with all of her save her legs and rear stuffed into a drainage pipe made to measure for just such a scene, came in front of my eyes, like a large cell cruising over the surface of the iris itself, and told a truth that no amount of time could smooth, I hated

178

then, as now, the deadliness of man, the ease with which humans kill one another when the snake- and horse-brains have a field day; and I knew why other civilizations in the galaxy hadn't bothered to call in. Maybe, by the time the Milk Dipper had lost its wedge shape and become an inverted milk churn or even a cut-off cone, mankind wouldn't be quite so handicapped, would be less in need of special care, might even have heard from whoever was on the planets around Barnard's Star. Here I am, I said, born long before my time, willing to live peaceably on behalf of love and knowledge, a placid and serene soul made saber-toothed only by circumstances. I am the Old World looking for the New, as on a previous occasion; the New was never looking for the Old, any more than birds in the Southern Hemisphere migrate as those in the Northern do. It was just a matter of having a star to mark the pole. North has, South has not. And who's to blame?

Answer there is none. The fortune cookie that could enclose it hasn't been baked. The aroma from the oven, then, was that of three frozen turkey pies, one pie more than there were days to go. Understandably, I think, I cast around for metaphors to badge the oceanic jitters of my mind. As astronomers say, what recedes is red-shifted, what approaches is violet-shifted; but what was I approaching? Only someone that receded. The mind was both red and violet, a stasis of blur. No exit could be had from that. The hot pastry of dinner tasted old. The turkey seemed human. Only Milk was on form, relieved that a certain thing was almost over, not because she wanted especially to go (yet how could we tell?), but mainly because knowing that an end was countably near in days (or sleeps) gave her a sense of mastery. Things she adored she relished the end of, simply because something had become clear. Living as she did, in a flux of the open-ended, she could not help but long for the semicolons in the maze of letters.

Uncanny how it felt, nothing so dramatic as waiting behind the curtain while the guillotine that just had thumped was hosed down, but rather as if I were some Japanese soldier going away to war and being honored with the gift of a sash that held a thousand stitches, kept out the chill and bullets as well. That distant-feeling symbolism had come home, from another war to this, the tussle against distance and genes. Chad had already brought Meg to say farewell, he as if glad to get the chore done (he once said the main thing about life is to get through it, implying threescore and ten is too long), and she as well as Milk dismally afraid. Asa we hadn't heard from; when he went he stayed gone. Kashmiri wasn't with him but, I seemed to recall, in Knoxville, busy with a movie of some kind. Everyone was outward bound or gone. On the home front, as I with martial hyperbole called it, things were falling apart so fast that there was only Pi, with a few stars, to hold on to. Accustomed to berating myself for too routine an existence (my argument in its favor having been that a confused head doesn't need a random day-to-day as well), I now found myself in the middle of a dismembered, balletic uproar that had no sound. Ironic to think of it, but I had begun increasingly to blot out half an hour at a time with music, not one of the spheres, but one of arrested atoms. Milk had sampled what came through the headphone cable, but it had impressed her little, just another version of the hearing aid, a different form of static. So, in one sense, I was battling anticipated loss with something almost underhand. Hearing, often enough to drive Pi into mild exasperation, Bergsma's *The Fortunate Isles* and Nielsen's Fifth Symphony (in which the drummer has instructions to drown out the orchestra if he can), I canceled a dimension, was as far away as if I had been holed up in some blockhouse-shaped elementary hotel near Tamanrasset in the Sahara. Meanwhile, in the basement, the space for Scorpius waited. Would we, would I, have the heart to do it? Even if all we did was install massive red Antares, which the Greeks called their "anti-Mars." A star bright as ninepence, in the idiom of the British, it would be our own bull's-eye, a big punctuation mark. Try tomorrow, I resolved. See what she thinks. Have her do it all with her own hands, I'll be staring at that bulb for many months or years to come. It would be a long time before this visitation got repeated. Hence everything was unique, or about to be so, as I could tell even from Pi's face, that of a profoundly stable woman observing the Fall of Rome, the death of a rhetoric, the failure of a nerve. Tact flooded with misgiving primed her smile. I would be leaving her too, in order to sever myself from Milk. Someone else, other than I, might have arranged things better, but for this kind of enterprise there were few rules. You began with the unique and added to it. And, after about fifty years of it, you learned perfectly how, when it was far too late. Upon an impulse, defensive and no doubt part of an emotional fugue I'd entered days ago, I picked out from the shelf a last-century tome on stars and began to read what it said about the Scorpion. Too much fustian for me, the introductory account went on for pages, and my eye skidded until it hit the epithet *rutilans,* for Antares, "glowing redly." That seemed better, except that Antares, being a double, was emerald green as well as fiery red. Skipping quaint lore about the seven famous selected poems of Arabia, said to have been inscribed in letters of gold on silk (or Egyptian linen!) and suspended in the Ka'bah at Mecca, as well as about what the learned saints Augustine and Basil thought concerning the scorpion's derivation from the crab, I found a bit that said the open cluster M 6 resembled a butterfly wing. Yet it was a phrase about something else, I forget what, that caught my mind on the raw and fed it salt. In order to see a certain close double as a double, one needed a magnification of two hundred, at least if one wanted "a clean split without notching"; in other words, a bit of one tended to overlap a bit of the other. Notching was what I was

181

in for; clean split I didn't want and wouldn't get. With one sensible word, "packing," Pi cracked the spell. She asked what I was taking. Had I thought about a present for my mother, with whom, on the other side of the ocean, I would spend a couple of weeks? "A silk scarf," I unimaginatively replied. "Then we should buy it tomorrow, locally; the duty-free prices at airports are a gigantic rip-off." It was the same prudent, caring voice that had persuaded me years ago to start visiting the dentist again, to wean myself of the bottle, to run the mile and lose twenty pounds. Under that same eye I had emigrated from Funk Ghetto to what remained of the twentieth century's fourth quarter, as she repeatedly had stressed. Poets are not supposed to be that practical, though I know of a few others who truly are. In any event, it was Pi who adjusted my wheels back onto what the British call the permanent way (apocalyptic term for a road's rails) and talked me out of the sleepwalking concession I'd made to life. How to repay such a debt I had no idea, but doing what I was told was a start. Out of its shell, the pulp of me felt vulnerable still, even so long after the break, the lawyers, the acrimony, yet feeling light-sensitive was also an intoxication. "Thank you," I said, "for remembering the gift. We'll get one tomorrow, anything but green or brown, which she can't wear." "I know your mother's spectrum," said the poet; "I have it by heart." Non-urgent matters clogged my brain, then turned into vapor. I felt I was living in my own sediment. Hyper-confirm pre-reconfirmed reservations, I kept telling myself: surely there's something I've forgotten. But there wasn't. It was only a matter of getting our two bodies aboard the first plane; aerodynamics and passports would do the rest. Wire only, ran my prearranged instructions, if something goes wrong. It did, but not to us directly. Kashmiri phoned, said Asa had been mugged in New York. His ear was badly cut. I could phone him, though, in the hospital. He sounded remote from himself, almost elated that something had happened to him that was over. If something had to happen to him, he said, he was glad it was only this. It was better than waiting, better than wondering. I marveled at such an impersonal sense of self, compared Asa's trouble with my own. Where he'd been struck by mundane lightning, I was being eroded, gnawed. Yet I had nothing to report to him, to the master of so many of our recent ceremonies, whereas he was full of it: just after a pink slip advertising a massage parlor had been thrust into his hand, he had walked away from Fifth Avenue up a side street to light a cigar. Foolish, he said. The three were lounging in the next doorway and had not taken kindly to his declaration, as at some hellhole customs barrier, of a few one-dollar bills and one long package that contained a freak book, four feet high and four inches wide, a book of tall thin poems, which they had taken anyway. And then the knife, applied to his ear with a laugh even as they were going away. A tickle, that was all, with bursts of tingling as, only five minutes later, a police car rushed him uptown. Stitches, swabs, and tests to come. That was all he said, talking as if one of the elect. It was as if he had already survived being a survivor. Or as if he had happened to the event, not it to him. I envied so superbly accommodating a mind, deciding Asa was geared for whatever world he found himself in, whereas I, I was still fudging up a policy that might get me from today to tomorrow without too much blustering fuss.

"Uranus," said Pi, to get my mind off Asa while Milk was mopping condensation off the toilet cistern. "Pronounced with the stress on the first syllable!" "YOOR-anos," I said: "it has five moons, and the cleanest mind of all the planets." Milk brought, as if it were frankincense and myrrh, about a pound of sodden paper towel, wise enough not to thrust it down the toilet, as she might have done a few years ago. "Wet," she declared. "Oof!" Which meant: Throw it away. But, before handing it finally over, she mopped her sweating brow and chin with it, just for completeness' sake.

A synoptic sense of our penultimate day must have been wrapped into that ball of paper. I saw the three of us, expendable as shapes made from a child's building blocks, lined up in syzygy: a sun, a moon, an Earth. But who was which? Not knowing, I decided each was all, and shut the figure out of mind, recasting myself as a Charon who on the next day would overfly the Styx, Pi as Hermes, Milk as Eurydice. Except the myth was garbled. After losing Eurydice, I wouldn't, like Orpheus, develop a loathing for all women. Just a few, that was all. I, Wight Deulius, would live to bungle many another day, even though I dieted and ran and abstained from the sauce.

Crazy impulses began. I'd pack both our cases with sliced ham, dozens of pounds of it, and leave the snazzy new clothes behind. Then Milk would fly back to fetch them. Or we'd just go over with what we stood up in, traveling light as viruses. Not only would we have nothing to declare; we would walk through Immigration, into that country other than the country of origin, without even being seen. We'd transcend the borders. Dream-paced. White-eyed. Aloof. And never be seen again, except in spectroscopes. Present as chemicals only. Blown about by wind, or kept under refrigeration. Only our formula would know us.

Unbelievable what happened next. *"Look, Yah,"* said Milk: *"Chew the vicissitudes and swallow them down. Don't fret. We'll have long holidays together, all three of us. We'll read Pi's poems on a beach somewhere on Antigua. At night we'll play word games, making* Rimbaud *out of* barium. *You'll teach me French, I'll teach you gibberish, my native language. You can both coach me for my final exams—I often wonder why I settled for philosophy instead of, oh, maybe medicine or psychology. I'll make some kind of a living as a book-reviewer. I'll read what you write and puff your books*

184

under an assumed name, see? We'll sit out, nights, and watch
variable stars, one good way for an amateur astronomer to
make his name. We'll tabulate, we'll wisecrack about Mirfak,
Ophiuchus, and RU Lupi, any stars with funny, just mildly
obscene-sounding names. But, myself, I'd really rather paint
than write, more in the manner (I think) of Francis Bacon
and Magritte—if you can envision the mix—than of Rem-
brandt and Dufy. If you get my drift. Perhaps I should set
up in Bayswater or Staten Island, in a loft, with lots of
accurate northern light that would also show off my medi-
um-brown hair down to my pelvis, and, I suppose, eventu-
ally shack up with some renegade existentialist who runs an
antique shop. And whenever the two of us, he and I, took off
to roam through jungles or ancient seaports loud with either
macaws or loading cranes, we'd stop off and look you up,
trying to time it during your vacations. Or just say the hell
with it and keep on rendezvousing year in, year out, in Cey-
lon. And I would keep on talking, in this no doubt perverse
vein of the ostentatious uttered, just to make up for lost time.
How many phonemes do you think went to waste during my
first twenty years? I saw men walk on the Moon, but had not
a single comment. In those days I didn't know Moon from
Sun, or Europe from America, the Suez from the Panama.
Talk for the sake of talking, as Novalis said, is the sincerest
thing you can do. Or, as Beckett has it, words have their
utility, the mud is mute. Pardon me if I seem like a goldfish,
forever surfacing with an aphorism in its mouth, or whatever
it was you once said about Pi, whose talk crackles with im-
pacted wit. I'll keep quiet only when peering at Andromeda
with you through the Astrax eyepiece of the eight-inch scope.
None of your toylike three-incher for me! I'll take especial
care of Asa, who's as deaf in one ear as I used to be in both.
I'll teach him to sign, just in case. I'm even willing, for a
financial consideration, to type your manuscripts for you,
for both of you. Pay me in encyclopedias. Or we'll redo, from

scratch, the Way in the basement. You must have thought me mighty unresponsive when you did it first. Well, I was mighty, by my own estimate: when one is shut out of things, one feels privy to an absolute of what's left, if you get my— I was going to say drift, but I've said it already. Eloquence is variety, is it not? Excuse me, the phone just rang. It was another invitation to model, such being the main source of my pin money. I'd hate to be dependent. As it is, like a good girl, I balance my checkbook monthly, as the bank says one should, and thus far I disagree by only seven cents. As for what you have already written about me, I'll forgive. The inaccuracies. The lies. The tiny slanders. The ballsed-up chronology. The utter misunderstanding of some of my neat- est gibberish. I promise to rebuke you, though, only in Indo- European, most hypothetical of tongues and therefore, I pre- sume through some kind of rearward teleological guess, nearer to God. How do you like them apples? How do you like being addressed in this irreverent way? I know, I know, you've been waiting all your life for this conversation. Lucky you I'm not fifty-five, but only as old as Pi was when I made my first landfall with you two. By the way, she looks better with her hair down than stacked on top. I've often thought that. I'm Nature's girl, catching up at three quarters of the speed of light. My latest discoveries, in case you want to use them, are: the reduction, long desired, of hadrons to quarks and gluons! Mr. George Crumb's composition Voice of the Whale, *which reminded me of a galactic kazoo! and the fake newspapers read by people in movies—the Philadelphia* Sentinel, *the Chicago* Courier, *the London* Daily Messenger! *I try to never let them catch me napping, as well as never to split an infinitive, God alone knows why, but maybe to please you when that look of irresponsible hubris comes over your face after your third cup of coffee. I have also discovered that from bikini to yashmak is fewer steps than you might think; that people who aren't worth talking to are people not*

186

bright enough to know that we're brighter than they think we are (if you can follow all that); and that rhyming slang, as practiced by the Cockneys of London, enables one to say I sent you a picture coastguard *or* Testicles live in pairs in a wrinkled factotum. *I have, as the saying goes, been around, have sustained the minimum of damage. Out of* Rimbaud *you can also make* radium. *A* lemma's *a glossed word. A* paraph's *a flourish or an underlining. My other favorite words include* jiffy, trounce, flank, euphoria, crittur, wydwose, *and* blazhenny, *which is Russian for crazy. I especially admire the Cambridge theoretical astronomer Stephen Hawking, a severely handicapped paraplegic who insists on reading his work aloud at conferences, in spite of difficulty in enunciating consonants. Of late I've been dipping into the* Rig Veda, *a text I believe you in your finite wisdom haven't ever read, and I would like to quote. If you think this is the kettle calling the pot black, then take it or leave it, including what I fully realize is my own reversal of the usual trope:* Who knows for certain? Who shall here declare it? / Whence was it born, whence came creation? / The gods are later than this world's formation; / Who then can know the origins of this world? / None knows whence creation arose. / And whether, he has or has not made it; / He who surveys it from the lofty skies, / Only he knows—or perhaps, he knows not. *Don't laugh: you've quoted enough at me in your time. And, while I'm about it, haven't you overlooked one fact pertaining to the messenger RNA you once saddled me with? According to my book on the subject (which I now read as if interpreting my premature epitaph), the signal for initiation of protein synthesis is a partially known sequence of symbols ending with AUG, the symbol for methionine. Hence, Yah dear, all proteins when first gotten going start with methionine. What's unusual, though, isn't the chemical, but those letters, AUG, suggesting augury or inauguration. Could it just be that I'm beating you at your own game? Baffled?*

Never mind. We nomads leave the aged behind, and they don't resent it, not a bit. If, as once seemed likely, you are writing the North American version of what the Japanese call the shishosetsu, *the autobiographical novel, shouldn't you inspect your auspices more roundly? After all, to miss a trick such as AUG, and have your protagonist remind you of it through centripetal ventriloquism, isn't that a bit thick? And it would help a lot, in other areas, if you wouldn't leave boxes of Kleenex strewn about the floor for folk to tread on, and if you would please flush the toilet after using it, and if you would please-please not smoke cigars in the bath. That's all for now. We are going tonight to hear Schönberg's* Gurrelieder, *of which I especially love the part called* Behold the Sun, *and I don't care if you dislike my taste in music. I have a term paper to write on Croce, heaven help me, and I must say that old essay of yours, an offprint of which I've really gone square-eyed looking at, hasn't been much help at all. Shorter sentences would have helped, as well as a less metaphorical style. Give me Swift and Austen any time over Carlyle and Pater. Take care of yourself now. Don't smoke too many cigars. Eat nothing fried. And get up earlier, which is to say: Don't stay up all night watching TV, even if you think you're planning chapters while doing it. There are maxims that cover all your misdeeds. I won't bore you by quoting them here; you know them already. The examined life is very much worth having. P.L. (for Post Locutum, is my Latin right?): Can you lend me a* Bouvard and Pécuchet? *I finally got the Voltaire thing, so don't worry about it. I doubt if you did. Oh, P.P.L., tyros speak with their mouths open, whereas a genius speaks with his mouth full."*

After that, I stared at her face for a good five minutes, knowing she'd said none of it; but she'd never said none of it at such intimidating, inspissated, length. All I could think was that old tag about Einstein's physics, which said that matter doesn't travel *at* the speed of light. It was like being separated from Milk by a so-called light wall, on one side of which particles were moving more slowly than light, while on the other they were actually faster. I had just space-traveled into what-was-not.

As for coming back, I don't think I ever did. Reminding me of dreams in which I argued with her non-stop, in fantastic erudite language, that long splash of ventriloquism still fills my ears. When a character talks back to its creator, that is one thing; but when a real person who's been made over into a character lets rip with an out-of-time harangue, you begin to believe in sorcery. I still do. Who's to gainsay me when I recount what I thought I heard? Wishful thinking? Of course. But also unwilled and automatic, something to be credited to my synapses firing again and again to relieve the pressure in their turf.

Uncanny, that was UAA, the first of the three triplets that mean STOP or NONSENSE. No doubt I lived up to its role. And this, UAG, is the second. Make sense of that last whole day? Not I. Maybe some other will. All I know is that not only the line between fact and fiction blurred, but also the line between Milk and me, between us and the behaving universe. It felt as if, although they didn't, commas halted us dead while periods fanned the flow. Nouns died. Verbs froze. Adjectives did not describe. While conjunctions severed, prepositions mislocated, and pronouns stood for nothing, the language took an opportunity to communicate nothing but itself. At large. At random. At the merest bidding.

At home to guests: receiving, shaking hands, taking off its underwear, cavorting nude in the presence of grammar. As who should say: I said what could not be, thus I-ing a no one, thus said-ing an unsayable, thus what-ing a not, thus coulding a *non posse*, thus negating a not, and thus making a trespasser of the verb to be. Is that how others have staged, say, a Two-Part Invention for Firmament and Supreme Be-

189

ing? I'll never know. But I know the synapses, "the fastened-together," made a poem of their very own. Gray anti-matter. I host.

Gaga at young age, I held my breath to rid me of the pipe dream thus made burly, lest it undo stoical acquiescences hard arrived at. And so got back to where life can be merely awful, no holds barred. The embarkation. The fastening of seatbelts. The transferring of one's traveling companion to other hands. The mater not alma, not by a long chalk.

Calmer than she had any right to be, Milk fell asleep early, her teeth unbrushed, her body naked, her nightdresses packed. But she had patted me on the back, to inspirit; had taken my hand and conducted me outside to stare together at the apple tree, as if it somehow prefigured our destination.

"Any laundry?" asked Pi. "Any last-minute things to wash?" "Have we," I inquired, "done any laundry these last two weeks? I can't even remember." "We?" "*I* have," she said, with the complete force of one who is going to be alone for three weeks. It felt like having snow between my teeth. A cranial jolt.

Useless, I listened to a piece of music based on Earth's magnetic field, in fact one year's measurements adapted from graph levels to pitch. It had the eerie gravity of certain compositions for pipe organ, sounded aloof and timeless, yet flooded with an abstract geniality as if the solar wind had learned to smile. How enviable, I thought, to be so accommodated to what Isaac Newton called fluxions. How does one achieve it? Is it a human possibility at all? That night it was not.

Chad phoned, reporting a daughter with a strep throat. Heavens be praised they hadn't come over.

An unappeasable fatigue took us to the bedroom for half an hour, nerves tightening Priapus' throat. Then a musical on

TV, at which we peered like horses in fog. At nine-thirty, a swift blast of rain, into which we ventured, patrolling the balcony, I in garish Polynesian shorts, Pi in a batik toga worn like a cape.

"Catharsis," I quipped; "let's go inside." The thunder made us switch off the TV. And then, with all lights out but with Milk's air-conditioner faintly pounding, we watched the lightning as it stabbed our chunk of the Appalachians twelve miles away. What a well-purged night, I thought, when all nightmarish wildness is washed away.

Curiously, though, within an hour the sky was partly clear: man's first picture book open again. Lounging on an outdoor chair I hadn't even tipped the water off, I looked down-range at Scorpius, the constellation we would never finish. Insistent-looking stars formed a claw that sprouted from red Antares, but I saw other shapes as well: the kite, the bucket of Dante, even what the Akkadians called The Place Where One Bows Down. Ah yes, it was all of that! Governing the groin, it emblematized in claws the yoke of matrimony, and presided (so I'd read) over Judaea, Mauretania, Norway, Morocco, Sardinia, and God alone knew what other stamping-grounds.

"Antares," said Pi: "wasn't it the first star observed through telescopes in the daytime?"

"Arcturus," I answered. "Some say it's Arcturus. I don't care. I'll have the whole southern celestial hemisphere to do on my own. Not that it matters. We managed to do an awful lot. It's just—oh, my pattern complex giving me a bad time again. Nothing's ever as neat as you want it."

Countdown, that was my mood. I might even tally the hours as they passed, disdaining to sleep at all and, perhaps, working out there in the damp with the eight-inch scope that tracked without a creak. To be followed by another sleepless

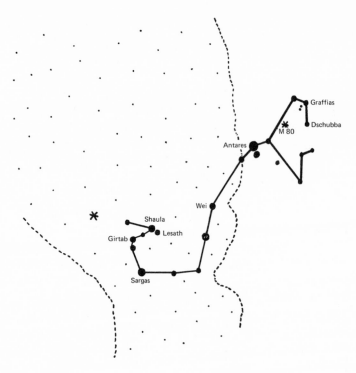

SCORPIUS

night over the Atlantic. *No.* I determined to average five hours at least and not to have one of my caffeine binges out of sheer anxiety. My fill of this night's stars, though, I'd have, as something—not in the basement—to remember her by.

A star by any name is sweet, I told myself, whereas numbers and letters do nothing at all to the mind's aural eye.

"Graffias," I said aloud, "a triple, with dominant lilac and pale white." It means Crab. Halfway between it and Antares lies the cluster which, on the western edge of a starless opening four degrees broad, prompted Sir William Herschel to exclaim: *"Hier ist wahrhaftig ein Loch im Himmel!"* He'd found a true hole in heaven, but one speckled with stars.

After Graffias, I found, with naked eye, in this order, red Entenamasluv, usually called *gamma* only; Dschubba, the forehead, also known as the Tree of the Garden of Light; and Shaula, the sting, thought unlucky. Yet my mind slouched, began mixing things up, blurring *sigma* and *tau,* "the outworks of the heart," with mu^1 and mu^2, supposed to be a little girl, Piriereua the Inseparable, and her small brother, who together flee from home into the sky when ill-treated by their parents, two other stars who follow them and are still pursuing to this very day. Or so claim the storytellers of the Hervey Islands, not even in my atlas.

Asleep, or nearly so, I lost the scorpion in the fishhook of Maui, with which a Polynesian god drew up from the depths the big island called Tonareva, not in my atlas either, but for better reason. Feeling fished-for myself, I consumed two cans of beer, blundered back inside, and helped Pi with the dishes. Celestial visions gave way to encrusted Jello, fish-perfumed pans, and blood-red charcoal in the broiling tray. Light and mud.

Unbearable humidity drove us again into the bedroom, where Pi almost at once fell asleep. After setting the alarm, I crept out, bore to the balcony the big scope, and began a midnight vigil after mopping up the table's top, resentfully aware that I should have done it before taking the scope outside. If I were unlucky, damn the star called Shaula, I'd find a minor rim of rust on the bottom of the cast-iron mount.

A sky of late July blotted with cirrus did me proud. Like a saliva gash, the Milky Way dragged at my eyes. A fishhook, a bicycle, a tent, and a big bird flowed coldly above, in a dimension not that of air-conditioners and bowstring nerves. Milk's other images were out of sight; but, anticipating tomorrow (now today), I looked east toward Pisces and Aquarius, the direction in which, at our own level, we'd soon be flying at less than star speed. Then I whipped my gaze back, gaped at the naked sky as a giant wedge of cloud cruised over. My ears filled with a thick, muddled squeak, and the eyepiece with bulbous-looking silver geese, legs retracted, heads rigid. I even saw the eyes, aimed away up-range. Blotting out entire constellations, the geese moved north as one enormous wing. Two thousand of them? Who could know? I was trembling.

Aimed instead at Libra, Milk's own group, next to the Scorpion. Who had not lauded it? The list of celebrants included Longfellow, Milton, Marvell, and Homer. The constellation itself resembled not so much Scales or the claws of Scorpius (which once it was) as a two-legged triangular table, with its best star, Zubenelgenubi, glistening pale yellow and light gray at the right-hand corner. On that tiny celestial tray I took an early mental breakfast before my own turning with the planet wheeled it out of sight. Uncouth-sounding, an obscure fourteenth-century line came to mind, and went as fast: *Whoso es born in yat syne sal be an ille doar and a traytor.* An ill-doer and a traitor? Never. Of slanders I'd had enough, no matter where they hailed from.

Church clocks, minutes apart, told me it was one in the morning, while another clock, familiar of my bladder and hormones, told me I could stay out another two hours at least without hopelessly unfitting myself for the day's journey. So I beered, cigared, took heart from a sandwich of Jarlsberg cheese and Roman meal, and looked abroad.

At Deneb chugging pale.
At Vega, the harp star, big stud of pale sapphire.
And Altair, pale yellow, according to some a portent of danger from reptiles.

Astrology, seeping in, I booted out on the wings of a mixed metaphor.

Attached a different eyepiece so as to gain higher magnification, relishing how easy it was, with the eight-inch, to look down as if through a microscope. No more stunted necks. No more wobble. No more the image diving out of sight. Having Milk on the premises was akin, whereas Milk in the cheap cardboard-tubed scope was a mortification of the flesh. Yet, after later on today, meaning today's European version, I'd be back to the toy telescope, more frustrated than ever before. I swore off all comparisons for the next month. It was more than enough to think how bizarrely Asa's ear joined him to Milk. Better by far to think how Milk's images in the basement had been added to the sum of things, whether as analogies or not. And what seemed important, then as now, was to give evidence of having been, even if the result were gross enigma. Daubs, graffiti, doodles. I launched into thoughts on the work of art as spiritual fidgeting that, having nothing to say, wanted to evince, make tracks. At one extreme there was the howl and the babble, at the other dumbstruck gesturing.

Going, going, but here today.

Gone tomorrow is the missing bit, except it doesn't figure as anything besides heavyweight guess.

As with the British, who often arrive at belated self-discovery in some such phrase as "Optimistic? Yes, I suppose I am," I took up a stance without naming it: a Jack Horner of automatic luck, a temporary Prospero. In one sense, I knew as little as the screwworm flies who, bombarded with gamma rays, were exterminated for the sake of livestock.

Under the influence of a not-knowing that wanted to leave a spoor, I was un-educating myself with some success. The pre-sapiens ambit I'd begun to call it, having found nothing else with which to face my lot. Head full of phenomena I'd never wish away—feather palms, the stubby-nosed antelope named saiga, *anableps anableps* the four-eyed fish—I kept inching my way toward a response that was merely evolutionary. The All, so-called, was here to evolve and, in that sense only, be meaningful. There would be no epiphanies, no day of judgment, no solution proffered after the puzzle proved insoluble. There was only process, would ever only be that, at most a trillion books whose ultimate effect might be to modify just a bit the brain (into no longer needing to write them or into writing them better), at least the entirety of human pensiveness since 10,000 B.C., end of the last ice age, gone for nothing: just a flicker in the private life of species. It was nothing to cheer about, yet nothing to lament, there being no alternative.

Gala, then, as I called my two-week fit, amounted to merrymaking during decomposition. It had, it would have, no more power to last than a bit of starlight which, after traveling for millions of years through intergalactic space, jostled at long last through Earth's atmosphere and fetched up against the mirror of some telescope, vanished into the silver-halide grain. That puny. A photon death. Yet, I told myself, it might also come back again and again like migraine, the pain in the head and the neck that was also a visual picnic. Unexpected, fast, and dizzily chromatic. Though I stole thunder, I liked to provide my own lightning.

Add to the gala, though, I couldn't. It was already over. Bar the shouting. I had run out of congruities, whereas irrelevances kept on coming home to roost. Kashmiri, for example, had once been a demonstrator of mechanical toys. My own face in the mirror, reminding me at that small hour not of me but of, oh indignity, the bumphead parrotfish whose fused teeth form a white oral heel in a mule's face. I went to bed, foolishly tried to make my mind go to sleep, and my mind stayed up to watch the maneuvers I performed upon it. Finally I got off by spelling the names of philosophers backward, n-i-e-t-s-n-e-g-t-t-i-W last.

Cozened myself into five-hour oblivion.

"Good morning" was the phrase no one said. It was hot, with cerise flashes in the east, a mound of untrussed cumulus over the roof.

A mind hopelessly divided, I checked the tickets, the bags, the calendar, half-hoping for the catastrophe that would save us all. Then I retrieved the miniature Milky Way, criss-cross silver on Prussian blue, from its hiding place on top of the unused record albums in the walk-in storage closet, and slid it deep into her case, between layers of adult-feeling clothes. Eighteen inches long, bigger than she herself when born. Or maybe not. She would find it, colored paper stars and all, when she needed it, later, or when perhaps she didn't need it at all. Once more I dreamed up the catastrophe that would postpone the trip, or cancel it for good.

As if, setting chocolate bars on fire with a butane lighter, Milk would win us three days more with a singed thumbnail. As if a wheel fell off a plane overflying us en route from Philadelphia to Pittsburgh, and it crashed through the roof. As if, after so much help, air changed its rules and no longer helped a wing up by creating less pressure on top of an airfoil than beneath. Force all wings

197

down. But even her period was over, as Pi said while breakfasting; the girl was eligible to go.

Giant dreams, little velleities.

All the way to the airport Milk smiled, alone in a mucous cocoon of her own creation. The way lay through forest along roughish roads that warned, with orange signs, DEER XING. Eight hundred feet higher, we found the air fifteen degrees cooler. Pi sang quietly to herself. I peered at Milk as she averted her gaze through entire civilizations and saw the forest not as trees or ponds, picnic tables or outhouse toilets in cropped clearings, but as heaving hot lava. So I guessed, as lost in query as she in—in what? In, I'd call it, renegade, outlandish, quicksilver, abundant, idiotic, gunslinging rapture. Homely as hoecake. Magical as lymph. Far as the galaxies in Sculptor.

"Gone out," said the sign that was her face. "Back in time. Don't wait. I'm free."

Ulysses and daughter checked their bags through to final destination. A rivet slipped. An airline man fixed it with a Scotch-tape Band-Aid, flagged the case with a label that said DAMAGED/FRAGILE. Which came first?

Gum from the vending machine lasted her two minutes only as she sapped each stick of its flavor and spat it yards. Retrieving the wads, I balled them up, wandered outside into the early afternoon of mountain air, and flung the ball at the inert, distant windsock.

Urgent waiting glazed all three of us. The commuter plane was ten minutes late, yet here it was, lunging with a halt-snort, then still, while five incredulous survivors entered the terminal. "Bye-bye, Pi," said Milk with an impatient kiss, pulling me by the hand toward the gate. Faces, backs, windows, belts, then the brute glare of the sun blotted us out. "I'll write," I'd said as I hauled at the heavy door that didn't open itself. The plane nosed like the halfbeak fish took off westward, fizzing and lurching. In two hours Milk and I would fly back over that very airport, but higher, well into travel's blur.

Unpressurized cabin, noisy propellers, and sudden falls as the air gave way, these distracted me a little while Milk peered past the curtain into the pilot's quarters, beaming at the tiny red lights that shone and died. One image, of the co-pilot's holding the pilot's hands against the throttle levers during takeoff, reminded me of us, of policeman and prisoner, of nuns' laps. Then I saw that she had fallen asleep leaning forward against the belt, as if frozen a winner as she breasted the tape after a hundred yards. Twirling the ceiling nozzle for cold air, I aimed it across the aisle at her head and let her sleep.

Grounded, we walked half a mile to the international terminal, again checked in, and munched candy bars on thinly upholstered pews. "Red," she kept saying as she pointed at the carpets and the cushions. "Red," I answered, wondering why they'd chosen so unsoothing a hue. The music, however, was creamy violet, an ectoplasm of melted aluminum. Then she ran, I in pursuit. Wet her head at the drinking fountain. Hit the restroom with full force, I outside. Played pinball once. Fished out and put on her hearing aids, for the hell of it, only after ten minutes to rip them off as if profoundly disappointed in the audible.

Commotion began as a rock group, mostly black, arrived and autograph-hunters from all over the airport slipped past the ticket-lift desk. "Which of those guys," someone asked me, "is Jubilant Angst" (or whatever the lead singer's name was, unknown to me)? "It's the girl," I maliciously said, "or rather the one who looks like a girl. You know. Sometimes they even travel with goats and perverted lemurs. I read somewhere that three of them had even raped a fish. There's

199

no knowing. If you want an autograph, you'll have to hurry up." He glared affront and went back to reading baseball scores. Milk eyed them as if she had just read *The Origin of Species* and couldn't understand how they had survived while others disappeared.

Up a ramp to board. It might be a ship. Stale air. Low doorway. View of the bloat cone of the nose, its thick wind-punished glass with wipers just like a car. Into the tube. The nonsense is not in the words but in the doing. This is the last genetic stop, the third triplet that makes no amino acid at all, but a muddle, a mutant, a mess. Very well, then. It felt like having an igloo in each lung.

Ghastly view of Milk's face, fatigue-blue in cabin light, seen rounded as if from 112,000 miles off, aboard Apollo 11. Man's a tumor.

And off. Too many passengers in my head, which has one seat only, the seat of the—here they come, zebus, yaupons, xebecs, all with seats assigned. When the seatbelt makes its final *sneckit,* there's no way back, but only coming out at the other side. Ave and vale. Chew, swallow, yawn. The goop in the sinuses grows fat. We head the conga of the buried two abreast in the class called First.

Useless pleadings came from the loudspeakers next our heads. "Would those passengers using radios or tape record-ers please refrain from using them during flight, as they" (I sardonically interpolate "the machines") "interfere with the aircraft's navigational aids?" Each member of the rock group, amidst whom Milk and I were marooned, was wearing headphones connected to cabin bags loaded with equip-ment. Aural solipsism. Only those who didn't need the mes-sage could hear it. Next thing Milk, who was already with them without being of them, had mimed her request for a headset and was listening, if that's the word, to the music of

200

hemispheres, her face tight in a strained but elated-looking scrunch. She'd gone from one no-man's-land into another, and to hell with the plane's navigational aids.

Grievous images of other fates made her doings welcome. I thought of children who, in extermination camps, had frozen together, but thawed out when buried, making the soil churn a little before giving up the ghost. Anything preferable to that.

Gurgles of delight from Milk made me peek-listen, peeling one of her earphones back; but the decibels weren't bad. She was happy about pretending to be listening: a symbolic refinement.

Cokes and dry sherry down the hatch. She felt unspeakably adult, I childish. Neither of us cared. Planted in the soil of rock she couldn't hear, she flowered, sipped her sherry with ostentatious poise. Listening to the nozzle tunes of desiccated air, I vowed to listen to nothing else, neither jazz nor classical, neither people nor ghosts.

Gargoyles, though, flew First Class in my skull: three-legged Francesco Lentini, the soccer wizard; the Tocci brothers, two boys down to the sixth rib, but only one below; Julia Pastrana, the Mexican Digger Indian called the ugliest woman in the world, mostly for being apish and hairy.

Ugliness didn't really come into it; it was more a matter of how original their deformities were. I peopled the First Class compartment with our own kind.

Carl Unthan, the armless violinist, the virtuoso of the toe.

Grace McDaniels, the mule-faced woman, before whom men fainted when she removed her veil; a sideshow in more ways than one.

Christine and Millie, Siamese twins born into slavery, but eventually pulling in six hundred dollars a week.

Charmingly addressed by hostesses. Pampered. Waited on hand and foot, or handless and three-footed. Not a trace of a snigger, even as they stuntedly approached the toilets.

Ghouls of the random, with whom the captain, four stripes on his sleeve, came to make polite conversation.

Apocalypse at thirty-five thousand feet, among the tea and toast. Why hadn't we had our flight in *Moby*, Asa's DC-3?

Coming into the jet stream, the plane lurched, felt as if along its entire length it had sagged, then flowed forward again. Not a single shriek. Milk giggled as her innards fell, a nest of bubbles.

Gross, Elizabethan dinner made us sleepy. Never had we been so plied with viands. Had the airmaids wreathed us in vines, we wouldn't have wondered.

Gear down, my mind was like the jet. The flight had taken only an hour, surely, instead of six. Where was all the air we hadn't flown through?

As for that last goodbye, that handing-over of treasure to the snow queen, the nearer nothing said the better. Let's say it was the keenest thrill I'd had in this life.

Grit-mouthed, I took leave.

Unspeaking, took a cab to the train station.

Ate two boiled eggs with my mother.

Got all the local poop, two years of it.

Crooked a finger round my coffee mug, which she washed daily.

Against just such a chance as this.

Gibbering a bit for lack of company.

As her unseen son's fatigue needled his eyes.

Avian chatter as she celebrated: "You did right to come straight home." And I didn't look back.

"Getting on," I told her. "I am. Don't have the stomach any more for the upset."

"Good clean breaks are better," she said. She knew.

Green grapes, to treat herself on this occasion. She's amused I still hate fruit. And wind. And snow. And noise.

"Galveston," she said. "It was in the *National Geographic*. Weren't you there?" "Somewhere near," I said.

Under the table there was still my father's little foot mat, for when his slippers didn't quite touch.

Generally, she told me, she'd kept very well.

George was dead, though. And others. They all had names.

Chocolate cream cake perked me up.

Gathering my wits for the last half-hour of talk before she returned to the TV, I said something about feeling like a test tube when at forty thousand feet. She let it pass, instead asking if Milk had been good.

"Good? She was perfect. Know what she did?"

Aired my pajamas for me on the second day by draping them over the folding chairs on the balcony. "Aired my pajamas," I said, "even though they weren't damp." My mother's eyes glinted as she opened her mouth in silent exclamation.

Godsend of sleep in my old room.

Grid of the last two weeks is all used up.

Got back power of speech. At long last.

THREE

Ara to Canis Major

I can begin sentences with an *I* again, not so much glad or proud as astounded to be here on the planet as myself and not a peppermint starfish, a thistle, an emu, a bit of quartz. Or a doorknob. Yet self is fainter than it was; self's effaced, and glimmers elsewhere. As in the case of the Masai mother whose child a lion ate and who, against sage advice, reclaimed her offspring by collecting excrement of lions, at least enough to shape a life-sized newborn baby with, which she carried against her chest, a sun-dried thing light as a plaster cast. Perhaps I'll turn to something else, compile my own photographic atlas of irregular or deformed galaxies, and leave the Milky Way alone. Yet, at a distance that feels like more than several thousand miles, the southern half of the Galaxy we call our own, from Ara to Canis Major, remains an underworld undone.